Call of the Cougar

Heart of the Cougar: Book 2

TERRY SPEAR

Call of the Cougar
Copyright © 2014 by Terry Spear
Cover: Tell-Tale Designs

ISBN-10: 1633110036
ISBN-13: 978-1-63311-003-8

Discover more about Terry Spear at:
http://www.terryspear.com/

DEDICATION

Thanks to Lor Melvin who worked with horses and gave me all kinds of great tips concerning the business, and helped me to brainstorm a lot of the book, which was a lot of fun! Thanks tons!

Also by Terry Spear:

The Highlanders Series: Winning the Highlander's Heart, The Accidental Highland Hero, Highland Rake, Taming the Wild Highlander, Her Highland Hero, (2014), The Viking's Highland Lass (2015)

Other historical romances: Lady Caroline & the Egotistical Earl, A Ghost of a Chance at Love

Heart of the Wolf Series: Heart of the Wolf, Destiny of the Wolf, To Tempt the Wolf, Legend of the White Wolf, Seduced by the Wolf, Wolf Fever, Heart of the Highland Wolf, Dreaming of the Wolf, A SEAL in Wolf's Clothing, A Howl for a Highlander, A Highland Werewolf Wedding, A SEAL Wolf Christmas, Silence of the Wolf, Hero of a Highland Wolf (Aug, 2014), A Highland Wolf Christmas (Oct, 2014); A SEAL Wolf Hunting (June, 2015), A Silver Wolf Christmas (Oct 2015)

Heart of the Jaguar Series: Savage Hunger, Jaguar Fever, Jaguar Hunt, Jaguar Pride (Feb 2015)

Heart of the Cougar Series: Cougar's Mate, Call of the Cougar (2014)

Vampire romances: Killing the Bloodlust, Deadly Liaisons, Huntress for Hire, Forbidden Love

Romantic Suspense: Deadly Fortunes, In the Dead of the Night, Relative Danger, Bound by Danger

Prologue

New Year's Day, Suburbs of Loveland, Colorado

After a harrowing case of nabbing two men in a scheme to sell jaguar body parts to prospective buyers, Special Agent for the U.S. Department of Fish and Wildlife Services Tracey Whittington was glad *that* ordeal was over, and settled down in her apartment to eat lunch early that Saturday afternoon. She worked side by side with the Colorado Department of Parks and Wildlife. And she took her job seriously.

The problem was that she'd take one rotten wildlife trafficker down and two more would slip into his place. Stiffer punishment might help. But until wildlife trafficking was taken more seriously, she figured it would continue to be a profitable deal for some criminals. Today was the beginning of a new year and she swore she wasn't going to think about the other case she'd been working on until Monday morning, bright and early.

She placed her plate of steak fajitas and a hot mug of cherry tea on the oak coffee table, curled up on her blue velvet couch, and clicked on the T.V. The snow was lightly falling, though the area was covered in snow from the storm they had last night, and she was looking forward to having a nice weekend off from the job. No investigating anything for the moment. Just enjoying the beautiful snowy day. The sky was a little gray, but at least she didn't have to go out in the cold weather for now. She was thinking about whether she should make New Year's resolutions, like— on New Year's Eve at the end of *this* new year—she should have a date and go to a party. *Right.*

She loved the quiet life when she wasn't tracking down the scum of the earth.

She started watching *3:10 to Yuma*, rolled up her first fajita and was just about to take a bite of the steak, bell peppers, onions, shredded cheese, lettuce, and her absolute favorite—guacamole—without it, it wasn't a fajita, when her phone rang. She glanced at the caller I.D.

Crap.

Honey. Her informant.

Last year, he had aided her in taking down a trafficker of rhino horns and elephant ivory, and helped to get the trafficker sentenced to nearly six years in federal prison and forfeiture of the $3.5 million in the monies he'd received in his smuggling pursuit. A lot of sentences weren't strong enough for these lowlifes, so she was glad he got as much of a sentence as he did. So she had no intention of ignoring Honey's call.

"Yeah...Honey?" She hated using his nickname, but he always seemed to be where the action was, and she needed him. She wasn't sure how he learned about the trafficking going down—though she'd asked, but he wouldn't say. She often wondered if he was playing both sides of the game—getting money from her and from trafficking. Maybe even putting his own competition out of business.

He was a good-looking guy—dark brown hair with blond streaks as the bangs flopped over one dark eye—fashion model material. It was sad that he was in a situation where he was around the kind of people who were involved in this seedy business.

"Happy New Years. Is that *3:10 to Yuma* playing in the background?"

She muted it.

"Love that movie. Got something for you, Agent."

"What do you have?" She set her uneaten fajita on the plate, afraid that was the end of her quiet weekend off. But if it meant finding evidence that could take down another trafficker, she wouldn't hesitate to give up her weekend. Crime didn't allow for breaks.

Whatever word he'd gotten about traffickers was seventy-five percent of the time on the money. She'd never had any trouble with making arrests or finding evidence when she investigated the leads that he'd given her that had led to a virtual goldmine. Only twenty-five percent of the time, the tips led nowhere. She had a much higher rate of success than many of her fellow investigators. Some of it she attributed to her enhanced cougar senses.

No matter what, she always checked them out. Her agency paid well for his time, when the job led to an arrest and conviction. All they needed was some good evidence and the proper handling of it to support their case.

"Do you know where the town of Anderson is?" he finally asked.

"The ghost town?" That was the only one she was acquainted with in the state of Colorado. And yes, she knew it well.

"Yeah, that's the one. Word on the street is that some trafficker was storing ivory in one of the old boarded-up buildings. But then he moved it. I know it's a longshot, but you still might find some evidence up there."

"Which building?"

"That's all I know. Sorry."

"Okay, thanks. You know the drill."

"Yeah. Good luck. My money's riding on you."

"Yeah. And the agency's riding on you."

They ended the call in the same way every time. There didn't seem to be any reason to change it.

She punched in her partner's number. A pain-in-the-butt, Bill Peterson was getting close to retirement from Special Agent duty. He hated that some women were now Special Agents in the field. Particularly her, because she was his partner and he had to work with her. She suspected some of his animosity had to do with his bitter divorce and him not liking any woman right now.

Surprisingly, he'd begrudgingly acknowledged she was damn good at her job. Having the senses of a big cat really helped. Though he was unaware of it. He'd given her an offhanded bit of praise every once in a while. His seniority on the job and his gruffness toward her appealed for some weird reason. He wasn't going to like being called on New Year's Day to back her up. He especially didn't like it that Honey always called her, refusing to talk to her partner.

"Honey called."

"Shit."

She smiled, expecting that kind of a response. "He says someone was storing ivory at Anderson, but it's been moved by now."

"Good. We can check it out at the end of the week." Bill sounded like he'd tied one on. Which, given that he was home alone on New Year's Day and had no work to do, not to mention he was still getting over his divorce, his condition was understandable.

But it didn't help her case one iota. "I'm going to go check it out. Since they've moved the ivory, there shouldn't be anyone there. I'll probably find nothing anyway. So no need for you to go."

Which there wasn't. She wasn't sure why she'd even called him. Force of habit, she supposed. And what if by some miracle he had wanted to go? She should have known better.

"End of the week, Whittington."

She wasn't waiting on this. "Get some rest. And...happy New Year."

Then she hung up on him, turned off the T.V., grabbed her plate of fajitas, and returned to the kitchen. Sometimes, a microwave was her best friend.

It would take her three hours to reach the abandoned silver mine town of Anderson, maybe longer in this weather. Then she'd have to hike in three miles from the point where the road ended. Not that the road was really a road. It had been a wagon trail at one time, now so badly eroded that she was glad she had a Hummer that could make it even that far.

She couldn't delay if she wanted to do this before it got dark and the fall of night hampered her investigation. She packed her gear in her field pack, including a high-powered lantern and a headlamp. Even though she could see in dim light with her cat's vision, she still wanted to have a little extra light for seeing small details if there was any evidence there at all.

She drove the three hours in the snow, admiring the trees coated in flakes, the view of the Rocky Mountains, and finally reached the landmark she knew from her youth—an old two-story wooden, white house. Mrs. Blasdell, widowed three years ago, had owned it forever. She was like a security force of one, watching all who traveled on the old wagon trail as if she was guarding the ghosts of the past. The back of the house faced the old wagon trail. Her new red Cadillac was parked in front of the garage. Tracey was sure that when she drove by the house, Mrs. Blasdell would be watching.

Sure enough, Tracey saw the woman peer through the blinds covering one of the windows. She was about Tracey's mother's age—in her mid-forties. Tracey thought she must be lonely out here by herself, and yet, Tracey was alone too, and it wasn't any big deal. Mrs. Blasdell probably just preferred it that way like Tracey did.

Tracey smiled, waved, and continued driving toward the ghost town and past two abandoned hovels from the same time period, miners' houses, where kids partied when they weren't supposed to. She and her twin sister, Jessie, had explored the old ghost town as teens when they were old enough to drive and loved to fool around in the old buildings, acting like they had time-traveled to the past.

She always thought about it in a good way because of all the fun they'd have, even shifting into their cougar forms and climbing the rocky cliffs to investigate the miners' houses clinging to the mountain. She hated to think traffickers were using it for their criminal activities now.

She reached the spot where she couldn't drive any further, the area surrounded by pinyon pines, junipers, and blue spruce, all dusted in white snow. She climbed out of her Hummer, grabbed her field pack, and locked up the vehicle, the bitter cold wind slicing right through her. She thought of how much warmer she'd be as a big cat. Or back home. She was often driven to catch the bad guys, but she wondered if Bill had been right. Not that she should wait a week to check on this, but at least she could have taken New Year's Day off.

Then again, she wouldn't have been able to stop thinking about it.

The scenery was beautiful, the trees and shrubs covered in white powder and encroaching on the path as she trudged through the four inches of snow, careful not to twist an ankle on the badly rutted trail.

After hiking three miles, she finally reached the ghost town. At one time, it had boasted a population of two-thousand residents—women, children, but mostly men—during the height of the prospecting business. She couldn't even imagine all the goings-on that had to have occurred here before, when now all she heard was the sound of the wind whistling through the town.

All of the wooden buildings were boarded up: two hotels, a school, two churches, four saloons, three dance halls, two gambling halls, and two parlor houses. She wondered what the people back then would have been doing on New Year's Day.

She took a deep breath of the snow-chilled air and began methodically checking the first of the buildings—a church, like the rest of the wooden structures, built in the early 1800's. Specifically, she was searching for any recent sign of breaking and entering, indicating someone might have used any of the buildings for illegal business.

After inspecting the first three buildings and finding no sign of forced entry, she discovered a loose board over a window at the old schoolhouse, the glass broken out long ago.

The sun was beginning to set, casting long shadows across the snow. She shivered from the cold, then readied her lantern, helmet, and headlamp. She climbed into the dark building, lit only by her headlamp and her lantern.

Inside the schoolhouse, she hesitated, listening to any sign of movement. Even the mice or rats or other varmints wouldn't be out this winter's day.

Her heart was thumping loud in her ears, the thrill of a potential find nearby, she hoped, as she began to search the bare wooden floors for any sign of footprints—when she saw dozens, or the same people had trekked back and forth across the dusty floors. Recent, too. Or new layers of dust would have covered them.

Then she heard movement outside. She pulled out her Glock and hurried to the window. She looked between the slatted boards, forgetting she had the damn headlamp on. Then she saw her partner, Bill, following her trail of footprints in the snow. He was frowning at her, his dark hair windswept, and his dark eyes narrowed because of the biting wind blowing his way.

"Way to go, Whittington. Good thing I wasn't one of the bad guys."

He was referring to her headlamp, shining through the slats over the window.

But she was pleased for the company, even as grumpy as her partner appeared to be. "Glad you could make it."

"Yeah, well, hell, I figured I'd be forced to retire early if I didn't watch your ass and you got it shot off. Did you find anything? Or should we have waited until the end of the week, like I said."

Which meant he was right and she was wrong. She could watch a movie anytime, but finding evidence to put these guys away? She couldn't risk losing the opportunity.

"Someone has accessed this schoolhouse recently and could have hidden something here. I haven't found anything yet. They could have been using another building to store stuff. The first few were all sealed up tight."

Bill pulled back the board and climbed inside. "You can be a real pain in the ass, you know?"

"Yeah, I know. But you didn't have to come. I was fine." And she had been the last couple of times too, when he'd had one of these mid-life—or whatever they were—crises again, and she had found evidence on her own, letting on to their boss that she hadn't been alone, covering Bill's ass. She'd felt sorry for him at the time. But maybe early retirement wouldn't be such a bad thing for him after all. His heart just wasn't in the business of catching these guys any longer.

When he moved closer to her location, he looked bleary-eyed, and she got a heavy whiff of the pungent smell of bourbon on his breath. She wanted to shake her head. He should never have driven here. She doubted she could talk him into allowing her to drive him home. Especially when they'd have to leave his Humvee out here in the boonies and risk having it stolen or vandalized.

He took a seat on an old wooden crate, making it creak. It was the only piece of "furnishing" in the building. She turned away from him, wondering why he was here in the first place. Then she began to search the floorboards, looking for any that might be loose, making for the perfect hiding spot.

Bill stayed where he was. He leaned against a wooden pillar, looking like he was about to go to sleep when she found a loose board.

With the discovery, she felt her heart beating a little faster. She set her lantern down and found a finger hold to lift the dusty floor board and peered into the cavernous hole. Perfect in the summer for a nest of rattlesnakes to escape the noonday sun. There, she witnessed the imprint in the dry soil of several elephant-size tusks.

Outside the building, rapid footfalls headed in the direction of the schoolhouse.

She whipped around to see a rifle pointed through the wooden slats of another broken out window. "Get down!" she shouted to Bill.

Getting out of the shooter's line of sight, she dashed for the window that she and Bill had entered. They were sitting ducks inside the schoolhouse.

Shots were fired. In slow motion, Bill barely stood before he collapsed on the floor.

Oh God, no!

She quickly put out her lantern light and head lamp, casting the schoolhouse into relative darkness. She heard the footfalls running for another window so whoever the shooter was could get a bead on her. She shoved the board over the window aside and looked out. No one. She quickly climbed out through the window, the sun setting, but it was still much lighter outside than inside the boarded-up building, the snow making it that much brighter. She headed around the building, listening for heavy breathing, footfalls, talking, anything.

Two sets of footfalls sounded, one coming around the schoolhouse from the north and another from the south side of the building. She was going to be in the middle of a shootout.

Praying Bill would make it, she couldn't quit thinking about him. For now, she had to draw the gunmen away, and she had to stop them before they killed her and finished off Bill.

She raced to the next building over, wishing she was in her cougar form so she could spring and attack. Though even at that, she would only be able to take down one man at a time.

A shot was fired. Instinctively, she ducked. To her surprise, a man cursed a blue moon on the south side of the schoolhouse.

The one on the north side poked his head around the corner of the schoolhouse, and she fired three shots at him, splintering wood on the corner of the building as he fell back. Then she headed for where the other man must have been hit. Bill had to have fired at him from inside the schoolhouse, which gave her hope that he'd be all right.

She reached the front of the building and saw a trail of blood. The gunman had been wounded. Good. But not fatally, or he wouldn't have gotten away.

She needed to get the other man. The uninjured one. Though both could be just as great a danger to her and her partner.

She peered around the side of the schoolhouse and saw the uninjured man heading for her. She fired several shots—stomach, chest, heart. Yet the man still managed to raise his gun to fire at her, and she dove behind the building. Rounds pinged off the edge of the wooden schoolhouse.

Her heart racing, she sucked in cold breaths of air. She listened, hoping to hell the two men would collapse, unable to shoot anyone any further, and she could see to Bill.

But it made her think of what her boss had told her once—how some men could take a lot of rounds and still kill someone before they went down for good. He'd learned that from real life experience. She couldn't chance making a mistake when she was outnumbered at least two to one, if the other man wasn't down for good.

She heard footfalls from the east and realized someone *else* was coming. The man she had shot had to be gravely wounded. The one that Bill must have hit, might have a minor injury, she couldn't be sure. Now, there was *another*? She couldn't hope that it was someone who would be on the agents' side.

"Where are they?" a man growled on the other side of one of the hotels.

"The woman's outside of the schoolhouse," one of the men gritted out, sounding like he was in pain. "The other agent is inside the schoolhouse. He has to be dead. I got him, but damn if he didn't graze me."

The gunman wasn't badly wounded then. *Damn it.*

"Where's Crowley?"

"He's badly wounded near the saloon."

"*Shit.* Which side of the schoolhouse was the woman on?"

"She was on the east side, but she could have moved by now."

She leaned her back against the north side of the hotel to steady her nerves. Then she came around the edge of the building, staying close to the wall before either man could move from their location at the end of the hotel. Running as quietly as she could on top of the soft snow, thankful that she could hear them with her enhanced hearing, while they couldn't hear her, she reached the corner of the hotel. She peered around the edge to ready a shot.

Dressed in an olive green parka, blue jeans, and cowboy boots, a blond man was holding his arm against his body, dripping blood all over the pristine snow while he was watching in the direction of the schoolhouse. He was a big man and she suspected it would require a lot of firepower and well-aimed shots to take him down. The other was dark-haired, blue eyes, and he was wearing a gray parka, blue jeans, and snow boots. She wondered where he'd been all this time while his buddies were involved in the shootout. The barely wounded man's parka sleeve was covered in blood. He appeared to be getting ready to move around to the front of the hotel away from her.

She needed a better angle, but as soon as she came out into the open, she'd have two guns blazing at her.

She had to take the chance. If either man reached the schoolhouse—if Bill was still alive—they could finish him off, wait for her to make an appearance, and kill her.

She came out from behind the building, fired several rounds at the two men, hoping to hell she hit some vital spots. With her cat reflexes, she dove behind the building while they leaped for cover and shot back at her. Their response was too late. She had already raced to the west side of the schoolhouse in case they hadn't been wounded enough and came after her.

She came around the end of the building to see the badly wounded gunman she had shot earlier propped against the wall of one of the saloons, his brown parka wearing a dark wet spot in the center of his chest, the snow beside him soaking up some of the blood. As soon as he saw her, his eyes widened a little. He raised his gun to shoot her, but his reaction was way too slow. *Damn it.* She wanted to take him alive.

She had no choice. Too many to still battle it out with.

Signaling her position—which irked her to the max—she shot him in the forehead. He fell over and planted his body sideways in the snow. Her heart thundering in her ears, she ran around the opposite side of the saloon before the other men came for her, and waited.

Her breathing still accelerated, she hated the waiting. When she didn't hear anyone coming, she hoped that meant her shots had injured the remaining two men badly enough that they had collapsed like this man had done.

But every minute meant her own partner could be dying. If she were wounded, she had the ability to heal faster than humans could, but her partner was strictly human.

She pulled out her phone. No reception. *Great.*

She peered around the saloon. She saw only the wooden buildings and snow caught up in the wind, making it look like a snow globe that had been shaken to scatter the snowflakes in the air.

No one was moving about anywhere. Then again, they could have left already, and she wouldn't have heard them because of her own footfalls, heavy breathing, and shooting.

She couldn't wait. Her heart pumping furiously, she crept as quietly as she could. She hated to be between buildings with nothing to duck behind. She finally reached the schoolhouse again, no one on the other side there. One more building to reach and peer around. Fingers crossed that the two men were lying in the snow bleeding out.

She held her breath, knowing as soon as she peeked around the corner, they could both be aiming for her, and she'd be dead.

Listening for heavy breathing, groans, or any other kind of movement that would indicate they were both still there, she closed her eyes and concentrated.

Nothing.

She peered around the church. The two men were gone. Red blood stained the white snow, and footprints and bloodied spots on the snow led away from the town.

They appeared to be on the run.

She wanted to take them down. God knew she wanted to stop them before they got away. But she couldn't. She had to go back to Bill.

She dashed to the schoolhouse and slipped in through the boards over the window. She grabbed her field pack and the lantern, and ran across the wooden floor to see to Bill. He looked ghastly pale in the light of the lantern. His pulse was thready, and she feared he wouldn't make it.

"Bill, damn it, you die on me, and I'll—"

He gave her a sickly smile. "Early retirement," he gritted out.

Damnable tears streaked down her cheeks.

"Are you puddling up over me, Agent?" he managed to get out.

"Dust in the room," she growled back.

"What of the men?"

"One's dead. The other two are wounded and ran off."

"Go...after them."

Ignoring him, she began to pull up his shirt.

He coughed up blood. "I'm not going to make it."

"Don't say it. You will, damn it. You're not going to leave me behind to fend for myself." As if that was her concern. She wanted him to think she needed his backup and just maybe he would hold on until she could get the paramedics.

He smiled a little. "You do good. Go. Get out of here. Get help."

She had to. She couldn't reach the police out here. She had to leave to get help. She patched him up with her medical supplies the best she could. But she knew just racing off to reach her Hummer three miles away, she could be ambushed anywhere along the route.

She had to take out the men. The best way she could in this terrain. As a cougar.

Chapter 1

Six months ago, Tracey had gone to investigate the ghost town of Anderson and had been in the worst gun battle she'd ever fought in and lost her partner. Now she was meeting with Tobias Mooney in Greeley, Colorado, close to her home in Loveland, at an old café decorated in western theme from the worn cowboy boots and Stetsons, to lassoes and pictures of cowboys hanging all over the wall. One of the signs on the wall caught her attention: I'm having a nice day. DON'T SCREW IT UP!

Tracey smiled as she was seated in a red-leather booth across from a covered wagon filled with the buffet for the day. She still believed Mooney had everything to do with her partner's death. Surprisingly, he had agreed to meet with her, as if he was the cat and she was the mouse. If he only knew.

She texted Mooney to let him know where she was seated. Then she saw him—tall, tanned, wearing high-priced clothes and looking out of place here. He nodded, gave her a half-smile and headed toward her booth.

"I'm only meeting with you because I have nothing to hide," Mooney said to Tracey as he joined her. His dark brown, curly hair was cut short, his dark blue eyes watching her, studying her reactions, like a hunter watched its prey—just like when he was on the hunt.

She wondered if he looked grungy when he was on a hunt, leaving chin whiskers to sprout and wearing old hunting clothes. She couldn't even envision him like that.

He'd refused to speak to her with her new partner present, which had irritated her partner and worried her boss. Did Mooney think she was just a woman and not as much of a risk as dealing with Anton? Her partner didn't have the wicked claws and teeth that she had. Or the enhanced sense of smell like she had either.

"So...exactly what do you believe I'm guilty of? I run an honest hunting guide business. I'm just as conscientious about wildlife conservation as you. The deer would eat down too much of the vegetation that's used by other wildlife to survive."

Tracey sipped her hot tea, allowing him to have his say. Maybe he'd incriminate himself. She was certain his lawyers wouldn't approve of him being here like this, but she thought it was worth a shot to arrange the meeting.

He drank his coffee." So, what do you think I've done, that is criminal in nature with regard to your area of expertise?"

She set her floral teacup on its saucer and looked him squarely in the eye. "We've had reports that you, or men working for you, have been maiming cougars and other prey, caging them right before the hunters arrive, then releasing them."

Mooney frowned at her, as if he couldn't believe anyone would do something that was so awful and unfair to the game. "I wouldn't risk losing my license over something so heinous. That's half of the sport. To hunt the wild animals down. If someone has been doing such a thing, it wasn't me or any of my men. Unless one of them has been doing some guiding operations on his own that I'm unaware of."

"Can you give me a name of any of the men who would be a likely suspect? We have had word that your guiding operations are involved. So if one of your men has gone solo, but is still using your good name in conducting this unlawful business, we'd love to hear of it and clear you and your operation of any wrongdoing."

"I can't imagine any of my current staff would be guiding on their own. But I did have one who left me last year and he might be. His name is Bear Tucker. I don't suspect he's doing anything illegal, but he's no longer working for me, so I can't really vouch for him.

He knows my operation, so he could possibly be using my name to build his own customer base." Mooney shrugged. "I haven't heard of anyone else doing that. Of course, it could be one of my competition. We usually stay out of each other's way. But occasionally a new guide goes into the business and who knows what tactics he might use to discredit one of the other successful guide operations."

"Anyone you might suspect like that?"

"No. They always have new guys cropping up in the business. But I could see where they're not getting enough clients. Word spreads if they're unable to catch sight of their prey on a hunt and exasperate the hunters who hired them."

"What do you know about illegal trafficking of animal body parts?"

Mooney sat back against his seat, appearing to distance himself from the new discussion. Had she hit a nerve?

"Nothing. I mean, except for hearing about it in the news periodically."

"What about the trafficking of ivory?"

"That's a hell of a jump from hunting deer and elk to hunting elephants."

"When there's no hunting for the season, what do you do?"

"You mean, how do I afford my house and such?" Mooney smiled. "Wise investments, of course. But I'm sure you already knew that. Anything more, Agent

Whittington? I have some other business to attend to."

Definitely, this was a topic he didn't want to get drawn into.

"Thank you for your cooperation in this ongoing investigation. If the rumors turn out to be falsified, I will push to have charges brought against the guilty parties." Tracey stood and so did Mooney.

He gave her a pleasant smile as if they had coffee and tea on a regular basis, but she smelled his nervousness, though he never showed any outward appearance of being nervous. That's what she loved about her enhanced cougar abilities. She could smell distress or other kinds of emotions, sexual interest, and more. It helped when she couldn't read an individual's facial expressions or body language.

Though in his case, he put on the air of being respectful, as if he was totally on her side and was eager to help her learn the truth concerning these false accusations. But the real truth was —as far as she was concerned—eyewitnesses were correct in what they had reported—three men, one fitting Mooney's description—and two hunters had taken off after two wounded cougars. Cages have been found nearby, according to these witnesses. But by the time she'd been called in to investigate, all the evidence was gone. Well, almost all the evidence. She had smelled that the cats had been staying in one spot for some time, smelled the blood from their wounds, speculated they'd been sitting in a cage and had left their panicked smell. But only her boss would believe her. No one else could use that as evidence.

Before she could leave, a man caught her eye, wearing a cowboy hat, boots, jeans, and a western shirt as he grabbed a coffee to go and headed outside. He'd caught her attention because she loved westerns and hot cowboys. All he needed was a pair of sexy leather chaps.

Mooney paid for their drinks, but Tracey declined and left payment also. When Mooney headed out ahead of her, she took in deep breaths as she tried to smell the scent the cowboy had left behind. He exuded confidence, but she wondered if he was a real working cowboy or just liked to look as though he was. But then she got a surprise. He was a cougar shifter! Who smelled of leather and horse and was sexy as all get out.

She peered around the parking lot and saw him climbing into a pickup pulling a horse trailer. Her natural cougar instincts were aroused. She sighed, reminding herself that the last cowboy she'd hooked up with had ended in a messy divorce.

She headed home when she got a call from her new informant, Ricky.

"Yeah, Ricky?"

"Got a new tip. Ivory is being held at Anderson. You know the place? The ghost town?"

***

Even now as Tracey trekked up the rocky incline for three miles with her new partner, Special Agent

Anton Genova, who had worked on several missions with her, she grew teary eyed.

She hadn't returned to her teenage haunt since the disaster on New Year's Day, and though she knew nothing would happen this time, she couldn't help feeling uneasy, like the whole situation could happen all over again—the shootout, her partner down, only this time *she* wouldn't be so lucky.

If her partner hadn't been so inebriated that day, things might have been different. Or if she'd just given in and said she'd do as he had suggested, and waited until the end of the week, maybe none of it would have happened. But he'd been in so many blue funks before that, she hadn't wanted to risk him saying no by the end of the week too.

Now, she wished she had let it go. The damnedest part of the whole situation was that they had found nothing. Sure, Honey had been right, like he usually had been. Someone had stored ivory there, right under the schoolhouse floor. The imprints in the dried mud proved that beyond a doubt. Casts had been made of it, and when they were analyzed, they not only had found the elephant tusk imprints, but fingerprints too. Except they had matched the perp she had shot in the forehead, so no help there. Her only satisfaction was that she'd managed to kill the one trafficker with her gun, and another with her cougar's teeth. But the third, despite being wounded, had gotten away.

She and Anton had worked so many cases

together—from undercover operations designed to infiltrate wildlife trafficking rings, illegal guiding operations, and even discovering a case of the intentional poisoning of bald eagles—that she knew her partner's every action.

Until today. Rattled by a recent divorce and custody battle over their two-year old daughter, Anton wasn't wholly in the game—when every bit of their attention had to be focused on the danger right here and now. Not that anything dangerous was about to happen, but then again, the last time nothing was supposed to either. It gave her a new perspective when dealing with traffickers.

With two partners who had marriages on the rocks that had affected their ability to do their jobs, she really was glad she wasn't in any kind of a relationship right now. She'd been there, done that, anyway.

Tracey couldn't help worrying about Anton, considering this was eerily like her former partner's lack of focus—in his case, due to liquor—when she had to remain just as alert about the possible peril all around them.

She'd thought Honey might have set her and Bill up, but when the police found Honey's body riddled with bullets in a downtown Denver apartment two days later, she assumed someone had learned he was a FWS informant. She felt badly that he had been murdered, even though some of her fellow agents had discovered he had been involved in wildlife trafficking, just as she had suspected. And he was attempting to eliminate his competition, which hadn't gone over well with them.

Now, a scrawny eighteen-year-old, by the name of Ricky, was her new informant and had told them a trafficker was using this place as a hideout for his ivory. She was certain it was old news. The same old news that Honey had shared with her six months ago. But what if it wasn't? She had to check it out. What if the trafficker had returned to the scene of the crime? Figuring no one would come here again, looking for his stolen goods?

Twice, Anton tried to get ahead of her on the path. Yeah, he was taller and had a longer stride than her. But he knew the rules. She went first. Her cougar hearing, sight, and smell dictated it. Neither he nor any of the other agents she'd worked with knew why her senses were so enhanced, only that her instincts were much better than theirs. After a few close calls and one death that could have been avoided, they'd quit being all macho or totally alpha and taking the lead when she was partnered with them.

Until today.

***

Sheriff Dan Steinacker called Hal Haverton, who worked as his part-time deputy for Yuma Town, Colorado, their official duties covering nearly 3,000 square miles of unincorporated territory. He asked him to check out widowed Mrs. Blasdell's claim that wild kids were off partying at one of the boarded up miner's houses on the hillside next to the old wagon trail that led to the ghost town of Anderson. As a kid, he and Dan and the rest of his Special Forces buddies who lived in Yuma Town, had loved to go up there and scare the spit out of each other. They'd climbed the mountains as cougars, sneaked into the boarded-up buildings, and even had a séance once in one of the saloons. Stryker, Yuma's full-time deputy, had even let on that he had communed with several ghosts—a couple of hanged stagecoach robbers, miners fighting over silver, a gunslinger, and others who had died violently in the town centuries earlier.

If kids wanted to play around in the boarded-up houses, Hal didn't mind. As long as they didn't vandalize the old buildings or hurt themselves. Or go down into the silver mines. The mines could be real death traps and many had lost their lives over the years when they had broken through the boarded-up mine shafts to go exploring.

The houses were close by and easy to check out. Only once did he catch someone in one of the houses. He and the other deputies and Dan never knew if Mrs. Blasdell was just lonely and wanted some attention, or if the partygoers had left before he arrived. Though when he'd investigated the other times, he'd never smelled anyone who had been in them recently, so he assumed it was just her imagination, or she needed a little company. Which he never minded.

On the warm summer day, he saw fresh tire tracks

on the washed-out dirt wagon trail, the grass and weeds growing there crushed by the tires of a vehicle. But the vehicle hadn't stopped at any of the miners' houses. He followed the trail up toward the point where it ended, assuming then, Mrs. Blasdell had been right. Maybe it wasn't kids, though. He called Dan to let him know he was checking out tire tracks leading up to Anderson. After the shootout here on New Year's Day, they were a little more cautious about assuming everything was fine.

"Do you want to wait for backup?" Dan sounded concerned.

"Nah. When I reach the vehicle, I'll give you the license plate number, and you can check it out."

The going was slow and Hal finally reached a silvery-blue Hummer covered in dust parked at the end of the trail. He called in the license number, make, and model of the vehicle and waited.

"The Hummer is registered to a Tracey Whittington, Fish and Wildlife Services Special Agent."

Hal frowned as he grabbed his pack. "Wasn't she the one involved in that shootout up here?"

"Yeah. January 1st, not a good way to start out the New Year. Do you want to wait for assistance?" Again, Dan sounded like he wanted Hal to hold up until they could get there to watch his back.

"No. If she's poking at rattlesnakes again without a lot of reinforcements, I need to be up there, making sure she doesn't get bit. If she's got more armed manpower this time, then we won't need anyone else." He smelled around the vehicle and frowned again. "Hell, unless it's someone else, she's a cougar."

"You're kidding."

"No. Call her boss." Mick Sorenson was a good friend of theirs, both a Special Forces officer and a cougar. But he'd never mentioned he had a she-cat working for him as a Special Agent.

"I will."

After all hell had broken loose up here on New Year's Day, Dan, Stryker, and Chase Buchanan, their other part-time deputy, had been up here investigating the matter. Hal had been out of town, picking up his horses stabled at another ranch, his own ranch finally ready for them. So he'd missed out on all the action. He still couldn't believe all that had gone down at their old childhood playground. Apparently, it had been like the old west shootouts all over again.

"Didn't you know she was a cougar?" he asked Dan, still pondering why none of them had known it or mentioned it to him if they had. He was certain his buddies wouldn't have kept the fact secret.

"I never had a chance to talk to her. It turned into a murder investigation. Feds were in on it and took over. The woman had been hospitalized for a nasty knife wound and was lucky she had survived. Mick never said a thing about it to me. As far as we knew, she and her partner were strictly human."

"Well, hell, Dan, now some of what happened makes more sense." Hal stalked up the dwindling remnants of the wagon trail, smelling a male human's and a female cougar's scents. "A cougar attacked the injured man up on the cliffs and killed him. You thought the cougar had smelled his blood because the gunman had been wounded, and the cougar came for dinner. But it didn't eat him. Just killed him. You assumed the cougar was saving him for dinner later then because he'd recently eaten. But if Tracey is one of us, she must have shifted and gone after him. Here we thought she had suffered a knife wound at the hands of the trafficker, which she had, but as a human, not a cougar." *A woman after his own heart.* "What does she look like?"

Dan chuckled.

"Well, we know she's up here. It's her vehicle. But we don't know who her partner is. So I need to know what she looks—"

The official agency photo came through on his cell phone. Hal studied it and smiled. *Hot. Damn.*

Long, dark blond hair, piercing green cougar eyes, sensuous lips meant to be kissed, but looking perfectly serious in the picture, meaning she was all business. But her green eyes captured his attention to such a degree, he tripped in a rut on the trail and practically fell on his face. He grinned at Tracey's picture.

Dan said, "She's unattached and appears to be married to her job."

Hal definitely liked the unattached part. "So, neither you nor Stryker made a play for her?" Not that Dan would. He was in sort of a relationship with Dottie Brown, their dispatcher.

"We didn't meet her, remember? And we didn't know she was one of us."

"Right."

Hal wondered if she had a new lead in her partner's murder now and that's why she was up here. Or if she had Post Traumatic Stress Disorder and was trying to come to terms with what had happened here. "Hey, ask Mick if they ever solved her partner's murder case."

"Mick says no. And before you ask, she's up here with her partner, Special Agent Anton Genova. She got a tip from an informant, but she believes it's an old tip related to the first time she was up here."

"All right." So far everything sounded above board, not like a woman having trouble letting go of the guilt that she might be feeling for having survived when her partner didn't. At least she wasn't up here alone being a Lone Ranger without her boss's approval. Hal was relieved she was doing everything by the book.

"Do you want a picture of Genova?"

"Of course I do. I'm a professional." Though Hal was certain he wouldn't be nearly falling on his face on the rutted wagon trail when he saw Tracey's partner's picture.

Dan sent him the agency photo. The man was dark-haired, large nose, nearly black eyes, the same kind of look that meant he could deal out the rough stuff if he got riled. That was good. The woman needed a man like that at her side, considering what happened the last time.

"Okay, thanks."

"Mick said he's glad you're going up there to check things out. He didn't want her to go, worried about how she might deal with the memories, but she insisted she was fine."

So maybe this wasn't all above board and she *was* still dealing with the issues. Frankly, he wouldn't blame her in the least. If he'd had to deal with that himself, he probably would have still been shaken up. Not that he'd admit that to anyone. "What's *Stryker* doing?"

Dan laughed. "I'll let him know what happened to you when you checked into Mrs. Blasdell's kid problem."

Hal smiled because whenever Mrs. Blasdell called, Stryker had a more pressing assignment.

"How's the mare doing?" Dan asked.

"Foaling in about a week."

"I bet you'll be glad when—"

Gunfire crackled a mile away in the vicinity of the ghost town. Hal abruptly stopped in his footfalls, surprised as hell.

"Shots fired!" His heart pounding pell mell, Hal took off at a run. He couldn't believe the woman could be in a firefight again—in the same ghost town, of all places.

***

Tracey and Anton had been systematically inspecting each of the buildings, as she'd done before, ensuring no one had entered one recently. She was saving the schoolhouse for last. Not because she feared going in, but because she didn't believe the traffickers would use the same place again, if Ricky's information *wasn't* out-of-date.

Unlike Honey, who had been older and she suspected had been working both sides of the equation, and then learned he had been, she assumed Ricky was in the midst of bad stuff going down, and he had a moral compass that said he'd rather be an informant than be involved in criminal activities. She normally didn't warn an informant how dangerous their life could be, but with him, being that he was so young, she had. They needed him, and he'd already helped bring closure to two cases, but he was the first informant who had worked for her that she really worried about. Maybe because he was so young.

"Here," Tracey said, surprised Anton hadn't found the opening into the second saloon first. He had passed this way just moments ago, and again, she worried about him—that he was too distracted to really be paying attention if they got into trouble.

With her headlamp on and her Glock readied, she climbed through the hole that had been covered with a single piece of plywood, aged, but only attached in a way that made it easy to swing to the side and up, like a secret door to a kids' hideaway.

She had her gun out, more for encounters with rattlesnakes taking refuge in the saloon, rather than being anxious that they might find someone in here. This was the time of year and a great place for rattlesnakes to take refuge from the hot summer's sun.

She heard no sounds, other than her boots walking across the creaking floorboards and then Anton joining her. Like the schoolhouse, she saw boot tracks, men's size elevens and twelves, tromping all over the dusty floor. Nothing real recent, but recent enough. Weeks, maybe? Days? She couldn't guess.

It didn't mean that anyone sinister had been here either. Just that a couple of men, or even teens with big feet, had been wandering around in here. She started examining the floorboards, looking for any that were loose, just like at the schoolhouse before this.

"Here," Anton said, breaking free from his gloomy mood for a minute.

She hurried to see what he'd found behind the old dust-covered bar.

"Fingerprints." He got out his kit to lift them off the scarred, oak countertop.

She turned to study the floor and just as she realized that brand new footprints had walked this way from what looked like a store room, she knew she and Anton were in danger.

She smelled the men's different colognes as they'd recently moved in this direction. Saw the business end of two rifles poke through the slats of a wooden door. With her enhanced feline vision, she easily caught sight of the slightest movement.

She was quick, her cat actions so flexible even when in human form, she turned and dove for Anton. It was the best she could do. But she was afraid it wasn't good enough.

Gunfire exploded from four different directions. Tracey slammed into Anton's six foot, two-inch frame, knocking into him. He went down like a wall of cement, hitting the wood floor hard. She landed on top of him, but quickly moved off him to see if he'd been shot.

He was staring up at her with his nearly black eyes focused on her, and then he began to get up, but she saw the stain of blood spreading across his black T-shirt. She grabbed his shoulder and shoved him down.

"You're wounded," she said, her voice hushed. "I'll take care of this. Stay there."

Rounds crashed into the solid oak bar that they were behind, providing Anton and her some protection. Splinters of wood rained down on top of them as rounds hit the countertop. Tracey hurried to pull out her medical pack, then jerked Anton's black T-shirt free of his black cargo pants. Blood spilled from his side. She fumbled to rip open one of the packages containing a sterile pad and bandage. Her heart racing a million miles a minute, she prayed Anton would live as she rushed to stop his bleeding.

The shooting continued and she hoped the rounds smacking into the solid oak protecting Anton and her wouldn't penetrate it and hit either of them. As soon as she had done all she could for Anton, she tried her phone, knowing she wouldn't have any reception, but she had to give it a shot.

Not enough of a signal. Damn.

Her skin was perspiring, her heart pounding as she felt the whole damn past catch up to her.

When neither she nor Anton returned fire, the traffickers—at least that's who she thought they had to be—ceased shooting.

She pocketed her cell, kept her gun ready, and hoped the men believed she and Anton were seriously injured, maybe even dead. Which could be a good thing, giving the perps a false sense of security. Even so, one agent against four armed men was no match if the men chose to rush their location. She and Anton would both be easy targets.

She glanced down at her partner. His face was ashen, perspiration beading his forehead, his long dark hair dusting the wooden floor. He gritted his teeth in silent suffering, trying not to make a sound. She was crouched beside him, facing the bar so that if the men tried to reach them from either end of the bar, she could see their movement and hopefully shoot them first. She reached over to squeeze Anton's hand. It was cold and clammy. As hot as the old saloon was this summer afternoon, that wasn't a good sign. He applied the slightest pressure while squeezing her hand back, and she feared she would lose him. Just like she lost Bill.

Her Glock readied, she listened to hear what was going on beyond the bar, her left hand still gripping his right. She couldn't let go just yet, wanting him to know she was there for him.

Barely breathing, she attempted to hear the slightest movement. Then hurried footfalls scurried across the wooden floor, creaking, headed away from Anton and Tracey's position—two men, she thought. They moved in the direction of the hidden entryway Tracey and her partner had used. She desperately wanted to take the two men out. But the other two remained where they were, waiting for the agents' response. She knew as soon as she came up to take the shot, she'd be gunned down.

The men staying behind probably thought if she and her partner were all right, they would chase after the men departing the area.

No matter how much she wanted to take them all down, her place was right here at her wounded partner's side this time. They had some cover, unlike the last time where they were sitting ducks inside the schoolhouse. Anton had a dark-haired, pigtailed daughter waiting for him back home. Tracey couldn't let him die.

No one was talking, so she assumed the men were communicating with hand signals. Running footfalls took off outside and headed away from the saloon.

Damn it. She hated that any of the bastards had gotten away. Further silence lingered on for what seemed like eons, but could have been only a couple of minutes, then the two men still there began to move toward Anton and her.

Every board-creaking footstep brought them closer.

She placed Anton's hand on his chest freeing up her hand. Then she used both her hands to steady her gun. As soon as a bearded, black-eyed man appeared around the end of the bar, his gun readied, she fired twice, hitting him in the forehead both times. He stumbled back into the other man, a smaller redheaded guy trailing behind him, using the bigger man as his shield.

As soon as the first man crumpled to the floor, the second man was exposed. The hideaway door across the saloon was shoved open, and a man with a deep, baritone voice full of command shouted, "Freeze! Police!"

She couldn't be that lucky that a police officer just happened to drop into a ghost town for the day. With her gun trained on the perp, she rose just high enough to peer over the counter and ensure it wasn't one of the gunmen coming back, pretending to be a policeman. Which was a much more realistic scenario than that a lone police officer suddenly dropped by to make an arrest in a ghost town.

The redheaded man jerked his attention to the tall, blond-haired man standing in front of the hideaway door. His dark brown eyes narrowed, the self-professed policeman was dressed in jeans and a black muscle shirt, and had his .357 magnum trained on the perp.

The redhead swung around to shoot the police officer, confirming the new man wasn't with these men.

She fired three times at the gunman's hand, wounding him, and he jerked his hand to the side, forcing his shot to go wild. He dropped his gun as his round struck the wall near the secret entrance. With his uninjured hand, he went for a knife strapped at his leg and whirled around to face her.

Crap! Did the bastard have a death wish? Maybe he thought he could take her hostage. Fat chance he'd have at doing that.

"Hands in the air!" She didn't want to kill the bastard. They needed him for questioning.

The police officer fired a shot, hitting the man in the side of his kneecap.

Crying out in pain, the gunman collapsed, writhing on the floor. His cold blue eyes turned to her, and she knew before he even moved, he was going for his damn gun.

The police officer raced across the creaking floor.

"You've got backup, right?" she asked, praying to God the police officer did, even though he appeared to be off-duty or maybe he was undercover. She rushed to kick the wounded man's gun out of his reach and bumped into the officer, aiming for the same thing.

She immediately smelled the police officer's sexy

cougar scent. Her gaze shot up to his, and she took another deep breath, her lips parting in surprise. And then she recognized him. The man in the coffee shop, who had smelled of horses and leather…and cougar.

In the type of business she was in, she had made a lot of friends among the various law enforcement agencies because she had to work with the different agencies to get the job done. But running into a police officer who was a shifter? A cowboy? And hot?

This was a totally new experience. He gave her a slight smile, his dark eyes matching the expression. Then he frowned. "What the hell's going on here, Special Agent Tracey Whittington?"

***

As soon as all hell had broken loose in the ghost town, Hal swore he'd never run so fast in his life as he did trying to come to the agents' aid. Now, he secured the wounded man with a plastic wrist tie, ensured the other gunman was dead, then turned to look down into the prettiest green eyes he'd ever seen—tendrils of dark blond hair caressing the woman's shoulders, the rest of her silky hair still bound, her black T-shirt fitting around a nice package, cargo pants showing off some more curves, and boots, indicating she was a member of a law enforcement agency. She certainly had the weapon to back up her business, and she knew how to handle it. What he didn't know was what the hell was going on with her as far as her being in two shootouts in the same vicinity.

"What took you so long?" she asked.

That made his serious expression vanish and his mouth curved up. He couldn't help himself. The woman was a firecracker, but most importantly, she was a hot cougar. In this line of work, he had never met one, female-type, in either a military or civilian police capacity. He was more than intrigued. And he was damn glad Stryker had wanted him to take care of the business with Mrs. Blasdell's call.

She turned her attention from Hal and kept her gun trained on the wounded man writhing on the floor, and the other man, just in case. "How do you know me? And how do I know you're who you say you are?"

Hal pulled out his badge and showed it to her. With one hand, she tugged on the long gold chain at her neck and pulled out a badge from inside her shirt that had to have been resting against her breasts.

"I'm Deputy Sheriff Hal Haverton from Yuma Town, checking on a call from the woman who lives in the house near the end of the road."

"Mrs. Blasdell. Will you watch him?" She motioned to the wounded man.

"Ycah, you got it. Do you live around here?" He was surprised as he'd never seen her before.

"Used to come here when I was a teen. How are we going to get my partner out of here and get him medical attention?" She took hold of her partner's hand, smiling at him, looking worried sick though.

"I can get reception where our vehicles are parked.

I was talking on my cell to Sheriff Dan Steinacker when we heard the gunshots fired. He would have alerted everyone within a reasonable distance to come to our location."

That's when they heard someone call out, "Police!"

"Stryker!" Hal turned to Tracey. "Will you be all right with him for a sec?" He jerked his thumb at the wounded gunman. "I'll let the troops know we're here."

"Yeah, go. We need the EMTs STAT."

Hal headed out the secret entrance and shouted, "Stryker, we're here. Agent down, GSW. One of the perps also. One gunman dead."

Suddenly, the area was crawling with law enforcement, while two men were tearing down the boards over the old saloon's entryway, freeing the two swinging doors.

With the all-clear call given to the EMTs standing by, they quickly moved in to take care of the wounded men. A policeman read the gunman his rights, while Tracey explained to an investigator all that had happened.

Fascinated, Hal and Stryker Hill, the full-time deputy at Yuma Town, watched her, the way she motioned with her hands when she described where everyone had been, the guilty parties—some informant who had turned on them, and possibly the ringleader of the wildlife trafficking group.

Hal knew Stryker was just as interested in the she-cat as he was. He smiled a little at Stryker, knowing that his friend would realize that this was one time he should have taken Mrs. Blasdell's call.

Hal explained what he'd witnessed to a couple of the officers who were helping with the search and trying to identify the men.

"We saw fingerprints on the bar," Tracey said, "but we don't know if they belonged to any of these men or if they're even viable after all of the shooting that went on."

Two of the men went to check on it.

Tracey retrieved her field pack and her partner's. But one of the policemen, who told her he was giving her police protection to the nearest hospital, offered to take the bags for her.

She let him, and Hal damn well wanted to be the one carrying her bags. What was wrong with him anyway?

She reached over and held her partner's hand as the EMTs placed him on a litter that they would have to carry him out on, and then headed through the swinging doors as another two officers held them open.

Hal and Stryker walked outside and watched her leave with the EMTs carrying the litter.

Hal wanted in the worse way to go with her, to be the one to protect her, but he was needed here for the investigation. Four police officers were providing security for her and her partner.

Search parties were already combing the cliffs, looking for signs of the two men who had escaped. She glanced back over her shoulder and said, "Thank you," to Hal and he nodded before she disappeared past the rest of the buildings and headed down the remnants of the narrow wagon trail.

Stryker slapped Hal on the back. "Hell, now that's what I call saving the damsel in distress."

"Believe me, she's certainly capable of handling a gun."

A couple of men hauled out the dead man in a body bag.

"I can see. Sure explains a lot about what happened to the man who was torn up during that last skirmish." Stryker didn't mention that he was talking about the cougar attack, but Hal knew that's what he was referring to.

"Yeah. Did Dan and Chase make it here already?" With much anticipation, Chase had been sticking close to home, never knowing when his twins might decide to come into the world.

"They're both here, organizing the search up in the cliffs. Dan said that when we were through down here, to join the search."

Tracey had long since disappeared, but Hal couldn't get his mind off the way she had single-handedly taken on four gunmen, until two disappeared, and how she'd protected her partner with her life. And was a cougar to boot.

Now *that* was the kind of woman he wanted in his life.

Chapter 2

Pacing across the hospital waiting room, Tracey waited to hear the outcome of her partner's surgery. Seeing the blood from Anton's wound after seeing Bill die, forced an icy sweat to cover her skin. She was glad she had taken the other men down, well, with the intervention of Deputy Sheriff Hal Haverton, who helped nail one of the perps.

But two of the men had escaped and that pissed her off royally.

That was one of the hazards of having time to think about all of this over and over again, when she wanted to ensure her partner was going to make it, then go after the bastards who might have killed him.

It would take ballistics a while to see if one of the men who had stayed behind or one of the men who had gotten away had fired the weapon that had wounded her partner.

A stocky, gray-haired police detective approached her. "We've questioned the man we took into custody. He says he doesn't know the man who hired him. He said he'd never worked for the man before. He'd never taken any jobs that had to do with the killing of animals. He likes animals, he says."

"Just not humans."

The detective smiled a little. "He said he'd been paid for this one small job. He didn't know you were Special Agents with FWS. He thought you were buying illegal drugs, except you were holding out on them as far as the agreed upon price was concerned. Anyway, we're still questioning him. He's being held without bail. Several warrants are out for his arrest—attempted murder and armed robbery at the top of the list—so he's not getting out anytime soon. He had no compulsion about killing you or your partner because, according to him, you were the bad guys."

"Yeah, right. Not paying up on our end of a drug deal." She shook her head. "He really doesn't know who the ringleader is?"

"Doesn't appear like it. He just needed to get rid of the two of you because you knew too much about the operation, and the guy who hired him would sell the drugs to someone else. I'll update you if I learn anything further."

"Okay, thanks." She was beginning to wonder if the ringleader had even been at the old saloon as part of the whole setup.

CALL OF THE COUGAR

She couldn't tell the detective that one of the men who had been in this shootout this time had also been at the other. How could she when the only way she knew it for sure was because she'd smelled him?

When the police officer left, she paced some more across the waiting room. She'd already talked to her boss about what went down before she arrived at the hospital, and she didn't intend to call him again until the doctor came out to speak with her. But when her cell rang, she glanced down to see that it was her boss, a tough, thirty-year-old, Special Forces officer, who was no-nonsense, and totally by the book. She suspected he'd been talking to *his* boss, and now he had some bad news for her. Like the last time he did when she was involved in a shootout of this magnitude.

"Here's the deal," Mick Sorenson said. "After you lost your last partner and now Genova was nearly killed this time and this is the second firefight you've been in this year—and damn it, it's only June—you're off the case." Before she could object, he continued, "I'm placing you on administrative leave for two weeks, pending an investigation into what went wrong. *This time.*"

She swore under her breath, knowing Mick would hear her, but she couldn't help it. She wanted to nail these bastards in the worst way.

***

As soon as Sheriff Dan Steinacker got a call from his good friend Mick Sorenson and—head of one of the

TERRY SPEAR

branches overseeing Fish and Wildlife Service Special Agents in this jurisdiction that included Yuma, Colorado and the surrounding area—Dan assumed this wasn't a social call.

"Yeah, what's going on now?" Dan suspected it had something to do with the shootouts at Anderson or maybe someone new was trafficking wildlife in his neck of the woods, and he'd have to organize his deputies to aid the Special Agents assigned to the case.

But he wasn't expecting *this* conversation at all.

"You already know something about one of my Special Agents, Anton Genova, who is at the hospital in Rocky Tower Springs currently in surgery, with around-the-clock police protection. His partner is on administrative leave following the shootout and no one has caught the two perps who got away."

"I thought the Feds were all over this. What do you need our help with?"

"I have a special favor to ask you. I…could make other arrangements, but I think this will work out best for all concerned. I need one of our buddies to serve as Special Agent Wittington's pseudo bodyguard and do whatever it takes to ensure she isn't out there on her own."

Dan couldn't have been any more surprised.

"You want…a bodyguard for the agent?" Dan knew both of his deputies would offer to serve and protect, but he suspected more was going on here than that she needed a bodyguard.

"Yeah. She's damn good at her job."

Dan could just imagine both his bachelor deputies fighting to serve as her bodyguard.

"She has great cat instincts," Mick continued. "I don't want her killed. She's special—because she's one of us and has our natural gifts. I trust you guys to watch over her. You know how it is with really dedicated agents. If I tell her to back off the case—"

"She'll go looking for trouble." Dan rubbed his chin as he considered how to handle it.

"Right. So I need you to coordinate a few things for me. Get a cabin at Chase Buchanan's resort for me if you can. I imagine it's already booked for the summer, but I think that would be the best location for her. Maybe he can work out some arrangement that will accommodate her. I know Chase has got babies on the way, but he could be there kind of watching out for Tracey. Beyond that, whenever she's not up at the resort, I need her to be occupied with other stuff—other than investigating this case. I know you're busy running the whole show there, but if Stryker or Hal could handle it, I'd be much obliged. If neither of them are up for it, and you can't provide any other backup, let me know. We're really tight on staffing with cutbacks and now with one of my investigative teams in a shambles, it's even tougher."

"Are you going to let her in on this? Don't tell me it's going to be a sham case of one of the guys dating her and then she learns he's only there to protect her."

"No. I'll tell her what I expect of her. She hasn't dated in forever. Bad divorce. So she's not going to date anyone, per se. And she's not going for a bodyguard scenario because she's highly trained herself. But if I tell her it's either that or she moves in with me—"

Dan smiled.

"No one who knows me wants to move in with me."

Not as much of a perfectionist as he was. "Okay, but just make sure she understands what's up. Or this is on your head."

Mick chuckled. "Yeah, yeah. The guys will have my head. She's a nice woman, smart, funny, and she kicks ass. The only problem I can see you having is determining who's going to win the lottery to serve as her protection."

Dan shook his head. "I'll do what I can. But if she really wants to go after this case, I assume nothing's going to stop her."

"I'll owe you."

"Yeah. You will." They ended the call and Dan phoned Chase to see what they could do about the situation with a cabin next, knowing that at the height of the season the Pinyon Pines Resort was always booked. "Hey, Chase, I've got a bit of a situation."

***

When her boss called her at the hospital, Tracey was afraid he would put her on administrative leave, per regulation, but she was raring to get back on the case before it grew too cold. Her reasoning wasn't just because her partner was shot and could be fighting for his life. Or that one of them had been involved in the shootout that killed her other partner. But these men were dangerous to anyone and they had to be stopped.

"We went by the book." Which for them meant improvising a lot because there was never any way to know where their investigations might lead. She and Anton had no way of knowing they were being led into an ambush. And she had to find the damn informant who had set them up. *Ricky*. That's all they knew about him—dark brown hair and eyes, scraggly beard, slight build, nervous—always looking over his back, and appeared to be barely eighteen. But he'd fed them the best information before. Not this time.

The boss spoke up again, as if she hadn't said anything about going by the book. The problem was they could really go out on a limb and as long as they resolved the case without any dead bodies and no injured or dead partners, the boss considered the job done correctly—and by the book—no matter how off the book it might be. "Until you have a psychologist clear you for field duty again, you can't work anything but a desk job once you return."

Grinding her teeth, she choked back a response. She knew the drill. She'd had to go through this in January when she lost her first partner. She knew Mick wouldn't find anything wrong with what had happened. It was just two cases of misinformation, and certainly not enough to get search warrants, convictions, nothing. That was their job—to investigate the allegations that these men were up to their eyeballs in wildlife trafficking. The boss knew that. *Damn it.*

"I want you to take a vacation."

She opened her mouth to speak, and then clamped her lips shut. He was telling her something. Clueing her in. He wasn't telling her to take a vacation. She didn't think. "Where should I go on vacation?" She hoped she was right.

"Genova will be in the hospital for a time. Why don't you stay in the area? Good skiing."

"It's *summer.*"

"Hiking, I meant."

"Hiking." Yeah, the boss had to be trying to give her a hint. He didn't make mistakes like that.

"There's no cougar hunting season in the Rockies in the summer. Run…wild for a bit. Enjoy yourself."

"What…part of the Rockies?" she asked slowly.

"I know of the perfect place. Cabin resort, lake view, mountains. I've got a reservation there but can't get away, and it's already paid up. The place is booked solid, so I didn't want to have to cancel and lose it. You'll find something to enjoy while you're staying there if you let your hair down a bit."

"Is it…safe there?"

"As safe as it usually is for our kind."

When she didn't agree or disagree, he let out his breath. "I was going over your file."

Because she'd lost one partner and nearly another? She knew that if she didn't agree to do this, he was going to put restrictions on her movements. Maybe even lock her up in a safe house. That would drive her batty. There was no way that she was going to hide out while some other agents caught up with the traffickers.

"You haven't taken a vacation in two years. You don't date anyone—"

"What has that got to do with—"

"You need a break. And that's an order."

"All right." She'd go along with this, for now. But if she got any leads that took her away from the resort, she was following them up. "What else?" She knew he wasn't letting her off that easy. Not when she was sure he would worry about her working on the case again.

"I've got some friends in that location. That's why I stay at the resort from time to time."

"Friends." Already she didn't like the scenario. Male friends, she suspected. And if he wanted her there, it was because—no, he couldn't be considering what she *thought* he might be considering. "Special Forces buddies of yours?"

She'd remembered him talking about his time in the military, and he'd shared a couple of stories about some of his friends in the Special Forces.

"Yeah. Chase runs the resort and he's a part-time deputy sheriff. Dan Steinacker is the sheriff, Stryker Hill, his full time deputy, and Hal Haverton—"

"Of Yuma Town? And he's a deputy sheriff also?"

"Part-time. So you know him?"

"He was at the shootout, okay? He came and helped me. So *no*, I don't know him. Unless you count my saving his ass, his returning the favor, and talking for a minute—means I know him."

"He's a good guy. I want them to watch your back while you're in the area."

"Your friends can't have agreed to this."

"We're like brothers. And you're like....well, given you're one of us and in law enforcement, you're like our sister."

She doubted Hal saw her like that, not the way he watched her when she pulled her badge out of her shirt for him to see and his eyes hadn't focused solely on her badge.

"So do we have a deal?" her boss asked.

"Let me get this straight. I stay in the cabin resort run by your service buddy who happens to also be a deputy sheriff, but you don't expect him to date me, do you? Or to serve as my bodyguard or something crazy like that?"

"No. His wife's twins are expected soon."

Tracey felt her whole body warm with chagrin for thinking her boss was trying to set her up with a married guy in the family way. "All right. And the other guys are all married?" If Hal was, she'd punch him for looking at her like he was really interested in getting to know her better.

"Single."

She was relieved—in Hal's case—to hear it. "No bodyguard and no dating."

"It's up to you, but you're on vacation, and if you suspect anyone suspicious in the area, I want you to alert one of the men."

Then she realized there was more to this than just watching her back. They would try to ensure she didn't investigate the case. As if they could stop her while they were going about their daily business.

Footfalls headed in her direction and she looked over her shoulder to see the doctor stalking toward her. "Got to go. Doctor's coming. Update you in a minute."

Then she spoke to the doctor. Anton was going to pull through. Thank God. Relief washed over her and she hadn't realized just how tense she'd been. She couldn't take losing another partner like that. Agents didn't shed tears over each other—at least that's what she told herself as tears welled up in her eyes. She thanked God again he was going to make it.

"Thank you, Doctor." When he left, she relayed the news to her boss.

"I'm sending some of our men to watch him, but the police are supposed to be providing protection around the clock," her boss said.

Tracey glanced at the two policemen waiting nearby. "Yes, they are."

"All right. As soon as he's out of the recovery room and in a room of his own, I want you to head north to Yuma Town."

"Will you have me tailed?" Her boss would, if he was worried about her safety even if she was off the case.

"You're getting a police escort—not a tail. Drive straight to the resort. Patrolman Holland will follow you there. He's there at the hospital now. Just tell him when you're leaving."

She thought about how much she wanted to slip away and see the ghost town one more time. It was directly on the route to Yuma Town. Or maybe while Chase was busy taking care of his resort, she could slip out and check Anderson out. She'd be happy to take one of the men, if he didn't say no and report her plans to her boss. Which was just what she suspected any of them would do.

***

As soon as Dan gave Hal and Stryker the word about Tracey Whittington coming to Yuma Town, Chase had scrambled to make a place for her at one of the cabins he'd closed for renovation, though both Hal and Stryker had enthusiastically offered to put her up at their own places.

Mick, her boss, had thought it would be better if she had a little more freedom than that.

For now, Hal and Stryker were having their Friday night pizza and beer party while watching a movie with Dan. Only this time they weren't watching a movie.

They'd been anxiously waiting for four days for Tracey to arrive in Yuma Town. Hal was ready to go to the city of Rocky Tower Springs and escort her here, though he understood that she wanted to be at her partner's side should he take a turn for the worse. If her partner had been a shifter, he could heal faster. But no such luck.

When Hal went to the kitchen to grab some more cold beers, he heard Stryker talking to Dan about picking her up just like Hal wanted to do. He returned to the living room and passed out the beers. Hal would have beat him to it though. "Hopefully she likes horses. As soon as the mare foals, I can show it to her. She's sure to love it."

"Hell, pull out the baby animal card," Stryker said with a smirk.

Dan laughed. "Better you two vying for a chance with the woman than me."

Hal smiled. Dan was too wrapped up in their police dispatcher to be looking for any other woman in his life. At least for now, though he denied he was dating her.

"I'm going for a puppy." Stryker yanked off another slice of pizza.

Dan shook his head. "You don't have a puppy."

Stryker smiled. "I can get one before we go on a hot date."

"Puppies are overrated, way too common. A foal is...special." Hal finished off his pizza.

"If she *likes* horses. What if she's afraid of them? Not everyone likes horses." Stryker bit into his pepperoni pizza.

"She's a cat. Maybe dogs don't appeal." Hal wasn't going to agree with Stryker, but it did worry him. What if she didn't like horses? Maybe she was afraid of them? There would go any chance at getting to know her. On the other hand, challenges were the name of the game. And he'd sure aim to convince her just how nice horses could be.

"She can't cuddle with a colt or filly on her lap." Stryker smiled. "They're really not pets. Not like dogs are."

"A puppy can get in the way and need way more attention. You'd have to potty train it," Hal said.

"Housebreak." Dan laughed.

"Yeah, housebreak it, feed it, and play with it all the time. The puppy would want all this attention right when you're getting ready to kiss the woman. Then what? Well, hell, you think that she's going to ignore the bundle of fur? No. She'll forget all about kissing you and…" Hal smiled evilly. "Yeah, Stryker, get a puppy."

Dan and Stryker laughed.

"She isn't delaying coming out here because she has a hankering for her partner, is she?" Stryker asked. "I'm not into breaking up relationships. Though, with him being human…"

Dan shook his head. "He's got an ex-wife and she arrived yesterday morning. Apparently, she might be working things out with her ex-husband, and that could get the ball rolling with Tracey leaving. Tracey's been anxious about him. Just like any of us would be worried about an injured partner. Shows she's sympathetic to his situation."

"Right." Hal finished his beer, leaned back on the couch, and stared at the blank TV screen. "I'm going to pack it in. I've got to go home and check on the mare."

The guys laughed.

Standing, Hal frowned at them. "What? I've never done this before. What if something goes wrong?"

Dan slapped him on the back and headed into the kitchen with two empty beer bottles and the pizza box. "I can just imagine what you'd be like when you have your own kids on the way."

"Yeah." Stryker finished his beer. "I thought Chase was bad the way he's so anxious about his wife and the babies."

"Either of you guys would be the same way if you were raising horses, and this was your first foal. Dan, if you hear that Tracey's on her way, give me a heads up. Will you?"

"But me first," Stryker said.

Dan just laughed.

The party was over, the earliest any of them had ever closed it down. Hal swore that it wasn't because they were getting to be old men.

Chapter 3

Dealing with her first partner's death a few months ago had been awful, but Tracey had felt better working through it. Now with her second partner in the hospital, she didn't want to sit around taking a break when she could be trying to track down the men who could have killed her and her partner.

This afternoon when she'd checked on Anton, he was sitting up, looking much better, not as pale, and he was talking again. His ex-wife, Shirley, truly seemed to want to work things out between them, whether he continued to serve on this job or ended up in another. Tracey thought his wife's change of heart was another reason that Anton was looking so much better. She liked the wife and their adorable daughter, so she hoped it would work out between them. Which meant it was time for Tracey to get on her way.

It would still be early when she left for Yuma

Town. The ghost town of Anderson was right on her way. She had the greatest urge to stop there and walk through the town—to try to understand why the traffickers had been there twice and had shootouts with her both times. She knew she couldn't ditch her police escort without getting into hot water with her boss though.

Before she left the hospital, she said to the patrolman who would follow her to Yuma Town, "I want to stop off at Anderson to just—walk through it."

His dark eyes narrowed a little, Patrolman Howard Holland said, "You know your boss will want me to report this."

"Haven't you ever been in a situation before where you had to return to the scene of the crime to try and figure out the significance of it?"

"Yeah, I have, actually." Howard looked around as if the waiting room walls had ears. "Okay, look. You know what your boss said. Sorry about that. I'd feel the same if I was in your shoes, but my boss is in agreement with your boss. It's time for you to go on vacation. I'm escorting you to Yuma Town and after that?" He shrugged. "It's up to you as to what you want to do."

"Just for a few minutes? It's miles from Yuma Town, but we'll pass up the wagon trail along the way there."

"Sorry, no can do. Orders were specific. You need to step away from the case. I've been there, done that,"

Howard said. "Actually, I was the one who got shot on a case similar to this, different perps, but I was raring to take down the bastard who'd nearly killed me. I needed the time to recover, both physically and emotionally. You lost your other partner. And now this. You need the break."

She thought he was saying one thing, but meaning something else. That he was watching what he said because the police who were providing security for her partner might be listening in on their conversation, and he didn't want to get into trouble with his own boss.

"Okay, so if I just happen to take a little detour—"

She thought he was fighting a smile a little as he shook his head. "Come on. Let's drop by your hotel and grab your bags."

She wasn't sure if he would stop her or not. But she was going to give it a try. After saying goodbye to Anton and his ex-wife in his hospital room, Tracey returned to her hotel and picked up her bags, then headed out to Yuma Town.

When she was close to the old wagon trail that turned off to Anderson, she flashed her left turn signal. She thought if Howard was opposed to her going to Anderson, he would flash his police lights to let her know that he wasn't going to allow it. And she really expected him to do so. To her surprise and delight, he followed her up the rutted, dusty trail. But then, she felt a sudden chill race down her spine—a fitful apprehension suddenly filling her. If she hadn't managed to get herself killed the last two times she was here, why not try it again? Yet part of her said that the men would not be here again. The odds were totally in her favor.

Like she thought was the case the last two times she came here.

Howard followed her to the spot where they had to park and then walk. When she got out, he was calling someone, and she assumed it was her boss or his. Maybe just letting everyone know they could be headed into danger.

"What do you think you'll find?" Howard asked, as he walked with her up the trail, side by side.

"Nothing really. But I just have to see the place. See if there's anything I missed the other two times. Others combed the place for clues, but they hadn't been here or seen what I saw when I was here before. Like, for instance, I hadn't thought of it at the time, but those men came out of a storeroom at the saloon. They had to have had another way in since they had only left recent footsteps from the storeroom to the bar. Not that it means anything. And I'm sure that investigators would have discovered this, but I just wanted to see it for myself."

"Sounds reasonable."

"So who did you call?"

"My boss. Who will inform your boss and—"

Tracey's phone buzzed in her pocket. She ignored it. At least it was on vibrate, and Howard didn't hear it.

But when she didn't answer her phone, Howard got a call.

He answered it and glanced at her and smiled a little. He handed her his phone. "Your boss wants to talk to you."

She grimaced and took the phone. "Yes?"

"Don't you ignore my calls. I know your phone was vibrating in your pocket. What the hell are you doing going back to Anderson? The only way I want you up there is to go with a military escort."

"What would the odds be that I would run into these men yet again?" And if she did, she was killing them. Every last one of them.

"In your case—good."

She smiled a little at that, despite not wanting to agree that it was kind of true.

"You have one hour up there."

"But…"

"One hour, Special Agent Whittington."

He only used her title and last name when he was pulling the boss card on her.

"But—"

"Let me talk with the patrolman."

She sighed and handed the phone to him.

Howard smiled a little at her and stuck the phone in his pouch. Her mouth gaped for a second.

"What?" he asked, clearly not getting what surprised her.

"My boss wanted to talk to you. You just hung up

on him."

Howard's phone rang and he chuckled, pulling out his phone again. "Yes, sir." He glanced at Tracey and nodded. "Yes, sir. One hour. Or you send in the troops. Got it."

When he ended the call, Tracey frowned at him. "We can't get anything done in one hour."

"I've heard you're a bit of a wild card. I've gone along this far, but this is it. One hour and we're back on the road headed for Yuma Town."

She nodded, grateful she was allowed this much time, truly. She hoped maybe her boss would be so busy, he'd forget the time. Knowing Mick, he'd set an alarm.

Maybe her police escort would forget the time. Even better? The patrolman wouldn't get reception in town so neither her boss, nor his, could remind him of the hour.

They finally reached the first building in the town. She was about ready to begin inspecting the buildings all over again when movement on the cliffs caught her eye. She turned and fully focused on the rocky boulders. A cougar was standing on a boulder up near one of the decrepit miner's shacks, his tan coloration nearly blending in with the rocks.

Howard glanced in the direction she was looking and pulled out his gun.

"No," she said, laying her hand over his gun, pointing it toward the dirt ground.

"That could be the cougar that killed one of the gunmen. The same man who stabbed you. You were just damn lucky the cougar didn't come after you too, once you were bleeding."

"The cougar saved my life."

"You were just lucky." Despite his objection, Howard holstered his gun.

Was the big cat a shifter? Or a real cougar?

Howard was right if it was a cougar; he could be dangerous.

The cat sat down on the boulder and observed her. She was certain he was a shifter. An all cougar would most likely leave. If it was one of the shifters, was he looking for more clues like she was? She hoped so.

After not finding anything new at any of the closer buildings, she headed for the saloon and saw that the storage room did have a door that led to it from the outside.

She examined it. "No fingerprints. Nothing," she said, more to herself than to Howard.

She noted Howard glancing at his watch when she headed for one of the churches. No access anywhere there. She moved to one of the gambling halls and again found no entrance that she could see.

Twice more, she saw Howard look at his watch. But she was working really hard to locate any evidence they had missed the first time around. She knew it was getting later because the sun was beginning to sink in the sky. And the longer they were there, the more often

Howard checked his watch.

Then they heard two men coming into town, and both she and Howard ducked for cover behind one of the gambling halls.

"Special Agent Whittington? Patrolman Holland?" one of the men shouted.

"I know him," Howard said to her and shouted out to the newcomers, "Here! We're coming."

Relieved, she let out her breath.

Two male police officers joined them, the blond saying, "Hell, Holland, the boss was on our case, concerned you were in the middle of a firefight alongside the Special Agent, who has a reputation for being involved in shootouts."

Howard introduced them, and the darker haired man smiled at her. "I've heard you're kind of a maverick. But rough on partners."

She didn't want to tell him why her partners had such trouble—the one who had too much to drink, or the other who was distraught about his marital problems.

She glanced up at the rocks and saw a flash of the cougar's tail as he disappeared behind the boulders.

"Boss said you had an hour up here." The blond-haired Sanderson glanced at his watch as if emphasizing the time. "It's been four hours. If we don't get down that trail in twenty minutes and report back, a whole garrison of patrolmen are going to be here."

She thought the officer was exaggerating, but then

again, maybe not.

Four hours. And in all that time, when she'd chanced to observe the cliffs, the cougar had moved around, but he hadn't left. She wondered then if it had been Hal Haverton and he had decided to hang around to give her added protection.

She was dying to know. Cat's curiosity. She couldn't do anything about it while she'd been with the patrolman though.

When they got to their vehicles, she gave her boss a call.

"Well, did you find anything?"

"Some peace of mind," she said. The other lawmen were watching her, and she suspected they understood. Only she hadn't really found anything to give her any peace of mind. She needed to bring the men to justice for that to happen.

"You left me no choice but to send some other officers to check on you."

"I understand. I'm on my way to Yuma Town now."

"We'll catch these guys. You don't need to be the only one doing the job."

"Right."

"Stay there at the resort and behave yourself."

"Yes, sir."

Then they ended the call and she smiled at the officers who were probably wondering if her boss had chewed her out.

"Thanks, for coming to check on us," she said to the men.

"We'll all follow you to your destination," Sanderson said.

Not that she was making any other detours.

When she arrived at the rustic resort, she thanked the officers and then they were on their way. She didn't expect the owner and his wife—Chase and Shannon Buchanan—to both greet her.

"You know why I'm here, don't you?" She didn't want either his wife or him to be hurt if she ended up being a potential target.

"Yeah, we're here to watch your back. Or…I am," Chase said, rubbing his wife's back.

And she realized immediately that they were cougars.

Very pregnant, Shannon was a dark-haired beauty, and looked like she was due any day now. All smiles, she was eager to meet Tracey and shook her hand. "Come inside and have some cake and milk or tea—before you settle into your own cabin."

"It's so late now. I'll just unpack what I need tonight and—"

"No, no. You have to have some cake. I can't sleep. I know I need to, but the babies are keeping me awake. I'm so thrilled to see another one of our kind visit, well, be our guest. Everyone else staying here is human. So anytime you want to drop in and talk, just do," Shannon said as she joined them inside.

Shifters were used to being able to keep secrets and since Tracey was off the clock—on administrative leave—and wasn't undercover at the moment, she wasn't about to keep her job a secret. Not when it was important for her to ensure the Buchanans knew the kind of trouble she might be in or cause if she remained here.

"Okay, you know I'm a Special Agent with the Fish and Wildlife Service and we were investigating the town of Anderson when my partner and I came under fire a few days ago, and that I'm, well… on—"

"Administrative leave," Chase said. His hair a light brown, he had penetrating dark eyes, and a nice smile.

But she sensed his concern also and she knew if she had trouble he would be there in a heartbeat to help her out if she needed him to.

"My…boss must have told you when he gave up his reservations so I could stay here." She guessed, anyway. She was glad Mick had told the couple what they could be getting into.

Shannon smiled brightly. "Personally, I hadn't had real good luck with police officers until I hooked up with Deputy Sheriff Chase Buchanan. Well, after he shot me with a tranquilizer dart, and we had a few more ordeals to get through—I knew then some law enforcement officers were all right."

Tracey snapped her mouth closed, glanced at Chase, and then found her tongue. "You tranquilized your wife?"

Chase smiled a little. "Yeah. Long story. Certainly a different way to meet."

Dying to hear what had happened, Tracey smiled. "Okay, so how long have you known my boss?"

"I was Special Forces buddies with Mick. We didn't know each other before the service, but when he ran into me during a mission, and realized I was just like him, we buddied up. So yeah, he asked me to watch your back. He admires you greatly and doesn't want anything bad to happen to you." Then Chase lifted the glass dome sitting over a double chocolate cake on a platter, set it aside, and began slicing pieces for everyone.

"Like you, I'm kind of on administrative leave from the department because the babies are due in a week or so. So I'll be here on-call at any time if you need me for anything."

"Thanks. I'm sure I'll be just fine."

They sat down to eat the cake and drink their milk.

"At least, I really don't expect to need anyone's help. But also, congratulations." Tracey loved babies, but the way she was headed, there would be none in her future anytime soon. She had to find a man who could be a reliable father for that to happen. "Do you know how many you're having?"

"Twins." Shannon smiled, then sipped from her glass of milk.

"That's wonderful. You'll certainly have your work cut out for you." Tracey's mom had often talked about how much of a handful she and her sister had been when they were little. She turned to Chase. "Are you sure that you're not going to have any trouble with me being here?"

"If we do, between you and me, I'm certain we can take care of it. Your boss said you're one of the best."

She appreciated that he included her for being able to deal with trouble should it arise and not as someone who was incapable of helping herself. But then she wondered if her boss had mentioned she'd lost her first partner.

She enjoyed the delicious double chocolate cake, licking every speck of icing off her fork which brought a smile to Shannon's face, and Tracey felt her own cheeks heat a bit with embarrassment at being caught. But it was good! "Thanks for the cake. It was really delicious. I'll get out of your hair and go unpack now though. I'm beat and you must be too."

"If you need anything, just ask," Shannon said. "Our Yuma Town General Store has about anything you might need in town. Chase picked up a few non-perishable items your boss said you'd like. The store opens tomorrow at ten."

Tracey stared at her in surprise. She wondered exactly what her boss thought she'd like to eat. Though she appreciated his doing so since she'd arrived so late.

"Uhm, thanks."

"The whole place is a cougar haven. If a couple of wildlife traffickers come to town, someone will surely notice," Chase said.

No wonder her boss wanted her to stay at the resort. For the first time since he'd told her he wanted her to stay here, she truly felt comfortable about doing so.

"Oh, and...you know that Mick wants one of our other deputies to watch out for you," Chase said.

"Yeah, but I really don't think it's necessary." Then she had a brilliant idea. She shrugged. "Then again, both can, if they feel they have to." She smiled brightly. If both did, that meant they'd take turns and neither man would get the idea he was dating her.

Chase laughed. "Good show then. Can I ride with you to your cabin? I was having it renovated and—"

She frowned. "I thought my boss had already rented it."

"Yeah, like when he needed you to stay here."

She groaned. "I wish he hadn't put you both out so. I could have found somewhere else to stopover for a bit."

"The only other place you could have stayed was Stryker's duplex or Hal's ranch."

"Wouldn't work if both of the men are going to safeguard me."

"Right, well, you'll be staying at the last cabin in the string of them, farthest away from the main one."

"I'll be fine," she said. "I have a spare Glock."

Chase nodded.

"He'll go with you," Shannon said. "If he didn't, I'd

never get any sleep." She rubbed her belly and yawned.

"I'd feel the same as my mate."

"All right then." Tracey said goodnight to Shannon, then she and Chase climbed into her Hummer. "You know none of this is really necessary."

"If anything happened to you while I'm supposed to be watching out for you, believe me, it would be necessary."

"You know about both my partners, don't you?"

"Yeah. Mick filled me in. We're all here to watch out for you. If you get any feeling that something's not right, even if it's just a hunch, don't hesitate to call me. It won't be any trouble." He pointed to the last cabin beyond a stand of pine trees and high shrubs. "That's it straight ahead."

When she pulled up to the log cabin and parked, she smiled to see the lights inside were all on. She appreciated the Buchanans' thoughtfulness. Chase helped carry her bags inside and then they both checked the place out.

"All clear," she said.

"Same here," he said, coming out of another bedroom. He gave her a list of phone numbers. "We're really glad you're here. Shannon is thrilled and hopes you will visit her often. She's kind of been housebound lately and it's driving her crazy."

"Sure thing. I'd love to. Thanks for everything." She gave him her phone number.

"You're welcome. Don't hesitate to call if you need

anything."

When Chase left, she locked up and then checked the cupboards to see what Mick had thought she needed.

A bottle of cabernet, seven packages containing six chocolate bars apiece, and three bags of potato chips. She laughed. In the freezer, three packages of extra thick, T-bone steaks, ribs, chicken drumsticks, and a pork roast. Not one vegetable anywhere.

She didn't care what time it was, she called her boss. Chase had probably phoned him as soon as she drove into the resort and her boss was probably still awake anyway.

"Who did you buy all these groceries for?" she asked.

"I figured you'd like what I like. Don't tell me you're a cougar that is a vegetarian," Mick said, sounding relieved that she was there.

"I am human too, and I need my vegetables. Thanks, though. I thought you said you had already rented the place."

"I have a standing invitation. Get your rest, Agent. And take it easy."

Yeah, right. "Night. Talk later."

"Night. No more thinking about the case."

No way could she shut down her mind about that whole situation and forget it. After saying good bye, she put her phone away and unpacked her bags.

Now, all she had to do was conduct some

investigative work on her own and then, she'd track down the ringleader and ensure he received a lengthy jail term—though terminating him sounded like a whole lot better plan.

***

When Hal's phone rang, he stared at it for a minute before he realized Chase was calling him. What time was it? Three in the morning?

"What's up? Is Shannon in labor?" Hal was already getting out of bed in a hurry.

Chase said, "No." And chuckled. "Just wanted to give you a heads up like you asked me to. Tracey arrived a little while ago. She's settled in her cabin now."

"Do you need me to watch her place?"

"No. She's fine. She's got her Glock handy. Don't go sneaking around the place and getting yourself shot. I may need you when Shannon goes into labor."

Hal settled back down on his bed. "Have you got her number?"

"Yeah, here it is and don't call her tonight. She has probably already gone to bed."

"All right. Anything else?"

"She doesn't have any breakfast fixings. Maybe in the morning, you can ask her out."

"What about Stryker? Did you call him?"

"I'm calling Dan next. He'll call Stryker."

"All right."

"She said that you could both guard her."

"What?"

"That's what she said. I suspect she wants you both to know that she's not dating anyone. Which means you'll have to work a lot harder at it."

Hal smiled. "I'm on it."

Chase laughed. "She might just be worth it."

After their first encounter, Hal was certain she would be. He couldn't believe she had gone back to the town of Anderson when he was certain her boss had said she was through with the case. He wondered if she realized the cougar up on the cliffs was a shifter and not a plain old cougar. He suspected she did when she kept the patrolman guarding her from shooting him. At least he was glad to see she had some protection. But if Hal had any notion of leaving the area once she arrived, he'd thrown that idea out. *He* had been providing a big cat's backup too.

In the background, he heard Shannon say, "Come to bed, Chase. I think I'm finally ready to go to sleep."

Hal smiled. He was wide awake. As soon as he finished talking to Chase, he called Tracey's number.

***

With the lightweight, forest green, embroidered coverlet at her waist, Tracey rested in the bed in the log cabin, the sounds of an owl screeching and crickets chirping were soothing to her soul. She loved the sounds of nature, much preferred to running around in the city when her duty took her there.

She was still thinking about the case, wishing she

could have found some real leads to run down, disappointed she hadn't found anything further in Anderson. But she suspected she had rushed over things a little, when she wouldn't have had she been totally free to investigate the area, and not worried her boss would send reinforcements to make her leave.

What she needed to do was... She smiled. She needed to run as a cougar. That's what she needed to do. Early, before dawn, she would stretch her legs as a cougar. Wasn't that what the boss said? Time to kick back and relax? She hadn't had a chance to run in...well, way too long.

Her phone rang and she wanted to ignore it, but she couldn't. What if someone was calling about Anton?

She pulled her phone off the bedside table and looked at it. *Hal Haverton*. She smiled. Chase must have just informed him she was here. She liked a man who was eager to see her, even if she wasn't about to date anyone.

"I'm all tucked in and have my Glock right next to the bed, handy-like. No need to come over and protect me."

He didn't answer and for a second, she hoped she hadn't read the caller ID wrong.

"Well, hell, then what about breakfast?"

She chuckled. She liked a man with a sense of humor. "What did you have in mind?"

More silence. She smiled, wishing she could read minds and know just what he was thinking.

"My place and I can whip up a mean batch of hash browns, omelets your way, mimosas, bacon, ham, or anything else your heart desires."

"Anything?"

"Absolutely."

"And I don't have to clean up afterward?"

"Got a maid to do that."

"A maid."

"Yeah, believe me, you wouldn't want to see what the place looked like before I got a maid."

She laughed. "Okay. Eight, all right?"

"I'll pick you up."

"I could just drive over there."

"No way. You might get lost and I'm your bodyguard. I'll pick you up at eight."

Her phone beeped, letting her know she had another call. "Okay, got another call. Got to go."

"We can have lunch too," he quickly added.

"Let's have breakfast first and see where it goes from there. All right?"

He sighed deeply. "Yeah, okay." But he didn't sound like he was okay with it. He probably suspected her next caller was his competition, Deputy Sheriff Stryker Hill.

"See you in the morning."

"I'll be there."

They ended the call and she waited for the other caller to try again. When he did, she said, "I'm all tucked in and have my Glock right next to the bed, handy-like. No need to come over and protect me."

Silence.

She laughed. This might be kind of fun after all.

"Uh, okay, so I don't need to grab mine and head on over there then." He chuckled. "I'm Stryker Hill and I wondered if you might like to have breakfast with me. Chase said you didn't have a chance to get any breakfast food."

Now Chase was trying to set them both up with her? "Hal beat you to it. Sorry."

"Hell, I thought you hadn't answered at first because you were asleep."

"So you tried again?"

"Just in case you weren't asleep."

She laughed.

"How about lunch, and don't tell me that Hal already booked you in solid for the next several days."

"He tried. How about dinner? Just in case I can't get away any earlier? Where and when?"

"I'll pick you up. Take you to anywhere you'd love to go for dinner."

"You don't cook?"

Stryker didn't say anything for a moment, then said, "Ah hell, is Hal telling you about what a great cook he is? Next, he'll be showing you the new foal. Well, when it's born. What do you think about puppies?"

She laughed. "Do you have a puppy?"

He paused. "Would it make a difference?"

"No."

"Okay, well, if you change your mind, let me know. I'll pick you up at five."

"See you then. Night."

"Good night, Tracey."

She set her phone on the bedside table and closed her eyes. Now this was going to be interesting.

She suspected her run would be uneventful and she'd return way before she needed to shift, wash up, and dress for her first date of the day.

At least—that was the plan.

Chapter 4

Tracey hadn't realized just how much she needed to run until she was wearing her cougar coat, exploring her surroundings, running free and wild. She always felt a runner's high when she stretched her legs as a cougar.

Darkness claimed the forest when she left the cabin and a cold breeze stirred the aspen's leaves, making them dance around on the branches. A western screech owl sat inside a hole in a tree way up above, his eyes closed, his feathers a pretty gray color. But then he must have smelled her. He opened his amber eyes and twisted his head around to watch her, a predator of the night every bit as much as her cougar kind were. He must have been the one making the loud screeching noise last night.

She moved through the mountain mahogany, junipers, pinyon, and ponderosa pines, and, avoided getting close to the lake where tents were standing, and camping trailers beyond that.

She was certain no one would observe her in the dark, and that no one would be running around in the woods or mountains at this hour. The only problem she'd have was if she didn't return before dawn when hikers were about and someone spotted her.

She watched for any sign of either big predators like bears or wolves, but she hadn't smelled any trace of them. Just cougars. She wondered then if the shifters in the area had been leaving their scent trail all over, clawing trees, marking their boundaries with piles of dirt and twigs, or scrapes, left to warn other cougars that this territory was taken, and to keep other predators away. Wolf packs weren't intimidated by a lone cougar or bear. But a cougar could handle a lone wolf. A pack of cougars? Evened up the odds a bit against a pack of wolves. Though that would sure take them by surprise since cougars didn't run in packs.

Wolves and bears would probably leave a pack of cougars alone. She leapt onto the rocks, and landed nearly on top of a rattlesnake coiled up in the groove of one of them. The temperature proved too cold for him to react, but even so, her heart was pumping hard from the bit of a scare she'd gotten. She leapt away from him in a heartbeat, just in case he was primed to bite, and landed on the rock ledge above him. The trees thinned, then disappeared completely as she climbed above the timberline. She jumped to the next boulder and continued on up until she reached the peak and saw a faint glimmer of light on the horizon.

Crap!

She must have been so wrapped up in the scents and sounds that she had misjudged how far she had traveled and the lateness of the hour. Though for a minute, she enjoyed the beauty of the sunrise. She'd never get back to the cabin before the sun fully rose, though.

She headed down the rocky escarpment in a hurry, her balance, strong leg muscles, and large paw pads allowing her to be extremely adept at climbing. When she reached the ground, she sprinted through the trees. Though cougars could run at a top speed between 40 to 50 mph, they were much better able to accomplish powerful sprints. She knew she couldn't race all the way back and reach the cabin before the summer campers would be up and about.

Not that it would mean she would run across any, but mentally, she liked to be prepared. Luckily, no hunting was allowed right now. Though someone still could shoot her and say he feared for his life. Great story to tell to all his buddies, at the very least.

She still had plenty of time to reach the cabin, shift, shower, and dress well before Hal arrived to treat her to breakfast. Her stomach rumbling, she was really getting hungry.

Before she got very far, she saw movement to her right. Big movement and it was headed straight for her. Nothing but bad news would come after her. She turned to see three gray wolves racing in her direction ready for the kill.

Her heart thumping against her ribs, she did the only thing she could safely do as a cougar. She jumped into a pinyon pine tree, scrambling to get higher. She turned and looked down at the wolves leaping at the tree trunk, growling, and snapping their wicked canines at her. Thank God wolves couldn't climb trees. One of them let out a howl, calling for pack reinforcements to help them eradicate the cougar in their territory. Even up in the rocks, she realized she hadn't smelled any sign of cougars. She must have gone beyond their marked territory.

Flattening her ears, she snarled and hissed back at the wolves, wrinkling her nose as she bared her own, very wicked canines. Her posturing didn't scare them in the least. But the effort made her feel better. She climbed higher and laid down on a branch, settling in to wait them out. She might as well rest for the time being since she had no other option. Two more wolves ran through the underbrush and joined the pack. *Damn it.*

They lifted their heads and looked up at her, sniffing the air, verifying she was their enemy. Their amber eyes were beautiful. They were beautiful. But while she was in her cougar coat, they were deadly adversaries. Even if she shifted, most likely they'd still think she was a cougar because of the way she smelled.

No way in hell was she coming down from the tree.

She still had plenty of time to reach the cabin if the

wolves got bored or sighted some other prey in the meantime. But as the day dawned and the air warmed a bit, she was afraid that extra time she was going to have to get ready for her breakfast date with Hal was dwindling by the minute.

The wolves moved around at the base of the tree, sniffing the ground, not leaving. Every once in a while, one would look up to see if she was still there. And then every member of the pack would raise their heads as if mimicking the one wolf's actions.

She looked off in the direction of the cabin, wondering what would happen when Hal came to pick her up to take her to breakfast and she wasn't there.

She snarled in annoyance at herself and the wolves. She couldn't believe she could live through firefights with the bad guys and then be treed by a pack of gray wolves.

***

After calling Tracey to make sure she was up and about, Hal grew worried when the call went straight to voice mail. Not that there had to be anything wrong. She could be in the shower. Yet, given that Mick wanted her watched, Hal did worry about the guys who had gotten away at the scene of the gunfight tracking her down, and that she might be off investigating the trafficking ring—on her own.

Though it was a little early, he called Chase to share his concerns and headed on over to the resort.

"I'm supposed to be picking up Tracey and taking

her to my place for breakfast, but she's not answering her cell. I'm on my way over there now, but do you mind dropping by her cabin and letting me know that she's all right? It'll take me a while to get there from my ranch."

"Yeah, sure thing. I'm headed out the door right this minute. Hang on the line."

Hal listened as Chase said, "Shannon, I'm going to check on Tracey. Be back in a minute."

"Is everything all right?" Shannon asked.

"I'm sure she's just busy and not answering her phone."

"Okay."

The door opened and closed, then Hal heard Chase's footfalls crunching on gravel as he trucked it toward the furthest cabin out. "When were you supposed to pick her up?"

"In about forty-five minutes."

"She could be in the shower," Chase warned.

"Yeah, but I've been trying to reach her for an hour."

"Okay, buddy. No problem. Always better to be safe than sorry in this business."

"Agreed." Still, no matter how much Hal was trying not to worry about Tracey, he was concerned.

"I'm at her cabin. Her Hummer's here." Chase knocked on the door.

If her Hummer was there, that had to be good news, in a way. She hadn't taken off. Unless something else had gone down.

When there was no answer at the door, Hal worried even more.

Chase called out, "Tracey? Are you in there? It's just me, Chase Buchanan."

Hal floored the gas pedal, driving way over the speed limit, sure something was wrong. He didn't like that Tracey wasn't answering the door either. He assumed, considering the kind of job she did, she was punctual and on top of things. She would be ready to go ahead of time.

"I'm unlocking the door," Chase told him.

The door creaked open and Chase called out, "Tracey? Are you here? Hal called and he was just worried about you."

No response.

"Chase, I'm ten minutes from there," Hal said.

"She's gone. Her night clothes are sitting on the floor beside the door. Her phone is on the coffee table. It looks like she shifted. I'm taking a walk around the place to see if I smell her scent leading away from the cabin."

"She wouldn't have gotten lost," Hal said. Their instinct was too great. Though he'd had a dog once—mangy old, good-natured mutt—that took off after a rabbit, he guessed, and got lost. What kind of a dog would get so lost that he couldn't find his way back home?

"She's taken off through the woods."

"I'm on your road. I'll be there in a couple of minutes. Wait for me."

"I'm headed back to my place. I'll let Shannon know we're going for a run in our cougar coats, and I'll tell Dan we're going on a search, possible rescue, and to get someone up here for Shannon, in case she goes into labor."

"Ah hell, Chase. You need to stay with Shannon. Stryker or Dan can follow. You need to be with your wife."

"Two of us should be going in case Tracey's in trouble," Chase said, then the door squeaked open.

"I'm not waiting. Someone can follow me."

"All right."

Hal drove past Chase's cabin and headed for Tracey's. When he reached it, he pulled to a stop behind her silvery-blue Hummer, and jumped out. Thankfully, each of the cabins was surrounded by trees, giving them full privacy, so shifting out of doors was no problem. He began yanking off his clothes on her back deck, then called Chase back. "Getting ready to shift. Any last words?"

"Dan and Stryker are both on their way. They said to wait."

Hal smiled a little. They had to say so, but they knew he wouldn't. "Okay, out here."

The day being slow to warm up, he called on the shift, his body heating in the cool breeze, his muscles warming with the change. He welcomed the flexibility in his limbs, the fur covering his skin, and his ability to move swiftly and without a lot of detection.

His tail whipping behind him, Hal began searching for her scent and took off at a sprint.

***

Despite being in danger because at some point she'd have to leave the tree, Tracey worried more about Hal. She was certain he'd come in search of her eventually. Hell, he'd alert Chase and then she worried about him too. She feared if anyone came in their cougar coats they could be attacked if they were upwind of the wolves, didn't smell them in time, and the wolves smelled them first.

Even though she knew it was fruitless to feel this way, she hated the humiliation of being treed by a pack of wolves. Yes, they were deadly to her kind. And no, she didn't feel any animosity toward them. They were doing what nature dictated—keeping predators that had the same dinner menu as her kind out of their territory—if she'd been strictly cougar.

The problem was that even with two cougars, unless Hal had brought back-up, she and he would still be at a decided disadvantage against a pack of five wolves.

She stared down at the wolves. They had all laid down to rest—underneath the pinyon pine. Two had their heads down, resting or sleeping, while two were on guard duty, watching and listening. The other was lying on his side, totally sacked out while the others guarded him.

She knew if she even moved an inch, the sleeping or resting wolves' heads would snap up and take notice.

She watched as the day grew later and could imagine Hal coming for her and wished he wouldn't risk his own neck. But she was certain she couldn't leave here on her own if the wolves didn't vacate the area.

***

The farther Hal got from the resort, the more he worried Tracey was in trouble or he would have encountered her returning to her cabin. He was certain she wouldn't have forgotten their date. And even more sure that she wasn't attempting to avoid seeing him. He was fairly certain the guys she was after hadn't been in the vicinity and she was tracking them.

Which meant she was in trouble. He knew he shouldn't second guess what had happened, but he couldn't help it. If she'd been shot, or she'd somehow fallen and injured herself, well, he couldn't keep thinking of what-ifs.

She'd been all over the place, happily exploring, so up to this point, she'd been fine. But the longer he looked for her, the more worried he got. She didn't know the area, or where their shifters had marked the territory to warn other predators away.

Then he'd gone beyond their marked territory and smelled a wolves' scent trail. Their paws left a scent as well. He smelled...four, no five. A brand new trail.

Damn it. She'd continued on her way, so the wolves must have arrived after she had passed through the area. She probably climbed to the top of the rocks in the distance to see the view like he would have done, had he not known any better.

He knew he had to wait for backup. But he couldn't force himself to wait. What if she was injured or dying? What if the pack had moved off?

But the wind was blowing the wrong way. Well, hell, even now, the wolves could be smelling *his* scent.

Then he heard them. All of them like a stampede of horses running toward him. Ready to attack. Crap!

He leapt into the branches of a pinyon pine just in the nick of time as the wolves reached the base of the tree and snarled and growled at him, jaws snapping, teeth bared, though his were a lot more wicked than theirs. And his claws a lot more deadly. Still, against five, he'd never stand a chance.

Suddenly, Tracey called out. "Who's there?"

He shifted. Bare assed, he sat on the rough pine bark, worried still about Tracey, but she didn't sound as though she was in pain, and he was grateful for that. "Your breakfast chef."

"Oh, God, Hal. Are…are you okay?"

"Yeah, what about you?" He tried to envision her sitting naked in a tree, which took his mind off the fact that he was also, and the wolves were circling, so to speak.

"I'm fine. I'm so sorry that I've gotten you into this

mess."

"Well, I'd say we have a good start. First in a gun battle, and now with a pack of wolves on our tail, I'd say we have what it takes to make a winning team."

She started laughing.

He smiled, glad she still had a sense of humor, despite the circumstances. "You're really okay?"

"Yeah. I'm a fast climber. So, what are we going to do?" she asked.

"Dan and Stryker are bound to be coming any time soon."

"And then we'll *all* be in trees."

He laughed. "I'm sure they'll be coming with rifles and medical supplies, just in case there's a medical emergency."

"As humans."

"Yeah. If you were injured, I would have to carry you out of here naked. So I'm sure they're not going to shift before they search for us."

"Well, that's good news. What time do you think it is now?"

"I'd say, depending on how long it takes for everyone to get here and for us to head back, it will be time for brunch."

"Great. Well, good thing that I told Stryker I'd have supper with him and not lunch."

Hal took a deep breath and let it out. He knew he should have tried harder to talk her into having lunch, and then gone for broke and asked about the evening meal with him too. "How about we go out for drinks after that? A movie?"

She laughed. "Maybe tomorrow."

He really didn't want to think of what would happen if she decided to stay the night with Stryker. "Okay, supper, drinks, and a movie tomorrow. And I'll run with you as a cougar if you'd like and be your tour guide. No doing this on your own again."

"All right by me. I never wanted anyone to get into trouble like this on my account."

"No problem. It makes for the start of a really different kind of date."

She chuckled.

They lapsed into silence for a while and then she said, "Maybe I should get down and warn the men you're in a tree."

"No. It's way too dangerous for you. If the wolves realize you're on the ground, they could rip you to shreds."

"What if the guys don't come?"

He had worried about that. But he suspected they would, since they'd be concerned about the both of them when they didn't return to the cabin. "They will. They had to grab their gear. I was already headed to your location when I couldn't get hold of you."

"I'm sorry."

He smiled, thinking again of just what she'd look like in the tree. *Naked*. "Well, it wasn't quite what I had in mind to do before breakfast, but it sure will make for some interesting conversation when I get around to making it."

"What about the mare and her foal?"

"I've got someone there watching her. She'll be okay." At this point he was more worried about Dan and Stryker.

"I guess the wolves are still there, even though you're no longer a cougar."

"Yeah. They smell cougar in this tree and they aren't budging. Wait."

Two of the wolves stood, their ears twitching back and forth. Their noses wrinkling as they smelled the air.

"Someone's coming," Hal said. "Don't shift back just yet." He shouted, "Hey, is that you, Dan? Stryker?"

"Yeah, we're coming. What's going on?"

"Pack of five wolves are straight ahead of you."

"Ah, hell, Hal, don't tell me they've treed you." Stryker was enjoying this a little too much. "Where's Tracey? Have you seen her?"

"She's in another tree nearby."

"Over here." She sounded totally resigned.

The wolves wouldn't attack the men and neither Dan nor Stryker would shoot them, but they fired off a couple of rounds to send them on their way.

"Are they clearing out?" Dan asked.

"Yeah, but I think I'll sit up here until you get a little closer in case they come back."

"Everyone all right?" Dan wasn't just asking about everyone's health. He was making enough noise to keep the wolves away.

"Yeah," Hal said.

When Tracey didn't respond, he assumed she'd shifted back into her cougar form.

"I'm changing back before you get here." Hal shifted, leapt from the tree, and ran to the location where Tracey had to be.

Sitting high in the pinyon tree as a cougar, she was a pretty golden color. Her green eyes widened a little when she saw him, and she jumped down from her perch.

He rubbed his body against hers in a way of greeting, to let her know he was glad she was safe. He brushed his whiskers against hers, making her smile a little. When she did, she showed off a gorgeous set of cougar teeth. Then they ran off to meet up with Dan and Stryker.

"Hopefully, we won't run into anyone who isn't a shifter," Dan said as Hal and Tracey joined the men. "It's going to look highly suspect if I have to tell anyone the two of you cougars are under arrest, and I'm hauling you to jail."

Hal smiled.

Stryker was checking Tracey out, in part because they always learned what each of their own kind looked like in their cougar coat in case they chanced to run into them in the wilderness and had to know if it was one of them and not a cougar that was all wild cat.

But in part, Hal suspected it was because Stryker

was just as interested in the single she-cat as he was.

Dan was on his cell right away telling Chase that he and Stryker had found Tracey and Hal. He smiled at Hal. "I'll let him tell you exactly how we found them."

Chapter 5

As soon as Tracey and her escort arrived back at her cabin, Chase unlocked her door for her and opened it, saying, "Do you mind if Hal shifts and dresses inside your place for safety's sake as late as it is?"

She shook her head, grateful that they had come to her rescue and certainly not minding at all. In fact, she welcomed the opportunity to return a favor.

Until she turned to enter the cabin and saw her blue, silky, barely-there nightie on the floor next to the door for all to see. If a cougar could blush, she was blushing. What should she do? Grab it with her teeth and head to her bedroom, embarrassed not only that the four guys had witnessed it, but that she was such a slob? Which she wasn't. Not *normally*. She'd just been in a hurry to shift and run and would have been back *way* before she had to meet Hal. He would never have seen her nightclothes like that. Nor would Stryker, Dan, or Chase.

Or should she just run by it like it was no big deal? Her cabin. Her way. It was already too late to do anything about it. And she could just see herself trying to grab the slinky nightie in her cougar's teeth, fumbling with it as everyone watched, making it worse.

Screw it. Her place. Her business. That was now everyone else's business. Note to self: go for run, put away nightie, *first*.

She ran right over her nightie, rather than around it—which would emphasize that it was there—and headed for the bedroom, feeling overheated as Chase, Dan, and Stryker said their goodbyes and then one of the men closed the door.

In her bedroom, she shifted and quickly dressed in a pair of jeans, sandals, a short-sleeved blouse, and then she grabbed a sweater. As soon as she left the bedroom and headed down the hall, she looked first for her nightie, which wasn't there, and then at Hal, who was sitting on the couch dressed in jeans, a black T-shirt, and cowboy boots, her nightie draped over the arm of the couch.

Her face heated all over again, and she knew this time it had to be plain to see.

"Ready?" she quickly asked.

"Sure am. I'm starving. You?"

"Yeah. That run turned out to be a little more of a workout than I had planned."

"Do you want to run again tomorrow?"

She smiled at him. "Sure. Do you know of a safer area?"

He chuckled and led her outside to his pickup.

***

Before they reached Hal's ranch house, Tracey marveled at the pinyon pines covering some of the hills, the panoramic view of the Rocky Mountains, and four spring-fed ponds.

He pointed out one of the ponds. "Excellent fishing and if you ever want to take pictures of waterfowl, numerous different species make their home here during the spring, summer, and fall seasons. The creek running through the property is large enough to sustain brook trout and beavers. Massive rock outcroppings rise over 8,000 feet above lush treed forestland. Maybe we could take a run up there. I could show you something really special. The whole area is great for climbing in our cougar coats."

"Wow, I'd really like that." She was just so in awe. She noted the no hunting and no trespassing signs posted all over and was glad he didn't allow any hunting on his land.

"The four-bedroom, three and one-half bath home has over 4,000 square feet of living space, and I own over 1,500 acres. Large herds of elk graze on the ranch, using it as a passageway between mountain ranges. I've seen mule and whitetail deer also. A bear and an occasional mountain sheep have passed through here also. I try to avoid running through the meadow area as a cougar."

"You live there all by yourself?" She had a studio apartment, no need for anything else. She couldn't imagine roaming around in a place that big all by herself.

"Yeah. I'm finally ready to set down roots."

Wife? Babies? She wasn't ready to settle down anytime soon.

"On the western 800 acres, it's more heavily treed, but has some grass meadows. The ponds are great for fishing and birdlife, but it's also great for other wildlife passing through. We're surrounded mostly by a national forest park, so it will remain in its natural pristine state."

She continued to gaze at the breathtaking vista. "It's like a beautiful wildlife sanctuary."

"It is. And I aim to keep it that way."

She thought how wonderful that was. She was attempting to put wildlife traffickers out of business while Hal was giving the wildlife a safe place to stay.

"Do you ever have problems with poachers?"

"Not often. Everyone knows a deputy sheriff owns the ranch and surrounding lands. Or at least, most do. I caught three men one time out here hunting. It really isn't a good idea to poach on a cougar shifter's land. I heard the gunfire, got in my ATV, and tracked them down. And promptly arrested them on the spot. It helps to have a badge too. I got them on so many charges, they won't be doing that again for a while."

"Good. I love to hear it." She only wished it was that easy to catch *her* perps.

As soon as she saw an old bunkhouse and corrals, the weathered gray wood, and no glass in the windows on the bunkhouse, Hal said, "That's the original bunkhouse and corrals, which I've preserved for historical sake. They're not used, except by wildlife. It's the perfect refuge for a variety of birds that nest in there. The old building and corrals are just a nice reminder of how long this ranch has been here."

"That's wonderful. I love old history. Reminds me a little of the ghost town of Anderson, except instead of it being a mining town, it was an old ranch." Then she spotted a two-story log cabin on top of a ridge, a wrap-around deck that afforded views of the forest, mountains, creek, and the hay meadows below. A round pen was off in one area for exercising and training horses, stack yard for hay, a horse shed, and a large barn.

Six beautiful paint horses and an all reddish-brown horse were eating grass in a corral.

"The mostly red bay with the all-white face is Fanny. She's an old, retired pony that's had several foals, and she will act as a nanny for the new foal. She can teach the foal acceptable behavior."

"And the others?"

"Breeding mares. And four trail horses for riding."

She studied them. "Are any of the breeding mares foaling?"

"Both. They're not as far along as Misty. She's in the barn. I'll take you out to see her after I serve you up some breakfast." He pulled into a garage, then got on his cell. "How's Misty doing? Okay, be out there in a bit." He guided Tracey into the house. "Ted Weekum, my ranch hand, has been watching Misty for me this morning."

"And he's a shifter?"

"Yeah, most of us in the area employ shifters. It makes it easier that way. He was working on another ranch down south of here that was human-run. When I decided to go into this venture, I asked him if he'd like to work with me. We've known each other since we were kids. He calls me boss man, which took some getting used to. He's a little rough around the edges, so you never know what he might say. Just wanted to warn you."

"I'm sure I can handle it." At least she thought she could.

Feeling like her head was riveting like an owl's, she took in as much of the home as she could see, the carpeted living area sporting floor-to-ceiling windows and a door to the deck. The tiled dining area, with the same kind of windows through which she could see the blue sky, a smattering of clouds and mountains off in the distance. The kitchen had a white marble-topped counter with an extended bar, perfect for quick meals or visiting with the cook while he or she prepared the meal.

"Take a seat, and I'll fix the breakfast."

"Do you need my help?"

"Nah. If you'd rather have a look around at the view, feel free."

It seemed rude not to keep him company while he was fixing the meal, but she really wanted to see the views from the deck. "Thanks. I'll be right back." She headed through the dining area and opened the door to the deck, then walked outside. Nice temperature. Maybe seventy degrees. Perfect.

She shut the door and walked all the way around the deck, seeing the view from different angles. Just amazing. A stone outdoor barbecue sat nearby, a stone fireplace on one corner and it looked perfect for roasting marshmallows on a starry night. She could stay here forever and enjoy this.

Returning to the house, she smelled bacon sizzling on the grill. She climbed onto a stool and watched Hal fill the omelets with shredded cheese, chopped ham, fresh chives, and lemon and pepper seasoning, then masterfully flipped them closed. "Are you sure you don't want me to help at all?"

"No, too many chefs in the kitchen—you know the saying."

"I can be a good little helper."

"Nah, you're my guest. My treat."

She couldn't sit still and got up to pour them cups of coffee. "Cream in yours?"

"Extra cream, just like the big cats would like. Half

and half."

Yum.

"I serve it with whipped cream in the winter," he said.

Even better. Typical cat. She smiled.

"So, tell me about what you do on your job exactly." Hal served up the omelets and then the bacon.

"Well, a little background first. The U.S. is the second-largest retail market for selling illegally obtained ivory. China has the dishonorable spot of being number one. For the U.S. to be that high on the list? It's shameful."

They sat down to eat and Hal said, "Yeah. The problem is that it's a big moneymaker for some and they don't give a damn about the animals."

"Right. You probably heard about Colorado destroying the stockpile of elephant tusks they'd confiscated in raids—six tons worth! Once they'd used the evidence to conclude the cases against the men on trial, they destroyed it so no one else could get hold of it and use it to make more money. The wholesale slaughtering of animals for profit is just so awful. Makes my stomach turn."

"I so agree."

"Being that you're with law enforcement, you probably know that a wildlife repository is located at the Rocky Mountain National Wildlife Refuge outside of Denver. The Fish and Wildlife Service stores most of the illegal wildlife they seize there. What you might not know is that stored on shelves, rows and rows of dead animals are categorized by species. A million specimens are there! It's just unbelievable. And that's just of those that have been seized. Can you imagine how many more never are? Heads of tigers, leopards, lions, jaguars, cougars, and that's just some of the feline species. But you name it, they're there. One was a tiger fetus, stuffed, that an American woman had been trying to sell for $1,500. In one case, a man and his son are up on charges of poisoning bald eagles so that they don't hunt the animals he wants to hunt. As if a couple of bald eagles are going to eat off all the animals and he won't be able to go kill his own! So you have a lot of different kinds of people involved in this. Any of them who kill wildlife for greed are sickening."

"Who the hell would want to buy a stuffed tiger fetus?"

"Agreed. The thing of it is—a lot of criminal networks and terrorist organizations across the world are finding animal trafficking is a great way to finance their future terrorism. In the Congo, rebels murdered wildlife officers and took over their eco-tourism facilities to serve themselves instead—since so many high-paying tourists were paying for the service. Can you imagine being a tourist, paying all that money, and not even realizing that the men running that particular operation are doing so illegally because they murdered the real wildlife operators?"

"You're right. I didn't know it either."

"Exactly. Most people don't. The same situation exists in Nepal. Maoist rebels did the same when they took over legitimate eco-tourism business and also trophy hunts. The attacks on the wildlife is widespread, orchestrated by criminals. If it's allowed to go on, eventually no more of the animals that they're murdering wholesale will exist. Then what's next? They're not going to suddenly become legitimate businessmen. The other thing is that they're using those funds to murder people too."

Hal believed it, and yet, it was hard to imagine that people would buy dead animal parts for any reason. But the bastards who were selling the parts wouldn't be doing it if people weren't buying them. He couldn't even envision working in the business of trying to stop the traffickers. He had a lot of respect for the job Tracey did.

"So what about this case that you're working on now?" He finished off his coffee and noticed she needed a refill also. He got them both another cup.

"Well, the Colorado Parks and Wildlife requires that every harvested lion be presented for inspection within five days of the kill."

"Right."

"Outfitter and hunting guides usually obey the rules. They take the hunting party out, help them locate the prey, the hunter kills his quarry, and takes home his trophy. Nice and legal like. Hunting license, in season, right animal, correct limit, all above board. Then we have this guy named Tobias Mooney, outfitter and hunting guide, who takes his prospective hunters up to the Book Cliffs mountain range along the border between Colorado and Utah. But something's not right. We had reports that mountain lions and bobcats were being caught, caged, and maimed—shot in the paw or legs, and then released right before the hunters were sent out to chase them down."

"Hell."

"Yeah. What's the sport in that? Like, uhm, tranquilizing a big cat and saying, 'There! Shoot it.' Or chaining it to a tree and doing the same thing. Except we couldn't get any evidence to prove he was doing any of this. Just a couple of anonymous calls. Once we received that information, Peterson, my partner, and I began searching for substantive evidence. But we still didn't get any reliable witnesses who would attest to the crimes. Then we'd heard that when he wasn't guiding hunters on tours because the season was over, he was involved in the trafficking of elephant ivory. From an informant, we were told that evidence was possibly located at Anderson, though the man suspected that it had already been moved. We did find evidence that the elephant tusks had been stored under the abandoned schoolhouse floor."

"So was it a setup? Instead of finding only evidence, you were faced with a shootout? Or was it unintentional? Right place, wrong time?"

"We never knew." She finished eating her eggs and

licked the cheese off her fork.

He smiled, glad she liked his cooking.

"My informant was found murdered before we could question him. It looked like he was also involved in trafficking and he was trying to destroy his competition."

"It's a bad business to be in all way around."

"Right. And from what I learned later, no animal tusks, or other illegal body parts, were located anywhere else in the ghost town, though investigators searched all of the abandoned buildings."

He thought back to the way Tracey and her partner had gotten in. "From the way the window slats were configured, it appeared the traffickers had been using the place for their illegal business for some time."

"Exactly. But we couldn't locate any new leads. So we're back to square one." She sat straighter in her chair.

"Except this time, he tried to murder two investigating officers. That has to take more priority."

She let out her breath. "Oh, they're looking into it. Sure. One dead and then one wounded Special Agent. The traffickers could have taken even more of us down. But investigators combed the whole area and came up with nothing. The wounded man they took into custody said he didn't know the man and when the police gave him a picture to I.D. him, he couldn't. Said he didn't know the man, again. Neither my partner nor I actually saw Mooney at the shootout. But I smelled his scent at both places. I certainly can't say that I know he was there for sure because I smelled him, but didn't see him. The story the guy taken into custody shared was that it was a drug sale gone wrong. My partner and I were buying the drugs and wouldn't pay up. That's probably what Mooney told him. I suspect that Mooney set up his prey and then he came along for the ride to watch the hunters take the animal down—or in our case, hit men were paid to hunt down two Special Agents. And in this case, he was paying the men to do the job, instead of them paying him to locate the prey."

"You trusted your informant completely, I take it. The one who sent you into the second firefight, I mean."

"Yeah, I do. His information has always been correct. At least on the last four assignments, it's been on the money. I don't believe he's in the trafficking business like Honey had been."

"Okay, so where do you go from here?"

"I'm on administrative leave, remember?"

"Right." Hal took their empty plates into the kitchen. "No hunting is allowed again until November. How are you…were you going to learn more about his illegal hunting practices?"

"We really thought we had a lead this time. I thought of going after the informant who sold us out the first time, but I then learn he's dead. I can't get a search warrant for Mooney's place without more evidence, and I can't get more evidence…"

"Without a search warrant."

"Right. We believe he's got to keep the income flowing in so he's involved in the wildlife trafficking when he's not serving as a hunting guide. He's got a really beautiful place in Aspen, Colorado—seven bedrooms, nine baths, four-car garage, four-stall barn, with its own two-car garage. Breathtaking views of four ski areas and major peaks. Stone patios with fireplace. Separate guest wing. Summer stream on six acres. A full gym with bathroom and sauna, outdoor riding arena. And he bought it for fourteen million dollars."

Hal whistled. "I take it he doesn't have a lot of income?"

"Not that we could tell. No inheritances. Nothing that he reports other than his hunt-guided excursions. Sure, he's got investments, and he pays taxes on them, so we can't get him there. We really have nothing to backup what we suspect in a court of law. Of course, we've questioned the hunters who paid to go on the excursions, but they're all saying they hunted the cougars out in the wild. None of them were close by, and none had been injured."

Hal nodded. "They didn't want to get charged with conspiracy to commit illegal acts. So what made you go into this line of work?"

"My sister is a wildlife photographer and she was in Hawaii filming the fish at one of the reefs while two divers were poking at the coral and collecting fish. They were at about fifty feet of water and one of the fishermen attacked Jessie, jerking the air regulator out of her mouth. Thank God she was an experienced diver. I've gone on dives with her, but I am totally inexperienced. If someone had done that to me, I probably would have panicked, become disoriented, might have tried to quickly return to the surface, and died. It could have killed her if she hadn't reacted quickly enough. You know what the fisherman said? He was scared of her! She had been taking a video of him! Then he said he might have to carry bang sticks to protect himself from the eco-terrorists. She's not the one who grabbed his regulator from his mouth! He should have been brought up on charges." She took a steadying breath.

Hal could see the notion that her sister could have died still bothered Tracey. He didn't blame her. If any of his close friends had faced such a dangerous action, he would have felt the same way.

"Anyway, my dad was already a FWS Special Agent, and I had been wanting to do my part too. I figured this was my calling."

"You have an affinity for getting the perps." Hal admired her all the more.

"Yeah, but I'm not always successful."

"I understand your frustration. We hate it when one of the lawbreakers we're after gets away with it also. Is your father still in the service?"

She shook her head. "Retired. And no, I didn't tell him what happened on this case—the shooting and all.

He'd want me to quit. He's testified on a number of cases in court, put away a lot of traffickers, but he never was in a firefight with any of them. At least that I know of. My mother, who has a cake decorating business, would agree with my dad." She sighed. "Enough about me. What about you? Being Special Forces first? Now a deputy sheriff? Having a horse ranch? Family?"

"As far as the military goes, we had a local hero, Special Forces, who told us his war stories when I was growing up. We all wanted to be like him, so we all joined. Deputy sheriff? Well, when Dan became the sheriff, he pretty much told the rest of us we were his new deputies." Hal smiled.

Tracey chuckled. "Sounds like you guys are real good friends."

"We are. Just like brothers. As to the horse ranch, my great grandfather broke horses for the cavalry during WWI, my grandfather broke them during WWII. My father wasn't interested in horses, rode them, sure, but he didn't want to raise them or break them. I used to sit on the fence and watch my grandfather while he worked with them. He knew how to talk to them. Knew how to let them come to him. He watched the horses' behavior. Saw how they greeted each other. Just like learning how to behave toward each other in our cougar forms, he knew how to commune with the horses. I was fascinated by the process. But...I had to run off and fight and serve in the army with my buddies. When we finally returned, Dan made me a part-time deputy sheriff. After that, I was busy getting ready to start my own horse ranch."

"You've been busy. So where's your family?"

"They live in town. Mom runs the newspaper and dad is one of her reporters."

Tracey smiled. "Any brothers or sisters?"

"Nope. Only child."

"Lonely."

"Not when I had all my friends in the area. They were like brothers."

"That's so nice. Can I see your mare?" Tracey loved the reason why he went into the horse business. Not just to make money, but because he really loved horses. "None of these are serving in the military though, right?" She couldn't imagine that the U.S. military still used horses for military missions any longer.

Hal smiled. "A few might. Maybe at the 1st Cavalry Division, Fort Hood, Texas. Seven mounted cavalry units are on active duty in the United States. No fighting for them. They're in parades, three presidential inaugural parades even, and drill and weapons exhibition. They get the best of care."

They walked out to the stable and a dark-haired man with smiling, equally dark eyes greeted them outside and took in Tracey's whole appearance. "Hell, is this the new boss lady?"

Hal smiled at him and shook his head. "Don't scare Tracey off." He made introductions, but she noted he didn't mention her occupation.

Ted grinned at her. "No way would I do that, if I can help it."

"I don't scare off easily," she said, and meant it.

"No, she's usually armed and dangerous," Hal said.

"Yeah, I can tell." Ted was smiling too broadly to appear to be taking either of them seriously.

"How's Misty doing?" Hal asked.

"Looks close, boss man." Ted turned to Tracey as they walked into the stable. "Have you ever seen the foaling process?"

"No." She hadn't expected to either.

"It changed my life around, first time I saw it happen. I was helping Hal muck out stalls when one of the mares went into labor. I'd been into minor scrapes with the law, but when I began seeing the foals born, taking care of the colts and fillies, well, it just gave me an appreciation for just how precious life is."

"Yeah, it was about time," Hal said. "Hell, I thought I'd never get off restriction after you stole Mrs. McCormick's hen so we could roast it over a campfire, when you'd said you'd paid for it."

"I did. For a long damn time. Who would have thought stealing one hen would have cost me in so much labor time on her farm."

"It was her best laying hen. Good thing you mended your ways."

"Yeah, well, I felt bad about that. I never realized that not all chickens were meant just to eat." Ted glanced back at Tracey. "So what do you do?"

"Take down wildlife traffickers, or others who harm wildlife for personal gain or profit."

Ted's jaw dropped. "Hell, boss man, why didn't you tell me what the lady did before I spilled the beans on myself?"

She smiled.

"I knew you'd be giving a tale about your bad boy image and how you were now one of the good guys."

Tracey laughed.

When they reached the 14 x 14 stall where the mare was, Hal said, "Misty is a blood bay and white tobiano paint."

She was a lovely color with white markings on the lower legs, white mane, the top half of her tail white, the lower half dark brown, her body large splotches of reddish-brown and white, her face, reddish brown. And very pregnant with a sagging belly. Tracey couldn't imagine carrying such a big baby.

"How are you doing, Misty, ol' girl?" Hal leaned against the gate and she came over and nuzzled his face with her own.

Tracey smiled.

The mare turned away and began to paw the ground. Sweat had collected around her neck and flanks. But she hadn't been exercising. Tracey was about to ask when the foal was due, but when she turned, Hal had already stalked off.

The mare paced and snatched small bites of hay,

then paced again. Tracey hadn't been around mares ready to foal and she was afraid of what this meant.

Hal returned with a package in his hand, and his cell in the other. "Yeah, Doc. She's sweating and..." He paused to look at Misty pacing across the floor. "Pawing at the ground. She just laid down. Got back up. All right. See you as soon as you can get here."

Tracey frowned at Hal. "Don't tell me she's in labor."

He smiled and winked.

"She's in labor," Ted said. "I've never delivered one myself, but I've seen enough of them foaled."

"Why isn't the vet coming sooner?" Tracey asked.

"She's delivering another foal that's turned the wrong way, and she's an hour from here, but it will take a while with the other delivery."

Great. "You watched your grandfather deliver a foal, right?" Tracey attempted not to panic.

"Yes, but I was young. Then I was in the army. My grandfather died before I returned home. My father had sold off the ranch, figuring no one was here to run it, and he wasn't interested in ranching. He didn't know when I'd return home, or if I'd make a career of the military. I wasn't sure myself, and I still had an army obligation."

"So what do we do?"

Hal's brows lifted a bit.

"You...do know what to do, right?"

"I watched some YouTube videos, I went to a

foaling class, and I've got a foaling kit." Hal began opening it up and seemed remarkably calm.

"And I'm here," Ted said.

She was worried stiff about everything turning out all right. "Can't the vet get here any quicker? Or can it take several hours for the mare to deliver like a human does?"

"Could be one to four hours."

"Okay, what do you want me to do?"

"How about you keep track of the time on each stage of her labor." He dug out a digital clock, marking pen, and foaling timesheet.

When he handed her the items, he was shaking a little. When she took them from him, she was too.

"I'll be right back. I'll get a bucket of warm water," Ted said.

Watching Misty closely, Tracey thought she saw the water bag, which was visible at the mare's vulva. "Uh, Hal? I think her water's ready to break."

He looked up from reading an instruction card. "Yeah, I see. This is the first stage of labor."

He joined Misty in the stall. She kept moving around, agitated. "She's having contractions."

"Better her than me." Tracey was really glad that she wasn't having a baby.

Hal glanced at her and grinned. Tracey was sure her face was beet red, as hot as it felt.

Ted brought him the pail of water and stayed with Hal and the mare. Hal took out a wrap, then proceeded to wrap the mare's tail.

For four hours, they watched her. She frequently urinated, kept switching her tail, and continued to eat erratically. Then the bag of water suddenly broke and a rush of about five gallons of fluid fell to the floor.

Hal, Ted, and Tracey just stared at the water before Hal read his instruction card again.

That done, he put on gloves, then washed the mare's vulva and hindquarters with the green soap, from the kit, that he added to the warm water. Then he rinsed her off thoroughly. He looked like he knew what he was doing. She swore her heart was racing faster than when she was shooting at the bad guys.

Strong contractions began and the mare laid down. Tracey thought the foal would be delivered at any moment. Then she witnessed the beginning of the miracle. The foal's front feet emerged as if diving, the foal's nose tucked between its legs, one hoof slightly in front of the other, soles down, the inner sac breaking. The foal was half out when the mare rested. Then fifteen minutes later, the foal was delivered the rest of the way.

"She still has to deliver the placenta," Hal said, as the mare stood and the umbilical cord broke.

The foal was a bay, reddish brown body, black mane, tail, ear edges and lower legs and an adorable white star on her forehead. A filly.

"What should we name her?" Hal asked.

Switching her attention from the filly to Hal,

Tracey looked up at him, figuring he'd already have a name picked out for her. She was really honored that he'd asked her. "Annie?"

He smiled. "Annie, it is."

Bright and alert and just adorable, Annie was making attempts to stand, breathing normally, and she was beautiful. Misty was curious and attentive toward her foal, which looked to be a good sign. She began to eat and Annie finally managed to stand after an hour. She began to nurse and it was the most wondrous sight.

Once the placenta was delivered Hal bagged it. Ted hurried to clean up the foaling stall, removed soiled bedding, and added fresh straw.

Then the two men just looked on in wonder, smiling, perspiration beading their foreheads, and she couldn't believe the marvel she'd just witnessed.

Tracey's phone vibrated in her pocket, and she set down the foaling chart and fished the cell out. *Stryker Hill.*

Ohmigod, she'd forgotten all about Stryker and her supper date with him! It was a quarter past the hour when he was supposed to pick her up at her cabin.

She closed her eyes and opened them and said, "Hello, Stryker?"

Both Ted and Hal turned their attentions from the filly and mare to Tracey. Hal quickly said, "Tell him we just foaled a filly. He can come over and see her, and then we'll all have a barbecue in celebration."

Chapter 6

Hal couldn't help it. He'd just had the thrill of a lifetime—foaling his own filly, and sharing the experience with Tracey, who looked awestruck and pleased. He loved that she had named the filly too.

But now? He didn't want her going off to supper with Stryker.

The instinct was natural—a cougar's tendency to claim his territory, and the female in it. For humans, it might seem archaic, but for cougars, it was an inborn condition.

In the wild, and as full cougars, he would fight off another male that encroached on his territory. In this case, he had to come to terms with his cougar half. Though he still didn't want to give her up for the evening, he'd go halfway.

He was still watching her to see her reaction, knowing the way he called out the barbecue invitation,

Stryker had to have heard it over the phone.

She looked up from the filly to him and said over the phone, "That would be great. She's really beautiful. See you in a little bit." Then she pocketed her phone and smiled, but it wasn't a sweet smile, more like she knew Hal had played a fast one on his friend.

Hal knew then, he'd won. Stryker would want to kill him for it later. In a good naturedly way, of course.

Unable to curb his enthusiasm, Hal grinned big time.

Ted slapped him on the back. "Way to go, man. Stryker is going to be…"

Hal gave him a quelling look.

"Thrilled to see the filly." Ted grinned. "Why don't you get cleaned up while I finish out here? Someone can call me when the food's ready."

"I'm going to take a shower," Hal told Tracey as he pulled off the gloves he'd used on the mare and foal, and disposed of them. He called the vet. "Everything's fine. No need to come out. The filly and mare are doing great."

"Okay, thanks. If you need me, just call. I'm still at Vander's Ranch."

"Bad case?"

"No, no, it's going to be all right. It's just going to take a little longer than we expected."

"Okay. I'll call if I need you." Hal ended the call and smiled down at Tracey.

"Wow, that was really beautiful. You did a great

job."

"Thanks. Misty did all the work, really. I'm glad no complications arose. Do you want steaks? Chicken?"

"I'm all for steaks."

"You got it. I'll be just a minute if you want to make yourself comfortable. Grab something to drink, if you'd like." He walked with her into the house, feeling on top of the world.

"I'm going to sit on your deck for a while." She slipped outside, and he thought life couldn't be any better.

Who would have ever thought coming to a Special Agent's aid when she was in the middle of a gunfight would lead to this? She had to admit, she was having the time of her life.

Washed up and dressed in clean clothes, Hal headed out of the master bedroom when he heard Stryker pulling up outside. He must have assumed she was still at Hal's place when he couldn't get hold of her at the cabin and driven faster than the speed of a bullet to get here.

Hal headed Tracey off to get the door. Hal opened the door and let Stryker in.

Giving Hal a look that said Stryker would get him back for this, his friend said, "Thanks for the invite. I'll have to start calling you Slick."

Hal chuckled. "We've been meaning to have a barbecue out here since I moved in, but all of us have been busy. With the new foal's arrival, it seemed the perfect time to do so and celebrate at the same time."

"Yeah, like I said—Slick. Did you induce the mare?"

Hal laughed. "Come on. Let's get some drinks and have a barbecue."

When they settled to eat on the back deck, it couldn't have been more perfect. Unless, Hal had been enjoying the evening *alone* with Tracey. But given that she would have been out with Stryker tonight, this was great.

Even Stryker had to admit Annie was cute. And Tracey had been all smiles again.

The air was still warm enough, and the food and chardonnay, absolute perfection, the company and conversation, even better.

Then Tracey got a call and all conversation stopped.

She quickly answered her phone, glanced in Hal and the other men's direction, and said to the caller, "Anton? How are you doing?"

"Her partner," Hal told Ted, since Stryker would already know who he was.

All of them were watching her facial expression and body language. She was tense, her posture stiff. She was probably concerned about Anton's health and why he would be calling her.

"Just a minute." She said to Hal and his friends, "Do you mind if I take this in the house? The breeze is making too much static on the line and he can't understand me."

"Sure, go ahead." Hal hoped everything was all right. She seemed serious, but not anxious, so he suspected everything was okay. He was thinking of asking everyone if they'd like to run in their cougar coats tonight. Not into the rocks though. He'd love to take Tracey there alone—to show her his special spot.

As soon as she went inside and shut the door, Stryker turned to face Hal, "I'm taking her home tonight."

Hal wanted to object, but what could he say? She was supposed to be eating out with Stryker tonight, and he would have taken her home after his date with her otherwise. Plus, Hal was home. Stryker wouldn't have to make much of a detour to take her to Chase's resort. No matter how much he tried to come up with a way that would work, he knew Stryker had outmaneuvered him this time.

"Did everyone want to take a run as cougars tonight?" Hal hoped Tracey would want to. Not that he wanted Stryker along for the run. Ted would say he'd stay to watch Annie. But he figured Stryker would say yes, just to ensure he was able to take Tracey home tonight.

"Sure, if Tracey wants to run again," Stryker said. "I'm game."

"I'll watch Annie." Ted looked highly amused at their antics.

They all looked back at the glass door. Hal hoped

everything was all right, concerning the call Tracey had received, surprised it was taking so long, and hoped her partner wasn't giving her word about the case so that she could look into it.

***

Frowning furiously, Tracey wanted to kill the informant who had led them into a trap. She hoped Hal and the others really believed she was talking to Anton. She didn't want anyone to get wind of the fact that she had every intention of working this case if she could get some clues. With Ricky calling her, she hoped that's where the conversation would lead.

"Okay, tell me your version of what happened." She bit back the urge to call him every vile word she could think of. She could have lost her partner! Not to mention she had been damn lucky when Hal had showed up.

"I didn't have nothing to do with it. You know. I didn't call you. Someone else did. I don't know who."

"What do you mean you didn't call me?" She couldn't believe he'd come up with such a ludicrous lie. Of course, it had been him. She'd talked to him a number of times, and she would recognize his voice anywhere. "He sounded just like you."

"Hell, anyone can copy anyone else's voice over the phone. It wasn't me. You pay me good money, you know. Why would I screw that up?"

She had to admit that was true, and it was possible, she supposed. Anything was in this business. "Okay, let's say you're telling me the truth. They have to realize you're informing on them. It's the only way they would think to contact me, if they believed you were talking to me about them."

Silence.

"Ricky?"

"Yeah, yeah, I'm thinking, you know?" She heard him pacing around on gravel. "Okay. I've got a brother, you know? Kolby's twenty-one—three years older than me. I always looked up to him. But I'm thinking he heard something about what I've been doing. And then he might have set me up."

"You talked to him!"

"I didn't tell him. Not to his face. Maybe he overheard me talking to you. Maybe he got hold of this Mooney character, and he offered to pay him some big bucks to impersonate me and send you there. I swear I didn't know anything about it. When I saw the newspaper story that said that you had been ambushed in the old saloon in the ghost town, I figured it was some other case you were working on. So I didn't call you. But then a new story got out and it said your informant set you up. I got to thinking about it...believing it was some other informant because *I* didn't call you. And then I got to wondering more and more. Did you think it was me? I didn't know how you could because it wasn't me. But if you did, I wanted to straighten you out. I had nothing to do with it."

"All right. So what do you know?"

"Well, since my brother, Kolby, thinks I'm still clueless about who your informant was, because I *was* until you said you thought it was me, I believe he's the one who did this. We do sound a lot alike."

"Okay, so now you're going to sell out your brother?"

"Hell, yeah. If he set me up to take the fall if the two of you survived. Either of you could have come after me and killed me for it."

"We apprehend wildlife traffickers. We build cases against them. Put them on trial for their crimes. We don't go after anyone with the intent of killing him." Though she was sure rethinking her philosophy on that one.

"If I were you, I'd want to kill them for that. I mean, *you* could have been killed. Sure pissed me off." Then as if it sounded like he was coming across as too soft, he added, "You know, because I wouldn't get any more work from you."

She smiled a little, then frowned again. "Well, I don't kill for revenge. So what do you know?" She wanted to get this conversation over with in a hurry. She worried that her supper companions would be concerned that she was taking too long. Maybe worried something was wrong with Anton. She had no intention of telling them she was on the case again. She was a Special Agent, and now? A Secret Agent. On her own. She knew if they got word of this, they'd really watch her and try to stop her. And probably report it back to her boss.

"Nothing."

"Come on, Ricky," she said, irritated to the max. "After what happened, I need to know something. Anything that will help the case."

"Really. Nothing. I had to make sure that you knew I wasn't the informant who set you up. That this was a case of Mooney trying to have you killed. The papers didn't say who was involved. Now that I know for sure you thought it was me and we cleared that mess up, I'll make some inquiries, you know. But you don't kill bad informants, right?"

In case it was his brother? "No. But watch your back, Ricky. In these cases, normally we don't have the traffickers shooting back at us."

Silence.

Okay, so for her, this was the second case. Did she just tend to land really bad cases? Or was she just lucky? *Not.*

"Thanks. That's the first time anyone's told me that, you know? I'll get back to you when I have word." Then he ended the call.

She stared at her cell for a minute. She realized then that Ricky wasn't just some lowlife informant with a name she suspected was an alias. He was real. Someone who lived on the scuzzier side of life, just getting by, who needed her as much as she needed him. She prayed he wouldn't get himself killed over this like her last informant had.

She headed for the glass doors to the patio and realized everyone was sitting there quietly, waiting for her return. Trying to listen in on the conversation? She wouldn't be surprised, being that both Hal and Stryker were with law enforcement. She suddenly felt exhausted—from her early morning run and trouble with the wolves, to all the excitement with the foaling—and she was ready to call it a night.

She opened the patio door and all the men stood.

"I've had a lovely time," she said. Hal's face fell a bit. She suspected he had hoped she'd stay longer. "But after the day I've had, I'm ready to say goodnight."

"I'll take you home," Stryker said quickly, as if he was worried Hal would get to it first.

She smiled. "Sure. Thanks."

"Tomorrow morning, we'll go on a run like we talked about?" Hal asked.

"Yeah, sure."

"And you'll wait for me?" he asked.

She laughed. "Yeah, you can show me the safe areas to run as a cougar."

She said her goodbyes to the men and climbed into Stryker's black Jeep, then they drove to the cabin, the stars lighting the night sky. She loved it out here.

"I had a really nice time visiting with you tonight." Stryker was tall, maybe six-one, with dark brown wavy hair and a genuine smile. At least when he wasn't looking all serious like earlier when she was running as a cougar and had been treed by a pack of wolves.

Golden highlights streaking his hair said he was out in the sun a fair amount, as did his golden brown skin. Green eyes glanced in her direction, and she knew he wanted to see more of her.

But she seriously wasn't on the market for heavy dating with anyone.

"It was a lot of fun. Lovely company, great vista, wonderful food. I just had a really lovely time."

Out of the blue, Stryker asked, "Is your partner all right?"

"Anton?"

When Stryker glanced at her, she quickly said, "Uhm, yeah. He's fine." She screwed that up big time. She had to remember that no matter how nice these guys were, as officers in law enforcement, they were used to watching for people's actions and reactions.

"So... he just wanted to let you know he was recovering all right?"

"Yeah."

"That's good to hear. When is he returning to duty?"

"I'm not sure. He'll be in rehab when he's released from the hospital. Could be months before he's recovered enough to go on another assignment." She hated to think of it. She really liked working with him, but she suspected she would get a new partner when she returned to work herself.

"So who called you?"

Blast it all. That was the problem with people in

law enforcement. What had the men been discussing all this time? Who the caller really was? Just because she'd taken the call inside? Though if she'd been in their place, she would have considered the same things.

When she didn't say, Stryker cleared his throat. "I was wondering. What kind of dog do you like?"

He probably didn't think he would make points with her if he kept questioning her about her caller, but it didn't mean he'd totally let it go, she was certain. "Is this about the puppy again?"

He smiled.

When they reached her cabin, the whole place was dark. She normally wasn't afraid of the dark—it certainly wasn't a cougar weakness—but having a firefight in the ghost town twice now had put her on edge a bit, and she really hadn't thought it would.

"I hate to ask you this," she said, as he parked his Jeep in front of her door. "Would you mind coming in with me?"

"Hell, no," he said, smiling. And then he frowned a little, as if he realized *why* she wanted him to come in with her. He quickly sobered. "Yeah, sure." They both left the Jeep, and he offered to take her keys.

She wasn't going to go that far, but it was too late to say she was okay with opening her own place up.

He reached in and turned on the light, and they both went inside. "Do you want me to check out the place?"

"Uhm…"

"Listen." He took hold of her hand and looked down at her, frowning a little, looking concerned for her well-being. "I fully understand what you're going through. I've been there. No one's going to think any less of you if you need a little backup."

"I don't want this to get back to headquarters."

"As long as you're not returning to duty, no problem."

She appreciated him for saying so. "Do you want a drink?"

He smiled.

"My boss asked Chase to buy some wine for me. Probably so I'd have a little fun and quit thinking about the case, knowing him. I'll get us some."

"Sure. I'll check out the place while you're doing that."

"Do you want to watch a movie?"

"Hell, yeah. I'd love to."

She took a deep breath, smiled, nodded, and went to get the wine and a couple of glasses. She really was tired. But she felt guilty for having forgotten about her supper date with Stryker. And she felt bad that Hal had outmaneuvered him with the barbecue. After the foaling, she really had loved the idea of sitting on the deck and having the meal, enjoying the view, then watching the beautiful sunset. So when Stryker was agreeable, she'd been glad. And she'd really appreciated him for it too. Not only that, but it had indicated she wasn't *dating* anyone.

She headed for the couch, saw her blamed nightie resting over the arm, where Hal must have laid it, and quickly shoved it beneath the couch cushions. Then she took a seat and Stryker joined her.

She didn't want either man to think she was setting up housekeeping with him. Best to keep this on more of a professional basis, spend some time with both men, while they sort of served in a bodyguard capacity.

She and Stryker agreed on an action thriller, and after she started the movie, he said, "Have you got popcorn?"

"Chips."

"Do you want some?"

"Sure."

Despite wanting to keep this on a professional basis with both men, she ended up tucked under Stryker's arm, watching a doozy of a thriller, sharing chips and wine and wondering what she was getting herself into.

When the movie ended and they called it a night, Stryker carried the half empty wine bottle and bag of chips into the kitchen, while she placed the wine glasses in the dishwasher. She wondered if he was just being sweet, or he was delaying his departure. She wasn't about to have him sleep over for the night. She didn't even want to consider what would happen if Hal showed up for their morning run and found Stryker eating breakfast with her here.

"I had a lovely time," Stryker said, holding her

hand, caressing it with his thumb, waiting for her to indicate she wanted something more.

"Me too. I'm so sorry about standing you up earlier."

"No problem. The night turned out even better than I could have planned. The barbecue at Hal's place was perfect. And I was glad I got to see Annie."

He sounded sincere, and she appreciated him for it. The next thing she knew, she was kissing him. She wanted to blame it on the past, the present, the future, the wine, but the truth was she needed this. Nothing more, just a little bit of tenderness.

He was a nice kisser, she thought, his mouth warm and agreeable, and eager, but she kept it at sweeter, no tongues, just melded mouths, for a precious moment in time.

She knew she really couldn't do this again. She had to keep this professional, and she was afraid as soon as her informant, Ricky, got back with her on any scuttlebutt he'd heard, she was going to be investigating the case again, and she didn't want either Stryker or Hal getting in her way.

Chapter 7

When Hal got a call from Stryker at two in the morning, he sat bolt upright in bed. "What's wrong?" A million thoughts were running through his mind. Chase, the babies. A need for a deputy. Top of the list? He worried something was wrong with Tracey.

"Okay, Tracey was afraid to go into the cabin tonight," Stryker said.

Hal looked at the clock again. "And you're telling me this *now*? At this *hour*? Why couldn't you have told me earlier after you dropped her off?"

"She was worried about her place. So I went in to check it out for her."

Hal narrowed his eyes. Now, he knew where this was headed since Stryker was calling him at two in the morning.

"She invited me in to have a drink and to watch a movie. To make up for forgetting about our supper date because she was helping you with the foal. So I said sure. But it was more than that. I think she needed someone to stay with her for a time. I think she's kind of spooked."

"Okay, good to know." Hal was trying to quell his annoyance because Stryker was right. She'd missed her date with him and then Hal had outmaneuvered him with the barbecue. He was glad that she was nice enough to try to make up for it with Stryker. But he hoped that didn't mean he'd won a bunch of points with her. And then he began worrying about her being alone out there if she was feeling spooked.

"There's more."

Hal knew it before Stryker even had to say anything. "It was about the phone call, wasn't it?"

"Yeah. When we'd discussed it on the deck, we figured it was either bad news for Anton, or something else was going on. When I asked her how Anton was doing, at first she wasn't sure why I had asked her."

"Because it wasn't him."

"That's what I suspect. I figure she's working the case. I thought Anton might be feeding her information, but I doubt it. From the way she talked, he's going to be in months of rehab, and he might not even be working as a field agent any longer."

"So someone else in the organization called her?"

"Maybe. Or another informant. I just wanted to give you a heads up in case you can learn what she's up to before or after you go running with her tomorrow."

"Thanks," Hal said.

"Yeah, remember, we're working on the same team here. Protect the lady at all costs."

"You didn't kiss her did you?"

"Some costs run a little higher than others. Hey, you don't have any more mares that are about to foal, do you? I don't want to have that conflict with my dates with Tracey in the future. Still need to learn what kind of dog she likes best. Better let you get your beauty rest for your run tomorrow morning. Night."

"Wait! You kissed her?"

But Stryker had already hung up on him.

Now, Hal couldn't sleep. He couldn't believe Stryker had kissed her!

He stared at the clock. It was fifteen minutes later than the last time he looked. Maybe she was still scared. He stared at his phone. It wouldn't hurt to call her, would it? If he didn't, he wouldn't get any sleep. But what if she had finally fallen asleep?

He pulled up her phone number in his list of contacts, but before he touched it, he hesitated. What if she realized Stryker had let him know that she was scared?

Hell, he didn't want her to know that.

He considered the phone. He wouldn't let on. He'd have to pretend he thought Stryker had dropped her off lots earlier, and he was just checking on her to see how she was doing.

He punched in her number and took a deep breath.

And waited for her to answer.

She didn't answer. This felt like *déjà vu* all over again. Hell. She could be showering. She could be sleeping.

He called Chase.

"Hey, it's Hal." As if Chase didn't have caller ID and very well knew just who it was.

"What's wrong?"

"Are you up?"

Chase didn't say anything for a minute, as if he was getting his bearings. "What time is it?"

"Two-fifteen. I talked to Stryker, and he said he's worried Tracey might be looking further into the case that she was working. Anyway, he said she was also feeling uncomfortable when they first arrived back at the cabin. So he suspects the call she got tonight at my place—"

"Your place? I thought she was having supper with Stryker last night."

"Yeah, it's complicated. Anyway, so she got this call and said it was her partner, but both Stryker and I were suspicious. Then he asked her about Anton's health when he was taking her home, and she didn't know what he was talking about. With the business of her being worried about entering the cabin on her own and not telling us the truth about who she was talking to—unless she was just really tired, which I doubt—we believe she might have had news about the case, but she's keeping mum about it."

"And?"

"Well, I tried calling her, and she didn't answer her phone."

Silence.

"Stryker just left her cabin a little while ago."

"How long ago?" Chase was moving about now, zipping his pants.

Hal looked at the clock. "Probably forty-five minutes ago."

"Hal, she's probably sleeping! Like I should be doing. Like *you* should be doing."

"Will you check on her? If you don't, I'm heading over there and she's got that Glock, remember?"

Chase chuckled. "Yeah, so she'll use it on me instead of you. I'll check on her. You owe me on this." The door opened and shut.

"How's Shannon?"

"Asleep for once. Which I should be. You know before long, I won't be getting any sleep."

"Sorry."

"No problem."

Chase's boots crunched on gravel. Even though he moved quickly, it wasn't quick enough for Hal. "Hell," Chase said.

"What?" Hal was off the bed in a heartbeat, trying to tug on his clothes.

"Her Hummer is gone."

***

As soon as Stryker left her place, Tracey got a call

back from Ricky. It was eerie, as if he had been watching her cabin, waiting for Stryker to leave. Thinking back on the earlier conversation with Ricky, she remembered him saying how similar he and his brother's voices were, and she knew that could be true. Whenever she or her twin sister called anyone, they always asked which one of the twins it was, if they knew both of them. Even their parents got them mixed up.

But what if Ricky hadn't called her? What if his brother had instead?

He knew her phone number and had reached her before. Or what if Ricky didn't even have a brother?

And now he was calling her to set her up again.

Which meant? She had to ask him about another case they'd worked on where the outcome was good. Except, would his brother have known about that also?

"Okay, remember the case you helped me with, concerning the goat that had been stolen from the reserve?"

Ricky took a while to respond, and she worried he was doing an Internet search. It probably would be easy to find too.

"Yeah, pretty brown goat. You caught the traffickers on that one."

"Right, but if you hadn't given me the clue about her and where she could be found—that was really amazing—and we might never have located her. Certainly not as quickly as we did. Worth every penny of the $500 I gave you."

He didn't respond.

"You there?"

"Yeah, just making sure no one's eavesdropping."

Or didn't know that she had paid him $750 for the job? "Hey, do you remember that time we met at the zoo and you were wearing—wait, can't think of the movie."

"The Dark Knight."

Which he could still know if he was the brother, if Ricky wore the shirt all the time and it was the only one he wore that had a movie theme. But she hoped Ricky would only know about this. "Yeah, and I slapped your chest in annoyance?"

Ricky laughed. "Yeah, cuz you hate mosquitoes and one had landed on my chest. Wondered what the hell you were doing."

She smiled.

"Didn't you pay me $750 for that donkey job?"

She chuckled. "Yeah, you're right. You kept calling it a donkey. It was a goat."

"Damn, you're *testing* me. Wow, that's too cool. And good idea. Okay, so I was hanging around with my brother and his friends, acting like we were all friends and I didn't know he'd turned on me."

"Be careful, Ricky. I don't want you hurt."

"I know how to handle myself, 'k?"

He might think so, but in a business like this, no one was really safe. Often, there was way too much money involved.

"Anyway, I was drinking beers and just hanging out, being my usual self, cracking jokes, not wanting anyone to think I was aware of what had gone down."

"Good. And?"

"Benny, he's one of my brother's friends. Been in jail a number of times. Twenty-four, got a ton of rattler tattoos. Anyway, he had a good buzz, and he was spouting off about getting in on some new action. Course, if it means money, everyone was listening. Me? I figure I'll earn my money in another way."

"By informing on them. What if they know that you are? What if they're setting you up? Me up again?"

"Yeah, I've thought of that. Okay? Give me some credit here."

She smiled.

"So here's what we do."

***

Hal rushed to tell Ted where he was going to be, not that he knew exactly, but just to give him a warning that he was going on a search for Tracey if anything came up with the foal, and to call the vet.

He couldn't believe that Tracey was off working on the mission again—and this time in the middle of the night, God knew where. While he was flooring it, trying to reach her cabin to see if he could find any clues, he called his good friend Mick, her boss. He didn't want to get her in any trouble with her boss, but they had to lay down some new ground rules. Like—Hal was going to help her hunt down this Mooney bastard before she ran off as the Lone Ranger again and got herself killed.

It took forever for Mick to answer the phone, and Hal recalled a little too late that Mick was a really sound sleeper.

"Damn it to hell, Hal! How could you lose Tracey that easily? I thought one of you guys was going to be safeguarding her."

How the hell did Mick already know? "Dan must have called you."

"No, he didn't. If you're calling me at..." Pause. "Three-thirty in the damn morning, she's missing."

"And so is her Hummer."

"Good thing we put a tracking device on it. Just in case."

Hal was damn glad Mick knew her so well. "Where is she?"

"Checking in with the office right now. Hold on."

Hal was practically holding his breath as he sped way over the speed limit to reach the cabins. He wasn't worried about anyone with law enforcement stopping him because *they* were the law enforcement out here, and he knew all of them would be rushing to meet up at her cabin in the same way that he was.

All at once, all hell broke loose. The dispatcher was on the radio letting him know a shooting had gone down ten miles south of there, near an abandoned gold-mine shaft at Pine Ridge—and Tracey was the one who had called it in. And needed backup. ASAP!

Damn it to hell!

Everyone was responding to the call, saying they were en route and where they were coming from. Hal was the closest, being that he lived the furthest out. What the hell was she doing at the old gold-mining shaft?

Mick got on the line and said, "Here are the coordinates where her vehicle stopped. Not sure what's out there. Nothing but…national forest and—"

"And a damn gold mine. She's called into our dispatcher for backup. She's in a shootout. Again. Who the hell are these guys anyway? This sounds damn personal."

"I'm going to have to put her in protective custody."

"Yeah, mine," Hal said.

Chapter 8

"Keep your head down!" Tracey snapped as she and Ricky crouched behind an outcropping of rocks inside the gold mine. She didn't want Ricky killed. But he kept trying to shoot at the shooters while she and he used the cover of the rocks. Three shooters, she thought.

They were hiding in the trees, another ambush. She was surprised they didn't catch them out in the open. But maybe they had planned it this way. Wait until she and Ricky entered the gold mine, then once the shooters killed them, they would dump their bodies down a mine shaft. That way they wouldn't have left bloody evidence outside the gold mine, nor would they have to carry their dead bodies far.

Glancing at him hunkered down behind the boulder, she said, "You probably don't even have a license for that gun."

"You need backup. You called it in, but nobody's here. I don't want to get killed either. If they kill you, where will I be?"

"In protective custody, if we get out of this alive."

"No way. Cramp my style."

"Yes way. Until I solve this case."

"You think they're going to let you back on the case after this?" Ricky looked at her, his expression obstinate, chin jutted out, lips pursed.

"I'm not supposed to be on the case in the first place."

Silence.

Then he smiled a little. "Cool."

Hoping the cavalry would show up soon and take out these bastards, she let out her breath. At least she had phone reception in the entrance to the cave. "Tell me again how you made sure they didn't know we were meeting."

"I did a ton of switchbacks. You know. Just like in the movies. Batman did it."

She rolled her eyes.

"I'm not clueless."

He had been really good at this before, but this time, she was afraid the guys involved in the operation were too close to her, him, and her investigation.

"They can't have bugged my cell. I changed it out." He smiled at her as if he'd fooled them.

She was certain no one had bugged his phone.

"Where were you when you were talking to me?"

"In my *car*." His eyes widened. "Hell, you don't think they bugged my car, do you?"

"I don't think so. Have you been here before?"

"Yeah. That's how I knew to meet you here."

"How…how did you know it wouldn't take me much time to get here? Have you been watching me? Do you know where I'm staying?"

Another volley of shots were fired from the trees, the rounds pinging off the rocks inside the cave, splintering chips, and sending them flying everywhere as she and Ricky instinctively ducked again.

"Wish I had a rifle with a scope. I'd nail every last one of them." She turned to Ricky. "Answer me. You knew where I was or you wouldn't have suggested meeting me here. If I'd been in Denver, and you knew that, you would have met with me somewhere closer."

Rick's eyes were round, then he nodded. "After they tried to kill you, I figured I'd stick close to you. You know, because I thought I might learn something about who they are. How else could I get you any new word? They're going to be holding their tongues around me."

"Okay, so you know where I'm staying?"

"The last cabin at Pinyon Pines. Sure. And they do too. It's not a safe house, is it? Because if it is, I'm going to tell you right now that it can't be all that safe if I know where it is."

"A deputy sheriff runs the resort and lives on the

premises."

"Right. But when you went off with that other deputy sheriff, and came home with another..." He smiled at her. "That was a pretty cool move, I tell you. But anyway, I watched your place. You know. Just in case anyone planted a bomb there or something."

"You watch too many movies."

"Yeah, but they're nothing like what you're always getting into."

That seemed to be true of late. "Okay, so you said you have evidence."

"Yeah. Well, not real trial kind of evidence. But—"

"Not more rumors. You said you had real evidence."

"Not me. I mean, I didn't want to say. Not over the phone. It was too dangerous. You know, because it has to do with your sister."

"Wait, you know about my sister?" Her heart began to race even faster. It was one thing for Tracey to be involved in this. It was her job. But her sister was a total innocent. "What's her name?"

"Jessie. She looks just like you. I saw the article about the guy who tore off her diving regulator in the islands. I put two and two together. At first, I thought I was looking at you. But then I saw the name and realized she had to be your twin. Or a double. Or you were undercover doing another spy mission."

"Why would you be looking at stories like that?"

"I research this stuff. Like you. Only, I'm looking

to see if I might know something about the mission. In case I overhear something. In her situation, her name caught my eye. Well, her picture. She looks just like you. If I were her, I'd want to kill the guy who pulled off her dive regulator. He could have killed her. Everyone even knew who the guy was. Why wasn't he brought up on charges of attempted murder? If it had been me, I bet they would have locked me up and thrown away the key."

"What about my sister?"

"She was taking pictures in Hawaii, right? But she took some in Colorado too. Didn't she? I'm wondering if the guys behind this—"

Another five rounds pinged off the rocks, and she and Ricky instinctively ducked again.

"What? The guys behind this what?"

"They thought like I did. That you were her. That she was you. That you were being your secret agent self."

"Special Agent."

"Right."

"How do you know Jessie took pictures in Colorado?"

"She posted them on Facebook. You don't have a Facebook account. I looked. So I figured that was you. Only you had this other name. And you were posting the pictures to show them off as part of your undercover operation. To bring the trafficker out in the open. You really have a twin sister who looks identical to you?"

"Yes." Tracey knew that Jessie had been in Colorado, since their parents lived in Loveland. She hadn't known she'd been conducting some of her wildlife photography there. Tracey should have known. Jessie always had her camera with her. "What exactly had she taken pictures of?"

"This gold mine shaft."

Tracey just stared at him. "And that has to do with what?"

"I figured we'd come here and find the clues. If they're coming after you, maybe it had something to do with the pictures she had taken of the gold mine."

Tracey closed her gaping mouth and turned her attention back to the trees. *Un*. Real. Maybe her boss was right. She needed to take a break from this case.

"Don't you agree?"

"No!"

"Okay, so maybe not *those* pictures, but I figured it would be safe to talk about them. I didn't want to blow your Jessie cover. If you and she were the same person. Maybe some other pictures she took are the reason they're after you."

"Or none of them at all."

She heard movement then, and was afraid the shooters were trying to reach the cave.

She heard a ping that distinctively sounded like a pin being pulled from a grenade. And then a grenade landed inside only a foot away from her and Ricky's location. *Crap*!

She seized Ricky's arm and hauled ass toward the mine shaft. They didn't have any other choice.

When the grenade started spewing gas, she realized it was tear gas and not a grenade that would explode. Thank God. She'd worried the whole opening would cave in if it had been a grenade.

They could either run out of the cave, coughing and hacking, their eyes teared up and unable to see as they were gunned down, or go down the shaft.

"Down," she said.

"I don't like heights," Ricky said, choking on the gas.

"Yeah, well if you don't move now, you're going to be too blind to do anything else. *Go. Now.*"

She was fighting tears, coughing, choking, craving fresh air.

She wanted Ricky to hurry it up, but not so much that he fell. Then she started down after him, thirty feet into the shaft. Once they reached the bottom, she hurried into the mine where they coughed and hacked, and crouched down together in the dark. "Don't move," she whispered.

"Why? Is something down here? I've seen those alien creature movies and in the dark cave something bad always lives."

Shaking her head, she couldn't believe what he would come up with next. "There could be a shaft nearby. We'd step into it and fall to our deaths. Much more likely than aliens."

"Oh." He bumped up next to her, coughing, trying to fill his lungs with fresh air. "You think I could be an agent like you someday?"

"Do you like animals?"

"Yeah. Never got to have one of my own, but yeah. Cats and dogs always like me."

"In this business, you see the ugliness when it comes to wildlife traffickers and others who kill the animals for greed or other reasons. Our findings can be really gruesome and horrible."

"So why do *you* do it?"

"To hopefully give some of the wildlife a prayer of a chance."

He nodded. "Me too."

She liked Ricky, wishing he wasn't in this business.

Gunfire erupted outside of the cave.

Shouts up above had her heartbeat quickening. It had to be their backup.

"Tracey! Are you in there?"

Hal! Come to the rescue. Again. He probably would be pissed to the max at her this time.

She tried to call out but her voice was strained from all the coughing, and yelling wasn't working. "I've got to climb back up there."

Ricky grabbed her arm. "No, you can't go. You can't breathe up there."

"They can't hear me down here. They don't know if we're all right. Wait." She pulled out her phone and tried calling. No reception. They were too deep in the mine.

She stood and Ricky grabbed her leg. "You can't go."

"I'm just going to get closer to the ladder." She used her cell phone light to reach the ladder and looked up. "Hal! Ricky and I are down here! In the shaft!"

The problem was, she figured, he couldn't reach her any more than she and Ricky could reach him. Not without gasmasks.

"Getting gasmasks! Everyone down there all right?"

She heard the relief in his voice and was glad he'd heard her and knew they were unharmed so no rush—which would cause them to be at more of a risk to themselves—to get them out.

"Yeah, Ricky and I are fine."

She turned around to rejoin Ricky and saw a chip of something white next to the side of the rock. She moved toward the item and crouched down, examining the chip. *Ivory*. That *shouldn't* have been down here.

"What is it?" Ricky practically bumped heads with her as he pointed his own cell light at the object.

"It looks like a piece of ivory—to a tusk."

"Something ancient?"

She shook her head. "Something recent. Like they might have been storing the tusks down here."

Ricky swore under his breath. "See? I knew we'd find a clue in the cave."

Right.

"What exactly had my sister shown of the cave?" Tracey knew she was a bit reckless on her photographing adventures, but Jessie had never told her she'd been climbing into old mine shafts. Here Jessie thought Tracey was a daredevil.

"Pictures of the cave." He shrugged. "I was going to show them to you on my cell so we could compare the pictures with the walls where she'd taken the photos. Then the shooting started. Didn't you 'like' your sister's Facebook page?"

"What?"

"Oh, yeah. You're not on it. You should be. They catch a lot of criminals that way. Other places online too. When you set up your page, you need to 'like' hers."

"Did one of her pictures show this?" She pointed to the ivory fragment.

"I don't know. It looked like a bunch of pictures of rocks to me."

"Tracey!" Hal shouted.

She moved back to the ladder. Even though her throat was irritated and her voice rough, she was feeling a little better. Tears still filled her eyes though. She was glad she saw that tusk fragment, but she was totally pissed off that they hadn't caught the culprits when they had hidden the tusks here.

"Yeah?"

"What the hell are you doing here? At this hour. And why didn't you ask for backup?"

"I'm spelunking. And I think I might have found some evidence of a crime."

Hal didn't say anything to her, but she heard him talking to someone else at the mouth of the cave.

Then he shouted, "What kind of evidence?"

"A fragment of an elephant tusk."

***

Police were all over the place as Hal and Stryker helped get Tracey and Ricky out of the mine. Some of her fellow FWS Special Agents went down into the shaft to secure any other evidence that could be related to the tusk, smiling, and giving her a thumbs up.

She smiled back.

Hal had called Mick to let him know as soon as he learned she was safe down in the shaft, and assured Mick that she was coming home with him until someone caught the bastards who were responsible. Or else she was stuck staying with her boss.

Ricky was being put into protective custody. Mick was seeing to that.

Stryker was shaking his head as soon as he heard Hal say, "Okay, we're packing you up and you're coming home with me."

Arms folded, Tracey raised her brows. "What if I wanted to go home with Stryker?"

Stryker smiled.

Hell, and Stryker had already kissed her!

"Stryker?" Hal asked.

Looking thrilled that he had a chance, Stryker

grinned. "Fine with me."

"He doesn't have a puppy. I'll stay with you, Hal. And you can serve as my bodyguard. All right?" Tracey didn't look real happy about it. Not because of the business about staying with him, he didn't think. But because she had to be guarded.

"All right. Can someone bring her suitcases to my place?" Hal asked.

Tracey shook her head. "We can drive back there. I'd really rather pack my own things, if you don't mind."

"I've got to head back there anyway," Chase said. "I'll give you a deputy sheriff escort."

"Okay, I'll drive his car to the ranch," Dan said. "Stryker, do you want to follow me and then when Hal and Tracey get back to the ranch, you and I can return to the mine to pick up my vehicle?"

"Yeah, sure." Stryker turned to Tracey before Hal and she left. "You didn't say what kind of a puppy you like."

Hal and Tracey laughed.

"German shepherd," Ricky said, as if Stryker was asking him.

Everyone looked at him.

Ricky shrugged. "That's what I'd like, if anyone was asking. Do you have a puppy?" he asked Hal.

"He's got a new foal," Stryker said.

"A baby horse?" Ricky's eyes grew big. "I never seen a baby horse for real. You could be my bodyguard. I could help feed the baby horse. This line of work I'm doing is getting kinda dangerous. I think I'm gonna quit it."

"The mare nurses the foal."

"Oh. Well, I could feed the mare. I'm real handy. Just ask her." Ricky waved his thumb in Tracey's direction.

"Ah, come on, Hal. Give the kid a break. Let him work for you." Stryker was grinning.

Hal looked at Tracey and she was smiling.

Ah, hell.

"Can I have my gun back? I didn't use it to commit any crimes. And it's not stolen. But just in case you're not around—"

"No," everyone said.

"Okay. Just saying." Ricky shoved his hands in his pockets.

"What about your clothes, Ricky?" Tracey asked.

"Stuff's in a bag in my car."

Hal called Mick back. "Okay, I'm safeguarding both Tracey and Ricky."

Mick was silent.

"Ted will help safeguard Ricky. And keep him off the streets. He can stay in the bunkhouse with Ted."

"Cool," Ricky said.

"Tracey's staying with me in the main house. But she can watch out for him too."

"Who's going to be watching out for you?" Mick asked and he was serious.

Hal smiled.

Chapter 9

After explaining a million times to Hal why she'd joined Ricky in the cave, while she had packed her clothes and personal affects at the cabin, they returned to Hal's ranch. Tracey stalked off down the hallway to the bedrooms of his ranch house, trying to keep her annoyance under wraps. She wasn't eager to give up her freedom and certainly didn't like that she might have to be safeguarded. Mostly, she didn't feel the need to explain how she investigated a case. With her boss, yes? With anyone else? No.

"Which bedroom is mine?"

"Any of them. Master bedroom included."

She looked over her shoulder at Hal.

His mouth was curved up in a sexy way, his eyes smiling.

She smiled back. "And... you'll move out?"

"Of the master bedroom? Hell no. What kind of a

male cougar do you think I am?"

She chuckled. "Cute." Then she checked out each of the other bedrooms and found the one she wanted. All dressed in blue, view of the rocky cliffs in the distance, furthest away from the master bedroom for more privacy. Perfect. Each of the bedrooms even had access to the deck. Sweet.

"Did you want me to wake you up to go running in the morning?"

She gave him a get-real look.

He grinned. "Okay, we'll play it by ear."

"Do you think Ricky will be all right out here?"

"Yeah, he'll be fine. He was about ready to fall asleep on his feet when we were standing in the stable, until he saw the foal. Did you see his expression?"

"Yeah. He loved her."

"I think it's a good deal for him. Get some sleep and when I see you, I'll see you. But don't even think of going anywhere without me."

"The shower?"

He smiled.

She felt her cheeks heat. "Right." Then she entered the bedroom, shut the door, and headed for the bathroom. She wasn't getting up until it was midday, the way she was feeling.

She let out her breath. She hadn't really even thanked Hal for taking Ricky in. She'd already thanked everyone at the scene with helping to rescue them. But taking Ricky into his household? That was going above and beyond the call of duty.

She'd thank Hal in the morning. She took a nice long shower, then pulled on a silky green nightie, and climbed into bed, hoping that the Special Agents doing the investigation on the ivory tusk would find some other evidence to link the traffickers with the crime scene.

She closed her eyes, thankful that she and Ricky had gotten out of the main tunnel quickly enough to avoid breathing the tear gas for very long. She was feeling fine now.

She began to think about what Ricky had said about Jessie posting pictures on Facebook. She reached over, grabbed her phone off the bedside table, and searched for her sister's page. Over fifteen hundred photos?

***

Hal headed for his bedroom when he noticed a light on in Tracey's room. "Need something to help you sleep?"

"No, thanks... Would it be too late or too early to have a glass of wine?"

He laughed. Then he thought of Stryker having wine and a movie with her and he got a kiss! "Seriously?"

"Nah. Night."

"Night."

He stalked off to his bedroom, glad that she was fine, but not liking that this business with Tracey being shot at seemed so...personal. He turned around and headed back to her door. "Tracey, don't you think this is kind of personal?"

"Me staying with you?"

He chuckled. "No, this business with the traffickers."

"Yeah, I do. But I can't figure out why it would be. Hold on." The sheets rustled, the mattress creaked, then quiet, until he heard her light footfalls crossing the carpeted floor to reach the door.

She opened the door. "Want to watch the sun rise and talk about it?"

He glanced down at her fuzzy blue robe and slipper boots. "Will you be warm enough?"

"Sure. You can light a fire."

He grinned.

"In the fireplace out there."

"Yeah, sure. Let me grab a blanket in case you get cold, and I'll make us a couple of cups of cocoa, if you'd like. Whip cream on top."

"Okay. That's as good as wine."

Before long, they were sitting in front of the outdoor fireplace on one of the cushioned benches, Hal's arm around Tracey, the extra-soft brown blanket covering their laps, and she was snuggled against him while they drank cups of cocoa. He loved this and he was glad, despite that she'd had chips and wine and watched a movie with Stryker last night, she'd wanted to stay with him and not Stryker this morning.

"This is so nice," she said.

"Really nice. I'm glad you suggested it. I've never come out here to witness the sun rise." He rubbed her arm, covered in the soft, fuzzy robe.

"Love this. I think while I stay here, I'll come out here to watch the sun rise every morning. It's so peaceful. Like the cabins at Pinyon Pines, but different. The view, the scents, and sounds."

And you, he wanted to say. Just coming out here by himself would never have been quite like this, feeling her bundled under his arm, her robe and the woman so soft and huggable. She smelled of strawberries, whip cream, and chocolate, all sweetness.

"I wanted to thank you for taking Ricky in. I think he's a good guy deep down, but he just needs some parental guidance, even if he's now an adult. He needs some goals in life that don't include a life of crime."

"I agree. Ted's good with kids and animals. I know Ricky is an adult, barely, but I believe the same as you do, or I wouldn't have taken him in. I think he'd be a lot better off staying here for the time being rather than managing on his own. Ted got into some scrapes of his own when he was a kid. So I'm sure with Ted teaching him the ropes, it will help Ricky."

She suddenly looked up at Hal. "I didn't even think of the problem it could be as far as Ricky not being one of us."

"We'll be careful around him. It shouldn't be a problem." He'd already considered it and thought it would work out. When Ricky had waited for Hal to give his okay, he had looked at him so hopeful-like, Hal hadn't had the heart to say no. Besides, it seemed to help win Tracey over, and he was glad he could make her happy.

She settled back down against him. "Sorry about messing up our run this morning since we'll surely be asleep before long."

He shook his head and tightened his hold on her. "It gives me a better plan. I wouldn't have given this up for anything. We'll go for a run during the heat of the day. I'll take you up to the cliffs."

She nodded and finished her cocoa. He set the mugs on the table and they watched for the sunrise as a faint glimmer of light began to appear.

"So what do you think this could be about that would make it so personal?" Hal asked.

"Ricky said it might have to do with the pictures my sister took. And that the traffickers think that I'm the same person. I looked, but she's got so many pictures, I got too tired trying to figure out if any of them have anything to do with trafficking on the tiny screen on my phone."

"Other than the one that showed the mines."

"Right."

"Mick will contact Jessie for the photos."

"Right. I was trying to see if I might catch anything on them."

"Were you involved in any other cases where you

were investigating this Mooney, or maybe even someone else, and he's got it in for you because you're so dogged about bringing him down?"

"Maybe. I haven't seen a connection."

"Maybe a much earlier case?"

"I've thought about it since the first shootout. They hid the tusks in the abandoned building in Anderson, and now at this gold mine. The only connection I can see is they're both abandoned mining camps."

The sun began to rise—the vivid purple, pink, yellow colors painting the sky—breathtaking.

"Oh, now that's really beautiful." She sounded sleepy and he wished he could carry her to his bed and provide real bodyguard protection.

After the fantastical colors faded from the sky, she patted Hal's leg. "Time for me to turn in or I'll be useless for the rest of the day."

"Me too." He noticed Ted leaving the bunkhouse with Ricky, who was yawning and rubbing the sleep from one eye.

They both caught sight of Hal and Tracey sitting together in such an intimate pose on the deck. Ted grinned. Ricky's jaw dropped.

Hal waved at them, then Tracey grabbed the two empty mugs, while he carried the blanket and escorted her into the house.

After dropping the blanket over the arm of the couch, Hal felt his phone immediately vibrate, and he answered it. "Yeah, Ted, we haven't gone to bed yet.

Unless it's a real emergency, I would appreciate no calls."

"You got it, boss man." Ted laughed.

Hal smiled.

Tracey put the mugs in the dishwasher, then turned and smiled at Hal. "What?"

"I think Ted was really surprised to see me sitting out, watching the sun rise with a beautiful she-cat."

"Except for the she-cat part, Ricky looked a bit surprised too. Thanks for being the first to come to my rescue. We didn't talk about it, but I assumed you got a call from the dispatcher and your ranch was closer to the gold mine."

He could let it go, and just say that was what it was, but he had to be truthful. "Stryker had called me."

Her eyes rounded. "After he left my place?"

"Yeah. He was worried that the call you had received wasn't from Anton, and that you might be getting involved in the case again. I tried calling you, wanting to tell you that if you were even thinking about following up a lead, I wanted to be your backup. Your partner."

Her lips parted. She looked so incredibly appealing, and he wanted to take her in his arms, crush her body against his, and kiss her like he had never done with any other woman.

But he wasn't sure whether she was thinking along the same lines as he was, or ready to slug him for having checked up on her.

"And?" she asked.

"I couldn't get hold of you. What were the odds that you would be out running as a cougar again?"

She smiled a little. "And get treed by a pack of wolves."

"Yeah. So I called Chase."

"Before I even sent out the distress call?"

"Yeah."

"I could have been sleeping."

"Right. But I had to be sure."

"Poor Chase."

Hal smiled. "Yeah, he told me the same thing. But he's been in the law enforcement business for too long, and with your history of getting into trouble…"

"He checked and found I'd gone." She wrapped her arms around Hal's neck.

"Yeah." Hal rested his hands on her waist. "I worried about you. I warned him that if he didn't check on you, I'd be over there."

"Thank you, then, for worrying about me." She tilted her head up, and he was certain she was looking for a kiss.

Did she kiss all the men she had "dates" with?

He wasn't going to let the opportunity pass so he kissed her. He didn't want to push her further than she was ready for and turn her off, but when she kissed him back, wanting more, pressing for deeper contact, he wasn't sure just what she had in mind.

He was certainly willing to go as far as she wanted,

his hand gently cupping the back of her head, the other stroking her soft robe-covered back, their tongues colliding, teasing, stroking. His blood was on fire, and he was burning up as he pulled her harder against his body—his very aroused body.

He wanted to rub up against her like a big cat would, wondering just what she was wearing under the robe. The same slinky nightie she'd left by the door when she went running as a cougar? When he and everyone else had seen it, he had expected her to pick it up in her teeth and carry it to her bedroom. But when she didn't, he did the only thing he could think of, shifted, moved her nightie to the arm of the couch, and then dressed.

He'd seen the way her eyes had taken in the new location of her nightie. Knew he'd picked it up, felt the silkiness, and probably had guessed he'd admired it.

And now? He wondered if she was wearing that sweet bit of short silk to barely cover her beauty. He kissed her warm mouth, tasting the whip cream and cocoa and she-cat. He looked into her eyes, darkened with lust, and smiled.

She was so tired, and yet, she moved her arms lower and tightened her hold on him.

He had to ask. "Did you want to—"

"Hmm, yes. Go to sleep." She hesitated to pull away, and he was hopeful that meant she wanted to join him in bed, but then she said, "Night. And thanks."

"You're not going to be too cold, are you?"

She laughed. "No. But nice try."

"What do you want for lunch when we finally get up to enjoy the day?"

"Anything is fine with me."

"Beef stroganoff? I can whip up a batch."

"Sure. Sounds great."

"All right. Then we'll run."

He left her off at her room and continued on to his bedroom.

"What else did Stryker tell you?" she asked, still standing at her door.

"That he stayed over for a movie and wine."

"And chips."

Hal smiled.

"Did he tell you we kissed?"

Hal's smile grew. "I'm not competing with him."

She smiled back at him. "Sure you are. I like it. It's never happened to me before. Keep up the good work." She entered her room and shut the door.

He frowned. So what did that mean? She liked his kiss the same? Better? That she wasn't going to decide between the two of them? He thought when she stayed with him that had decided it. What if Stryker learned what kind of dog she liked best? And got a puppy?

He shook his head and reminded himself he was an alpha male cougar. Not a pussy-whipped beta. Well, that had some appeal too.

Chapter 10

As soon as Hal woke, showered, and dressed, he was raring to go. Not only did he have the most charming houseguest known to a male shifter cat, but he'd had the best sleep in years, knowing his first foal was doing well. And he felt good about taking in a wayward "kid" to help give him some direction and maybe keep him out of trouble for a while. Maybe even help to set him on a better path for the future.

When Hal walked down the hallway, he noted Tracey's door was wide open and a bit of panic hit him. She was fine, he told himself. He had to stop jumping to conclusions where she was concerned. Not that the last few times weren't warranted.

He listened for any sign of her moving around in the house, and he heard none. She might be sitting on the deck, enjoying the scenery and having a cup of coffee, or checking on the foal.

He wanted to force himself to relax, but damn it. When it came to Tracey, she kept him on edge. He went out to the deck, observed that she wasn't there, and was about to take a walk to the stables when he saw movement in the grassy meadow near one of the ponds, way the hell out. He squinted his eyes. A rider and horse alone. One of his horses. And if he had to guess, the rider was none other than Tracey.

He yanked out his phone, ran down the steps from the deck, and stalked toward the stables, calling Ted immediately. "Ted—"

"Morning," Ted said so cheerfully, Hal knew he'd let her take one of the horses for a ride. "Boss lady took Nelda out. She's a good rider. She might not know anything about foaling, but she's a natural in the saddle. Now, Ricky? He's another story. He's afraid of the horses. Though Holly, that's fearful of humans, has taken a liking to him. Maybe because she senses he's not pushy with her like some humans can be. Anyway, there's hope for Ricky still. Before you say it, I've already saddled Big Red. He's chomping at the bit to get outta here."

Wordlessly, Hal ended the call. He couldn't help being irritated with Ted. He should have asked him first. Hal worried about her being on a horse without seeing for himself that she knew how to ride, when yeah, normally he fully trusted Ted's instincts. But when it came to Tracey, well, Ted should have asked him first. Especially because of all the times she'd been in real trouble lately.

Ted was conveying his usual "take everything in stride" posture today. Ricky looked nervously from Ted to Hal, like *he* was in trouble for letting Tracey go.

When Hal reached the corral, Ted said, "Hey, boss man, she's fine. You know me. I wouldn't have put her on the horse, if she wasn't capable of it. She showed me just how much she knew, and I let her go. Horse and rider are perfect for each other."

"What about the terrorists who are trying to kill her?" Before Hal climbed into the saddle, he noticed that Ted had packed his bedroll, which Hal shouldn't be needing.

Ricky quickly said, "She's got her Glock, and she's a good shot." He sounded as though he was protecting Ted from Hal's wrath.

Giving him a stern look, Hal looked down at the young man. It appeared that he was going to work out just fine here on the ranch. It seemed he already had Ted's back. But Hal frowned down at him anyway because *he* was boss and he didn't want Ricky getting the idea that he wasn't. "I thought you were supposed to help protect her."

Ricky shoved his hands in his jeans pockets and gave him a hard scowl right back. "You took my gun."

Like Hal had any intention of arming the kid. He shook his head and rode off after the lady.

By the time he was able to ride beyond the house, she was gone. Again, he felt that same sense of dread of losing her skittering across his spine.

Then he tamped down his concern and got out his cell phone and called her. It took a moment for her to answer, and when she did, he said, "Where the hell are you?"

There was a significant pause and then she said, "Well, good morning to you too, Sunshine."

He smiled. Just that one little jabbing, but humorous, poke changed his whole view of the world and her.

***

Tracey supposed she should have told Hal that she'd ridden horses before. A lot. On her job and off. On several occasions she'd ridden into the backcountry on horseback to investigate a crime. But she hadn't ever been around any that had foaled. So that was a new experience for her. Riding like this, wasn't. She loved exploring all the meadows brimming with wildflowers, the evergreen forests, and the ponds. Now, she headed toward the rocks. Riding horseback was just the best way in the world to really see the layout of the land. She'd been up for a couple of hours, had a piece of toast coated in honey, visited with Ted and Ricky, and when Ted suggested she take Nelda out for a ride, she was all for it. He said he'd send Hal out to join up with her when he woke. But that had been over an hour ago. And she really loved riding the ranchlands just like this.

A red-tailed hawk flew up above the pines, and she watched him soaring high in the bright blue sky. She wasn't upset with Hal, who was displeased with her for riding alone. She understood his concern, but she wasn't going to be cooped up in the house all the time until he got his butt out of bed so he could go with her places.

Maybe some of it was taking perverse delight in proving he couldn't tell her that she wasn't going anywhere without him.

"Where are you?" he said in a much nicer tone, though it still bordered on hostile.

"I'm headed for the rocks."

"Wait for me."

"Did you have a good sleep?"

"Yes, the best ever. Having cocoa with you until sunrise agrees with me. Waking to find you had ridden off on your own when someone is trying to have you killed, doesn't."

"I love it out here." She sighed. She wasn't going to let him ruin it for her. She was thrilled. "I'm having the best time ever."

She could hear his horse galloping, at least on the phone. She was still a ways off and couldn't hear the actual sound of him getting closer.

"I'm glad. Sorry. Good morning."

She laughed.

He let out his breath. "It's beautiful out here. I often ride first thing in the morning—"

"But we slept instead."

"What time did you get up?" He sounded really surprised that she was out here already.

"Two hours before you did. I'm glad you got a nice rest."

"Sorry that I didn't get up any earlier. Couldn't you sleep?"

"I had the most wondrous sleep. Then I heard one of the horses whinny, and I was thinking how much I'd love to go for a ride."

"What kind of dog do you like?"

She laughed. "Any kind, really. I love dogs."

"And horses."

"Yeah. And animals in general. Which is why I do the job I do."

"Are you waiting for me?" He sounded like he thought she was still riding away from him.

"Yeah. When are you going to get here?"

"I see you, just through the trees."

"I hear you." She took a deep breath of the fresh air and smiled at him. He looked great, like a cowboy in an old western—jeans, cowboy boots, hat—except for the blue T-shirt. And the gelding, a beautiful bay. She thought the stud riding the gelding was pretty hot too.

Ted had told her the gelding's name was Big Red, best bomb-proof gelding they had. Tracey was riding a perfectly good trail horse. She noted also that Hal was armed like she was, only he was carrying a rifle and a handgun.

Hal was giving her a look that said he was still not pleased. She just gave him her cheeriest smile back. He was being an all alpha male, deputy sheriff right now.

But she was a Special Agent, and she could handle herself.

"So do you want to show me the rocks?" she asked.

"You said you weren't going anywhere without me. How am I supposed to protect you if you don't stay near me?"

"Okay, next time I'll come knocking at your door when I wake up, and then you can protect me all day long."

"How about you stay in bed with me the next time, and I'll change your mind about leaving me?"

She laughed. "You're too cute."

"I'd go for something a little hotter than cute. Foals are cute. Puppies are cute. Male cougars are not—cute."

She laughed again. She really liked him. She liked his protectiveness and his teasing her about staying with him, though she knew it wasn't all teasing. If she agreed, he'd have her in his bed tonight.

"Remember, just a bodyguard detail. Nothing more."

He didn't look like he bought it. Probably not, after she seemed so comfortable here. Loved everything about the area and the ranch, the horses, and even got along with Ted. Not only that, she'd kissed Hal. But she knew as soon as she went back to work, Hal wouldn't like it. Not when she had to run all over the place doing her investigations. She suspected, as she assumed most husbands would be, he'd want her home in his bed at night, there to share meals, not gallivanting all across the country.

He was watching her, smiling a little, and she thought he had the notion of changing her mind. She wasn't about to.

"Okay," he said, though he didn't appear to be agreeing with her, and he headed toward the rocks. "We'll go this way. There are several ways, but this has the most scenic trail."

Wild rose, bluebells, primrose, and some kind of yellow flower covered the meadows on either side of the well-worn horse trail. Way before she reached the rocks, she heard the sound of what she thought was a waterfall, the water rushing over boulders just up ahead. Ohmigod! Hal had to have been keeping it a secret from her. A special treat that he had wanted to show her when they ran as cougars. And she had almost ruined it for him.

But she would love to return as a cougar later.

A stand of junipers had hidden the view of the waterfall cascading into the creek. Now, she saw it in all its glory.

The waterfall rose several hundred feet, the water cascading between the rock walls of a narrow gorge, moss covering the rocks, giving it a pretty green cast. The water rushed over a stepping stone of rocks into a pool, before it continued on its way down the rocky creek.

The breathtaking spot was like a secret garden, only in this case, a half hidden waterfall with rock walls that jutted out in front of the falls to provide a glimpse of the shower of water.

On a hot summer day after horseback riding, no one could see all that tumbling water, and not want to at least get in and cool off a bit—but just her feet. She knew it would be cold. But she couldn't wait.

"You wanted to save this for me to see tonight when we ran as cougars, didn't you?"

"Yeah." He smiled. "This is good for now. You can see it in the daytime and enjoy the flowers in the meadow. I didn't know you could ride or I would have suggested we ride out here too."

"And visit it tonight as cougars. I'd love to see the waterfall by moonlight." She dismounted and tied her reins to a juniper.

He watched her.

"Are you going to join me?"

He jumped down and tied off his horse. "You know this can be awfully dangerous."

"What? Slipping on the moss-covered rocks? Falling? I'll be careful."

She sat down and took off her boots.

He sat next to her and began to remove his boots. He didn't say anything more, just began to strip off the rest of his clothes, all but his briefs.

She had removed her jeans, but she'd left her T-shirt and panties on. She wasn't that wild. He was so hot. Sculpted cowboy, cougar, and deputy sheriff all rolled into one sexy package—the abs, the tanned body, the erection already straining for release.

She stepped into the creek, carefully, so she wouldn't slip and fall. He quickly joined her, grabbing her hand and guiding her. As soon as she reached the pool of water, she slipped and fell, pulling him down into the five feet of water with her.

"Ohmigod, it's cold!"

He laughed and pulled her into his arms and began to kiss her. Now she knew what he meant when he said this could be dangerous.

Maybe because this was the second time they'd kissed, or maybe because he'd worried about her again, he was kissing her without reservation, holding her tight against his body, and hers warmed his enough that she began to feel his cock stir and grow again.

She felt so wickedly entranced by the setting, the rocks towering above, and the seclusion from the rest of the world. Then she thought briefly of how it would look when they returned to the ranch and Ted and Ricky saw they were soaking wet.

She smiled against Hal's mouth, just thinking of it. She kissed him back just as passionately, pressing hard against his crection, loving the feel of him wrapped around her body.

This was perfect. The ride here. The wildflowers in bloom. The waterfall. Hal.

All of it.

She didn't think anything could get more romantic than cuddling with him in front of the outdoor fireplace, cocoa in hand, while they watched the sun rise. This was the ultimate romantic spot though.

Nature surrounding them, wild as days gone by. Pristine, beautiful.

He began to lift off her T-shirt, pulled it over her head, then threw it on the rocks, out of the water's spray.

They began kissing again, his hands on her breasts, rubbing the lace bra against her nipples, so sensitive, she was in heaven and wanted to experience everything with him.

"Do you have a blanket?" she asked.

His eyes clouded with lust, he looked down at her, studying her as if he was trying to figure out what she had in mind.

"For heaven's sake, come on. The water's too cold to do anything else, and we need to dry out a bit." Except she wasn't planning on *just* drying out.

Unless, he wasn't ready for this. Fat chance of that, she figured.

She took his hand and led him out of the water, but when she slipped again, he quickly came to her rescue and helped her over the mossy rocks to the shore.

"You sure about this?"

"About drying out? Sure."

He pulled his bedroll off his horse while she brushed the water off her arms and legs with her hands. She wrung out her hair, observing him as he adjusted the seamless, down-filled bedroll from twin size to king size and spread it out among the wildflowers.

"I hate to get it wet. Wait." She grabbed up his sun-warmed T-shirt, still perfectly dry, and wiped down her body as he watched in fascination. She considered the bedroll, then put his shirt on the ground, not ready to let him use it, unfastened her bra, and dropped it on the flowers, then pulled off her panties and spread them out to dry. Then she used his shirt to wipe the water droplets off her breasts and smiled at him. "Sorry. I probably should have let you use it first. Since it's your shirt."

Not that she was truly sorry, nor that she figured he minded in the least.

He pulled off his sopping wet briefs and gave her a sinfully roguish smile. "Lady's first."

Smiling back, she handed him his damp T-shirt, laid down on the bedroll, and watched him dry himself like he'd watched her.

Between the mild breeze and the sun, she was already warmed up, and the bedroll was nice and comfy. She wondered if he'd thought it might come to this, and she liked that he'd thought of it. He dried himself really slow, working over his abs, letting her get an eyeful of every impressive inch of him—his chiseled muscles, the light dusting of blond hair on his chest trailing down to his blond curly hairs, his growing erection, jutting out proud and strong. Imposing. Smiling just a little, she swore she wouldn't blush, but she did.

He laid the shirt out flat so it would dry. Then he joined her. This was just perfect—dry, warm, well, now things were beginning to get hot, surrounded by wildflowers, the scent of junipers, and the water, the sweet fragrance of the flowers, the smell of him—man and cougar combined.

They kissed again under the blue, blue sky, only a smattering of white clouds high above as his mouth was hot against hers, his tongue quickly probing as if he wanted more, a deeper connection, to show this was only the beginning. Then he moved his leg in between hers, dominating, claiming, displaying his intent. She welcomed it—nothing permanent—just a special moment in her life that she would remember forever, instead of the real reason she was here, that her life needed protecting, that she had lost the bad guy, that her partner was in the hospital after what went down.

Hal paused in his kissing her, and their gazes collided. He was watching her, and she realized she'd stopped responding, her fingers on his waist, her mouth open to his, but she had become lost in thought about what she wanted and her intent was not anything permanent.

She took a deep breath and smiled a little, then tugged him down for another kiss. He must have thought she was rethinking this moment, and that she might not be ready for this now, if ever. But she wanted this, needed this, and was damn well going to have it.

She lightly scratched his back with her nails as he

stroked her breast with his hand, cupping, lifting, rubbing his palm over the sensitive nipple. His gaze trained on her breast, making her feel admired and beautiful.

Wanting more, she locked her leg around his and rubbed her mound against his thigh, encouraging him to go further. He groaned and moved his hand lower, and began to stroke her sweet spot. His tongue circled her nipple, the warm breeze blowing on it, licking the flames higher, making her all the more sensitive.

She loved it. Love being here with him. Loved the way he made her feel sexy and hot and totally desirable.

She hoped she did that for him, because *he* was sexy and hot and totally desirable as her hands combed through his hair, the length just perfect, rugged looking, outdoorsy, not cut military or cop short. But sexy, like he was.

As sensitive as her sense of smell was, she adored the smell of him—the way his hot and spicy pheromones kicked hers into a higher aroused state, the animal part of her that she valued, and she appreciated that it did the same to him.

He continued to stroke her, continued to work her into a frenzy of emotions from need to want to raging desire. She was burning up, felt the tactile pleasure of his strokes on her clit pulling her heavenward, up and up, until she thought she'd burn up in the flames of the sun's brilliant fire.

As if he knew she was nearly there, he stroked

harder, plunged his tongue into her mouth, saying he needed to be in her at that moment. She sucked on his tongue, just as she came, loving him and this instant and the intimacy between them.

The climax hit her like a burst of fireworks, hot, bright, and beautiful.

He pressed the broad head of his erection between her folds and pushed in. But then he held still and cursed under his breath. In that instant, she knew exactly what he was concerned about.

"Birth control shots. Don't you dare move," she growled.

His expression lust-filled, his eyes darkened, and he smiled a little.

Hal hadn't forgotten such an important thing as that since he began to experiment with sex as a teen. He was glad he didn't have to stop and delay the forward momentum as tantalizing as Tracey was. As eager as they both were.

He pressed deeper, allowing her time to adjust to his size, loving the feel of her heat and wetness wrap around him like soft velvet. He thrust into her, wanting this so badly, his body ached for her, their bodies moist with exertion, the smell of her sweet and sexy—the cougar half of her firing his pheromones into action.

Not that he'd needed the extrasensory assault to make him want this. Want her.

She wrapped her legs around his hips, opening herself further to his exploration, allowing him deeper into the sensual abyss.

And he took the invitation. He thrust harder, deeper, having to feed the primal need to conquer, to have her...to...to keep her?

It was in the genes when a cougar mated a cougar that he'd claimed her as part of his territory. And yet, it was also in the genes that they didn't mate for life.

Screw it. They both needed and wanted this. Now. Just the moment.

She purred and he valued the sensuous sound—a she-cat vocalization that was so right and engaging, but best of all? He had made it happen. Her eyes closed, her skin glistened in the sunlight like diamonds sparkling. Her breath was barely there as she looked to be absorbing the feel of him inside her. Her fingers clenched his ass, and he was certain when she arched against him, another orgasm had hit.

He was enraptured, his blood on fire, his breathing raspy as if he couldn't take her and at the same time breathe. She moaned softly. The beautiful sound added to the magic of the moment.

With the utmost control, he held still for a moment. He looked down at her swollen, well-loved lips. Her darkened green eyes opened, jade with flecks of gold, watching him with wonder.

"Perfect." He turned his gaze to her rosebud nipples, succulent to feast on, every inch of her stunning.

Then he thrust again, and again, desperate now. He

felt the end coming and couldn't hold back even if his life depended on it. The sweet-pain of holding on, and then the climax, letting go, the release, sharp and hot and wondrous.

He collapsed on top of her, wanting to pin her body beneath his, and wanting the closeness. He loved this miracle between them, this moment in time, her, the setting. All of it.

She still had her legs wrapped around his and her arms tightened around him as if she craved having his body pressing heavily against hers. That she needed it.

He obliged, not wanting to let go of her or the moment, either.

He didn't want to see anything more in this than that they had both needed this release. Maybe because of the recent shootouts with the bad guys. Maybe because neither of them had been with someone in a good long while. He shouldn't have cared. And yet, damn his hide, he was already thinking along the lines of her with him, as Ted had called her already, boss lady, his mate, his wife, helping him to run the ranch.

Yet, he knew how foolish the notion was. She was a highly trained Special Agent. Why would she give up her calling to live here with him? If he was married to her, he knew he'd want her with him, exclusive to him. Not running around, investigating wildlife criminal cases all over the world. Not in shootouts with damned wildlife traffickers.

He moved off her then and wasn't sure what to do

next. If she was in his bed, he'd pull her into his arms and sleep with her.

Out here, they were bound to get sunburned and if he pulled the bedding around them, they'd get too hot.

He rested on his side as she smiled at him. "I opt for letting our clothes and my hair dry before we head back in."

"Works for me." He was glad to see her smile, as if she was happy to have had sex with him, and was not in the least bit regretting it.

He pulled a wet blond curl over her shoulder and leaned down and kissed her mouth. "Let's move the bedroll into the shade. I don't want us to get sunburned."

"Hmm." She sounded too boneless to move.

He smiled. "Fine." He got up then, enfolded her in the roll and carried her into the shade of the trees. "You'll thank me for it later."

She chuckled.

He unwrapped her, returned to the bedroll, took her into his arms, and promptly fell asleep.

Until, he heard her phone buzzing and felt her stirring against him, her body soft and warm and so damned appealing.

She groaned and moved to get off him, but he grabbed her arm. "I'll get it for you."

Naked, he left the shaded bedding and went back to where her clothes were. He grabbed her clothes and his and returned, handing her things to her.

She fished out her phone that had stopped ringing and checked the caller ID. "The boss."

He figured Mick had waited to allow her some time to sleep first after their wild night with her attackers at the gold mine, none of whom they'd caught, but now he was ready to counsel her for her rashness. Which Hal was glad for. Someone needed to do it. And she wasn't listening to him.

"Yeah?" she said to her boss, her fingers straying to Hal's thigh as if she wanted more sex and wasn't ready to go back to the ranch just yet.

And he was eager to make her forget about her job all over again.

Chapter 11

Hal settled next to Tracey on the bedroll. This was probably the weirdest call she'd ever taken from Mick since she had started working for her boss. Outside, yeah, that was usual when she was working a case, with the birds singing and a breeze ruffling pine needles or leaves of trees nearby. The sound of a creek in the background, sometimes. A waterfall, never. But it was the image of one hot male shifter sitting naked next to her on a bedroll while she was naked—that was what made the situation so secretly tantalizing.

She didn't want Hal to get dressed just yet. She didn't want to give any of this up. Just yet. Though she suspected her boss was going to give her a lecture big time because she'd run off to meet with Ricky last night and got herself and him into trouble.

She figured she'd sidetrack the situation quickly. "Did the investigators find any real clues about the traffickers? Did my sister's photos show anything else of importance?"

"I need you to go home."

"What?" Now that was a real twist, but it worried her also.

"Your parents' home, I should say. Your dad asked me to call you—"

"Wait, *what*?" Her dad had called her boss and not her?

"Your dad called me after I asked Jessie for her photos. She's staying with them for the week."

"Yeah, okay, but if he wants me to come home, why did he ask you to ask me?"

"He figured I'd lend more weight in the matter. I want you to go home—to your parents' place. Jessie's there. You and your dad can safeguard her."

Tracey's heart began to race. "You think my sister really needs protection? That they could be after her now?"

"Your informant is right. The two of you look too much alike. And after she took pictures of the cave where the evidence was found, it appears you are one and the same person, and you're gathering evidence."

"That I would showcase on Facebook? Get real."

"To draw out the traffickers. You've been known to be rather reckless on occasion."

She couldn't believe they'd go after her sister. But then again, she could see the problem. "Why don't you put Jessie in a safe house?"

"Are you kidding? The two of you are as different as the seasons in Colorado, but this is one area that you two are identical. You and she refuse to be locked up for your own protection."

"So you've decided you want us both locked up at my parents' house instead?" Irritated to the max, she glanced at Hal. He was studying her, there for her, but keeping quiet so she could deal with this on her own, which she appreciated.

"Listen, this past Christmas, you were chasing down leads on the case of the piranhas smuggled into the U.S. You've been working nonstop since then. Take the time to spend with your family. They'd appreciate it, and you're close to them, so no problem there. And, oh, by the way, if I didn't mention it earlier, you are on *administrative leave*. You know what that means?"

She let her breath out in a huff. She wanted to stay here, but if she was needed to safeguard her sister, she'd leave in a heartbeat.

"Well, let me spell it out for you, if you don't recall since the last time you were on administrative leave."

"I don't investigate anything." She couldn't help sounding irritated. She wasn't a damn child. She was a topnotch investigator, and she'd solved more cases than any of the other Special Agents. Mostly because of her cat senses and because she was so doggedly determined to bring an end to a case, which meant the bad guys went to jail. And she didn't take a lot of breaks. Except when she was put on administrative leave. Even so, she'd continued to work on the cases.

Mick needed her. Which worked in her favor or he'd fire her butt for insubordination. But she'd never had a case thrown out in court based on her lack of handling the evidence correctly—which was the main thing.

"Right. So do I have your word that you're giving your dad a call and then returning home?"

"Yeah, sure."

"Tracey."

"I said I would, didn't I? Hell, if I didn't, my dad would call you and rat me out. Is that all you had to tell me?"

"One last thing, if your dad gets into investigating this, I want you to put a stop to it."

Her heart nearly quit beating. "Is he?"

"You know your dad. Retiring from the force was the hardest thing for him to do. I don't know anything for sure, but both his twin daughters are potential targets for these assholes, so what do you think?"

"I'll make sure." That's all she needed was for her father to get himself killed over this. Sure, he and his retired Special Agent buddies still went to the firing range and kept up their skills. But she could just imagine him calling them up and having them assist in the investigation.

What a nightmare.

The thing of it was, they were trained enough, albeit their age would hamper their reflexes some, that she could see them all getting themselves seriously injured or killed. A chance at reliving the old days?

You bet. She'd heard them share their tales for years—their glory days—which was another reason she had wanted to join the force. All of them had come to her graduation, as proud of her as if she had been their own daughter.

She loved them as much as she did her own family.

"All right. Is that it?"

"That's it. For now."

"Thank you." Then they ended the call and she looked up at Hal, lost in emotions anywhere from worry for her family and her dad's friends, to anger that these traffickers were drawing her family and friends into this.

"Do you want to bring them here?" Hal asked, stroking her arm, and she didn't believe he could be serious!

"No." She pushed him down and settled against him, wanting to have sex again, before she had to stay at her parents' home. "My mother has a successful cake-decorating business. She's got so many summer weddings, summer parties, and birthdays to plan for, that there's absolutely no way that she's leaving home. I can just imagine what I'll be doing when I go home. I just inhale calories when I'm in her kitchen. But it's never truly a vacation when I visit. Not that she forces me to help. It's just hard not to when she's so busy and could use an extra hand. And truthfully, it is a lot of fun decorating."

"So what's the deal with Mick wanting you to leave here?" Frowning, Hal didn't look happy about it in the least.

"Some of it is that Mick wants me there to help protect my sister because my dad needs backup. Mick's afraid the traffickers don't believe that I have a twin. But also, and I think a lot of it rides on the second part of the equation, his four buddies, also retired from the agency at the same time as Dad did, keep in touch and—"

"Mick thinks that they're going to investigate the case on their own, without agency backing."

"Right."

"So if you don't want your parents and sister to come here, what if I go with you and stay out there?"

"Stay with *us*?" She shook her head. "No way. My parents would think something more was going on between us."

He smiled as she felt his erection stiffen between their naked bodies.

She chuckled. "Yeah, but a lot more than that. It wouldn't be right. And it would be awkward. I'd have to scratch off my mother's notes on her calendar, giving a guesstimate as to when she needed to make a wedding cake for us. I could just see my dad making us be on our best behavior at all times."

Hal caressed her shoulder. "You don't think we would be?"

"We'd have to be. Or my dad might force you to marry me, shotgun-wedding style. Just warning you."

"I don't want you to leave. How could I come to your rescue the next time if I'm here, and you're in...?"

"Loveland. It's really not that far from here."

"A mile is too far." He sighed. "Loveland, Colorado. That's the city that's known for its Valentine Re-mailing Program."

She smiled at him. "I wouldn't think you'd know about it. Yep, since 1947 after the postmaster had received over two dozen Valentines with requests to have the cards postmarked from there to make the gesture all the more romantic. That's why my mom opened her cake business up there. It just seemed perfect for business."

"Yeah, I know about it."

"Why?"

He let out his breath. "At Valentine's Day one year, my mother sent a card to me from there when I was on a bad mission overseas. Of course, the guys all ribbed me about it, but..." He shrugged. "I've saved it to this day."

She couldn't believe the Special Forces, hot cougar could be so sentimental.

"That's really sweet." She began to rub up against him. "I have to go. I've got to make sure that my dad and his friends don't get involved. And that my sister is well-protected."

"What about you?"

"I'll be fine."

"I don't like it, Tracey. Not one damn bit."

She let out her breath. "I don't either. Okay? But I don't have a choice." She glanced back at her T-shirt. "It's still drying." Then she spread her legs over his and began to gently rub his erection with her body. "But *I'm* getting kind of wet. Want to do something about it?"

***

Hal couldn't believe just how so out of this world the experience could be in the wild with one hot she-cat. Tracey was unbelievable. Not only did he not want to give this up, or her, because of how fantastic she made him feel, but there was no way in hell she was going home without him.

He was protecting her back, her sister's, her family's, and the retired Special Agents' backs, if need be. But she wasn't going home alone.

If any woman had told him she was taking him home to see her mom and dad and that shotgun weddings could be involved, he would have said no thanks. But with Tracey, the notion had some kind of crazy appeal. Was it a case of him not having been with a she-cat in a long damn time?

No. It all had to do with one firecracker of a she-cat—this one. He hadn't known any woman who would have wanted to have sex with him in the woods by the waterfall like this. And twice? It only got better. But it was a lot more than that. Her love of animals, like his. Her determination to bring the bad guys to justice, like he was just as determined to do. Her need to protect others, just like him. She loved the ranch and though he loved it too, she brought something special to the experience. Watching the sun rise. If he'd ever have the chance—watching the sun set. And running with her as a cougar up in the rocks.

Though he never ever thought he'd consider such a thing, he was thinking how perfect it would be to have a wedding and reception out here. He couldn't imagine anything better. Was he nuts? If any of his buddies had said a while ago that he'd be thinking along those lines, he'd have told them they'd had too much to drink.

He'd already rolled up the bedroll when he glanced at her to see her pulling her still damp T-shirt on.

She shivered. "I shouldn't have worn it into the waterfall pool."

"You didn't expect to slip and fall into it."

She smiled. "Sorry about that. I didn't mean to take you for a dunking."

"Water kind of tamped down my libido for a moment." But only for a moment. After he pulled her close and her hot little body heated him up, his erection had all the encouragement it needed.

She chuckled. "I didn't think much would tame that wild thing down."

He laughed, then he grew serious.

He didn't want to discuss the next matter with her because they'd had such a lovely day, and he knew this wasn't going to go over well with her. But he had to because it needed to be said.

He helped her mount her horse. He was about ready to climb into his saddle when his phone rang. He glanced at it. And smiled. "It's Ted. He probably figured we got lost."

"I doubt it," she said. "He's just checking up on you."

Hal shook his head. "Hey, Ted, we're headed in."

"Okay, good. I knew you were fine, but Ricky's been bugging me for the past two hours, wanting to check on the both of you, afraid you fell off the face of the earth."

"Yeah, we did. But we found our way back. Talk to you in a moment."

"Out here."

He pocketed his phone and climbed into the saddle. "So, about you going to your parents' place…"

They started to head back to the ranch, and she turned her head to look at the wildflowers or the scenery. Or maybe she was just trying to avoid eye contact.

He finished what he had to say. "I'm going with you."

Her head whipped around. "No way, Deputy Sheriff Haverton." Her green eyes were feral, like a cougar's when she got ready for the kill.

He knew there was something really wrong with him when he found her annoyance with him appealing.

"Not only would my mother be penning in the

wedding cake baking date on her calendar, but my sister would be scheduling our Save-the-Date and engagement photo sessions. And Dad would be cleaning his shotgun. Maybe even practicing with it a bit more at the range."

"How many bedrooms do your parents' home have?"

She frowned at him.

"Three? Plenty of room."

"Didn't you hear what I said?"

"Yes. I'll clear it with your folks first."

"Don't you *dare* call them."

"Then *you* call them and tell them. Because I'm going with you."

"All right. Your funeral." She got on the phone and made a call. "Hello, Mom?" She cast an annoyed glance Hal's way. He watched her, giving her the deputy sheriff's look that said he meant business.

"Okay, so Dad called Mick and you all need my help there. Right?" She let out her breath. "All right. So Dad thinks he's going to protect us all. But that's not the way this works. First off, I'm the one who has a badge—" She paused. "Yes, I know I'm on administrative leave. Sheesh. But I still have a badge. No, my boss didn't take it away from me. He knows better."

Hal smiled, thinking how much "fun" having the wild cat working for Mick had to be.

She nodded. "All right. But here's where we have a

problem. I've been staying with a deputy sheriff. No, not for a long time. Just since early this morning. Mom, no. Don't you dare put a date on your calendar for making a wedding cake. He was watching over me for a little bit. A few hours. Like a bodyguard." She glanced at Hal. "Yes, he's in great shape."

Hal smiled. He already liked her mom.

"He's a deputy sheriff. Hal Haverton. He has to be in great shape. What? No, I haven't seen him eat any donuts. How would I know he's in great shape?" Her cheeks grew red, and she again glanced at Hal.

He couldn't help grinning back at her. He *really* liked her mom.

"No, you do not have plenty of room at the house. Not with Jessie staying there. No. Bodyguards don't sleep with the body they're guarding."

Hal chuckled.

"So can he sleep on the couch?" She paused. "How tall is he?" She looked at Hal.

"Six feet."

"He's six feet. Yes, he's here with me now. We went for a horseback ride and are headed back to the ranch. Yes, he's a deputy sheriff, a cougar, and a rancher. All right? Why do you want to know the color of his hair and eyes? Mom. He can curl up on the floor if the couch is too short for him. As a cougar."

She bit her lip. "Fine. I'll sleep with Jessie and he can have my room. Who? Who is Stan? Oh, for crying out—all right. Are they getting married? No? And you're letting her sleep with him in her bedroom? Does Dad know?" She glanced at Hal.

He chuckled.

"Fine. I'll sleep on the couch. Hal can have my room then. Where is his ranch? Out in the boonies. Two hours from Loveland. South. No, I don't have the address. Sure, you can ask him when he gets there. No, I don't need to know his address."

Hal smiled. He suspected her father was going to do a search on him. Probably call Mick to learn more about him.

"I don't know when we'll get there. Tonight, I guess. We've got to get packed, have something to eat, and we'll head on out there. I can help you bake some cakes while I'm staying with you. Oh, all right. If it interferes with my guard duty, I won't. Love you, Mom. See you in a bit."

Tracey pocketed her phone and glowered at Hal.

He shook his head. "See, it's fine with them. Parents never cease to amaze me. When we're kids, they have one set of rules. When we're all grown up?" He shrugged.

"Not *my* parents. Jessie must have thrown a fit and said she wasn't visiting if Stan, whoever he is, didn't get to stay with her."

"You don't want my address?" Hal was smiling when he asked her.

"You know what they're going to do with it? Investigate you!"

"I can handle it. I like your mom." He called Ted. "We're headed back but we're going to be packing up and leaving."

"Las Vegas?" Ted asked.

"Everyone's a wiseass. No. We've got some more problems. Think you can handle Ricky all right?"

"Yeah, sure thing. He's a great help, and he loves it here. Do you want me to fix us something to eat?"

"Yeah, go ahead. I've got fixings for beef stroganoff in the fridge, if you don't mind making that. We're going to pack up while you take care of the horses. You've got my number if anything goes wrong with Annie."

"Gotcha."

Then Hal called Dan. "I'll be pulling some guard duty at Tracey's parents' place in Loveland, so I won't be around for a little bit."

Dan didn't say anything for a couple of heartbeats.

Hal smiled. He knew he was going to get as many questions from his buddies as Tracey's mother had asked her.

"Mick called," Hal explained.

"Ahh, and he wanted you both at her parents' place?" Dan sounded confused.

"No." Hal further explained the situation. "Tell Mick, if you wouldn't mind, that I'm going to be at their house also."

"Okay, will do. What do you want me to tell the rest of the guys?"

"I'm serving as her bodyguard."

"Yeah, okay. Right. I'll...let them know."

Hal pocketed his phone and glanced at Tracey. She was watching him. "So, sounds like they wonder about what's up with this as much as my mother does."

"Dan never said anything about us going to Las Vegas."

Her eyes rounded, she said, "Who said anything about us going to Las Vegas?"

He chuckled. "Ted. He's a wiseass. Didn't I warn you about that already?"

Shots rang out near one of Hal's ponds off in the distance and Hal and Tracey turned around, knowing the shots were fired too far off to be anyone shooting at Tracey. "Damn it to hell," Hal said as ducks, geese, a swan, and herons took flight. "I'll meet you back at the house." He galloped off, but she rode after him.

He glanced at her. "I don't need backup."

"I'm giving it to you anyway." She was frowning so hard that he figured she'd take a cavalry-strength force of hunters on and arrest every one of them single-handedly, she was so mad.

He was glad she was on his side.

Chapter 12

Hal and Tracey continued past one pond, then through a stand of pine trees to make their approach a little less obvious, though the hunters would hear them riding through the area. She suspected they'd try to run off with their illegal catch before the landowner arrived.

Riding on horses to the scene of the crime with a hot deputy sheriff was a totally new experience for her, and she felt as though she was in an old western. She just hoped no one began to shoot back at them because she feared for the horses, most of all.

As soon as they saw the two thirtyish-aged men stalking through the grasslands away from the pond, rifles in hand, making a hasty retreat, Hal hollered, "Deputy Sheriff Hal Haverton! Drop the rifles and put your hands behind your heads."

One of the men looked at the other and the black-haired man swore. "You said that it was all right to hunt here, damn it."

"Put your weapons down *now*!" Hal said again, his voice stern, like he had been a military commander.

This time the men did as he said. "Walk this way, gentlemen."

"Can we see a badge?" the lighter-haired man asked as he glanced at Tracey.

"Don't need to because you're trespassing on private property, *my* property, and no hunting and no trespassing signs are posted all over the place. You can't help but see them." Before Hal could show his badge anyway, Tracey was showing hers.

He fought smiling at her.

"Special Agent with Fish and Wildlife Service. Hope you weren't shooting any protected birds on top of killing waterfowl on private property," she said. She didn't have as commanding a voice as Hal had, but both men's eyes bugged out. Which silently told her what she didn't want to hear. "You shot the birds and left them to rot?" She turned to Hal. "Did you leave food out for the birds?"

"Yeah, I put some seed out every three days. Which means, if the area *was* open to hunting, you still couldn't legally hunt here until ten days had passed since the seed was all gone. That means the timing would never be right, and you wouldn't have the right to hunt them." Hal holstered his rifle and dismounted. He handed his reins to Tracey, but she was ready to pull her Glock out if the men tried anything.

"Let's see some I.D. and hunting licenses, and then we'll return to the lake and see what kind of luck you had."

The black-haired man narrowed his eyes at Hal. "We couldn't have reasonably known the area was baited."

"So you know the law enough that you think you can say the right words and get around it." Tracey was dying to check out the birds, but she didn't want to leave Hal alone in case the men pulled anything.

Both men glanced at her, probably surprised she knew the situation as well as she did. They must have forgotten the part about the job she did.

Hal made a call. "Sheriff, I've got a couple of poachers on my land. Here's the information."

She assumed he called Dan by his title, which she hadn't once heard him use, to impress upon the men the trouble they were both in.

"They're both from Denver."

That said it all. They weren't cougars from the area or they would have known not to trespass here.

"All right. We're going to check out the birds they killed." Hal continued to eye the men with irritation.

She noted that not once had they denied they had killed any.

"Nope. They didn't take them with them. They heard us riding up on horseback and figured they'd take off on foot and pretend they didn't know anything about this. They just didn't realize that they'd not only have to deal with a deputy sheriff, but a FWS Special Agent also, who's trained in investigating poachers and more when it comes to the harm done to wildlife."

Watching the men's reactions, and knowing they wouldn't get much more than a tiny fine and a slap on the wrist if they'd just shot some ducks illegally, she suspected more was going on here. Hal cast her a look that said he thought the same.

So what *had* they shot?

Hal handed them back their licenses after taking down all the information, seized their rifles and secured them, then remounted his horse and motioned for the men to walk with them.

It was killing Tracey not to ride ahead of the men, but she stuck with Hal, ensuring the men didn't decide to take off. They were both sweating now and looking nervously about.

"So what did you shoot?" Tracey finally said. "Couldn't have been birds."

Neither man said anything.

"What else visits the pond?" she asked Hal.

"Everything. Big game, when it gets hot and dry like this. Bull moose, mountain goats, bull elk, pronghorn antelope, bighorn sheep." He paused when the men looked guilty as sin. "You killed a bighorn sheep?"

"Jail time and damn big fines," Tracey said, furious, but glad something would be done about it. She suspected that because of the cougars running things here, they'd give them the maximum sentence they could.

Hal gave Ted a call and told him they were in the middle of apprehending a couple of poachers. "No, Ricky can't help. I'm sure he's got chores he's doing for you. All right. Out here."

When they got beyond the stand of pine trees, they saw the bighorn sheep lying dead beside the pond. Tracey was glad they hadn't wounded it and left it to suffer. She dismounted and measured his horn length. "At least one-half curl, twenty-five thousand dollar fine in addition to a fine between one-thousand up to one hundred thousand dollars, imprisonment of up to a year in the county jail, and an assessment of twenty points. If convicted, the commission may suspend any or all license privileges for a period of one of year to life. So who shot him?"

The animal had been shot several times.

Neither man spoke up.

"That's okay," she said to the men. "We'll determine who shot him." She glanced in Hal's direction. "Do you want to make the arrests or shall I?" That was one thing she loved about being a Special Agent. She had the authority not only to use a firearm in the apprehension of people like this, but she could arrest them.

"I'll do it." Hal dismounted and secured their wrists with plastic ties. Then he read them their rights. He called for backup. "I need a pick up. The hunters shot a bighorn sheep, not waterfowl as we had thought. Yeah, big fines and jail time, if we're lucky."

One of the men snorted. Hal cast him a small smile. Tracey suspected luck would have all to do with them having done so in the cougar territory. Word would spread that it was not a good idea to poach in the cougars' jurisdiction.

"Yeah, I'll head them on over to the road. You can pick them and the evidence up, and we'll head on out."

One of the men muttered to the other that they were serving no damn jail time.

Tracey hoped he was wrong. She glanced at Hal. He smiled at her. She liked that the cougars ran the territory. Too bad more didn't run other areas.

After waiting about forty minutes, Stryker picked them up in a police pickup. He and Hal loaded the animal in the back.

"What about my car," the black-haired man said.

"We'll have a tow truck pick it up."

"And I'll have to pay for that?"

"It's parked on my property," Hal said. "Remember the part about trespassing on private property, the signs posted all over, along with the no hunting signs?"

"Yeah, I forgot about that part," Tracey said. "Sounds like some more charges, more fines. Expensive hunting trip for the two of you."

Stryker looked like he'd rather be riding horseback alongside Tracey, but then she worried—did she look like she'd had a tumble with Hal? Great. When it came to her job, she forgot everything else.

After Stryker took the men in his vehicle and waited for the tow truck to show up, they visited for a bit, and then once the tow truck arrived, Hal and Tracey headed back to the ranch.

She wanted to ask if Hal thought Stryker knew about what had happened between the two of them. About how far they'd gone. But then again, she really didn't want to know.

When they got back to the ranch, Ted took the horses' reins. "Beef stroganoff is simmering on the stove. Ricky and I'll take care of the horses, and then we can eat."

"I'm going to pack." Tracey blushed furiously and hurried up to the house.

Ted smiled at Hal. "I heard she had a date with Stryker today. Did you...beat him to it...again?"

Hal smiled and slapped him on the back. "This time it couldn't be helped." He turned to head to the house and pack.

"Couldn't Stryker have served as her bodyguard?"

"Nah. He's a full-time deputy sheriff. Dan would have been shorthanded then."

Ted said to Ricky, "That's the way to get the girl."

"I offered to protect her. I was trying to shoot at the bad guys when they had us pinned down in the cave, but she wouldn't let me," Ricky said. "What happened out there?" He motioned in the direction of the ponds.

"We'll talk about it over the meal." Hal stalked off

toward the house.

As soon as he was done packing, he saw Tracey heading out to her Hummer with her bags. He headed her off. "We're taking my vehicle. I'm driving."

"I thought we would take both."

"No. Too dangerous. One vehicle. One driver."

"Has anyone ever told you that you're awfully bossy?"

He just chuckled and loaded her bags in his truck. Then they rejoined the others in the house.

When they were getting ready to eat at the dining room table, she said, "Can we sit outside? We can't watch the sun set this early, but I'd love to just sit outside and see the vista while we eat."

"Yeah," Ricky said.

"Sounds good to me." Ted grabbed his plate of stroganoff, and they all headed outside.

She really wished she didn't have to go.

"No shootouts this time?" Ricky asked Hal as if he was afraid she wouldn't want to tell him the truth. "When she's involved, someone's usually shooting at her. And at whoever's with her." He scarfed down some of his stroganoff.

"Not this time," Tracey said.

"I would've come and helped you out, but Ted wouldn't let me go. He said I couldn't ride yet, and I couldn't have my gun back."

"Maybe someday, if you keep out of trouble, you could do something like we do," Tracey said.

Then Hal told them all about what had happened, and Ricky kept asking more about laws and anything else he could think of.

Tracey hoped that meant he wanted to stay on the right side of the law and not learn how to ensure he didn't get caught breaking them in the future.

When Tracey finished eating her meal, she said, "This was so good. I'd love to have it again sometime."

"I can certainly fix it for you." Hal rose from the table.

"Are you sure that I can't go—" Ricky didn't finish what he was saying when both Tracey and Hal shook their heads at him.

"Fine. I'll just eat some more." Ricky went to the kitchen to serve up some more stroganoff on his plate.

Ted cleared his throat. "Is the agency paying for room and board for Ricky?"

"I'm earning my keep," Ricky said.

Ted shook his head.

They all laughed.

"Mind Ted while I'm gone," Hal said.

Tracey smiled at Ricky. "I'm glad you're here."

Ricky was still holding his plate, but not going anywhere. "But you're leaving."

"It's all part of the job. Watch out for anyone who might come to the ranch. Not that anyone might, but just be on guard." Tracey glanced in Ted's direction. He nodded. She was glad he'd be watching out for Ricky.

Then she and Hal headed out to his truck.

As soon as they were on their way, Hal said, "I still think this business with you is something more personal. Have you ticked off anybody lately?"

She gave him a get-real look. "Do you know how many traffickers I have put in jail or got hefty fines? Who lost their sales licenses? Hunting licenses? Who were given a black eye when it came to their friends and family? Of course, I've ticked off some people." Tracey folded her arms and leaned back in the seat as Hal drove her to her parents' home.

"A lot, huh?" Hal smirked at her.

"Yeah. A lot. I keep busy."

He sighed. "But no other case that might be connected to this one."

"What do you think would make it really personal?"

"You killed someone's brother or best friend?"

"That's possible. I killed three men in the line of duty during the shootout in Anderson on New Year's Day. One of them murdered my partner." She closed her eyes and remembered seeing her partner die, and she didn't believe she'd ever get over it. She was just lucky she'd managed to get three of them before they killed her also. "But one made a clean getaway. He was wounded also. My partner was still alive, I hoped, but I couldn't reach my Hummer to get phone reception. They were waiting for me up on the cliffs, and I knew I'd be gunned down by these men if I tried to make it through town as a human. And I couldn't carry my cell with me as a cougar."

"You suffered a knife wound," Hal reminded her.

Annoyed at herself for being injured, she scowled. "I shouldn't have been. *Stupid* mistake on my part. As a cougar, I tracked them up into the cliffs. The one who was wounded in the side, turned to shoot me. I leapt from the boulder and grabbed his wrist and bit down. He cried out and dropped his gun, which I expected. But then he reached for a knife with his free hand, which I hadn't expected. I had intended to incapacitate him and turn him over to the police so we could get some information out of him. But once he stabbed me, I couldn't risk that he'd cut me in a place where I'd bleed out before I could get help. And I still had to think about my partner. The other man had taken off. As soon as I went after his wounded buddy, who had stabbed me, the other guy was out of there."

"Okay, so what about him? Maybe one of the guys you killed was a brother or a really good friend. Partner maybe."

"I don't know. A cougar was up on the cliffs near the miners' shacks when I was on my way here. Was…that you?"

Hal snorted. "You were supposed to be on administrative leave, not looking into the case any longer. Mick said you were headed straight for Pinyon Pines Resort. I couldn't believe it when I saw you there with that patrolman. And just that patrolman. With *you*, you need a whole army to keep you safe."

She smiled a little. "So it was *you*. Looking for clues?"

"Yeah. But I didn't expect you to be there. I'd gone home to check on the mare, and found everything was fine, but I couldn't quit thinking about what had happened to you and your partner. I knew that if I climbed around the cliffs as a cougar, I might be able to smell something that everyone else missed."

"Did you find anything?"

"Yeah, that the cougar who had taken down the one guy was you. I'm sorry it had to happen—any of it. But I was glad you survived the encounter and the trafficker didn't. So what are we really up against?"

She couldn't believe he'd act as though this was his fight also. But if he was willing to help her, she was willing to let him. He wasn't just a civilian after all. And he was a cougar like her, so he could be a great aid.

"You have an elephant tusk smuggling ring. You found the fragment of the tusk in that mine tunnel. Maybe these men are hiding ivory in the tunnels on a regular basis. But there must be hundreds of abandoned mines all over the state, at the very least. On the last case where you were in the line of fire, that had been a ploy to get you there. It was only a way to set you up to take you down, don't you agree?"

"I believe so. Do you know if anyone checked out any of the mines?"

"Not likely. Just made sure they were secure. I do

that from time to time at Anderson to ensure that no one is crawling around in them. They're too dangerous for the average person to explore. Even trained spelunkers have died in them."

"Okay, let me talk with my sister and find out what she was doing in the mines." Tracey got on her phone and called her sister. "Jessie, did you take pictures of ghost towns?"

"Yeah. Did Mom and Dad tell you? I'm writing a book about them."

"Why were you in the gold mine taking pictures?"

"Which one? I've been to fifty or so."

Tracey couldn't believe it! "Are you crazy?"

"Hey, I always take a guide who knows the mine, and I've got another cameraman with me. I'm writing a different book about gold mines, since many of the ghost towns were related to abandoned gold or silver mines, it's an easy way to document both. I don't get shot at in *my* line of work."

No, just had her dive regulator ripped off her face, which could have killed her.

"Jessie, you know that whoever's trying to kill me might think you and I are the same person, don't you? That they might be trying to shoot you? Thinking it's me?"

"Yeah, Dad said I was restricted to the house. Good thing Stan likes to play video games. It's driving me batty though. You know me. I'm happiest when I'm out shooting something. With my camera."

"Who the hell is Stan?"

Jessie didn't date for months, then all of sudden, she had a boyfriend who was her nearest and dearest, and she knew they were soul mates. The longest relationship she'd had may have lasted a month.

"We're not soul mates. But hey, Mom said you picked up a live one. And he's really well-built."

"What?"

"Six foot? Great shape? Sounds like a winner to me. Besides, we looked up his profile on the Yuma Town sheriff's department page. Hot, hot, hot. If you don't like him, maybe he's my kind of guy."

"He's not." As soon as Tracey spoke, she thought she sounded like she had a vested interest in Hal. Which she didn't.

Jessie started to laugh. "Okay, Sis. Sounds like you got your hooks in this one. Great hunting. How long will it take you to get here?"

"Another hour and a half. Are dad's friends getting involved in this?"

"Secret meetings. *Check*. Late night shooting at the range. *Check*. The guys taking turns sitting in their cars outside Mom and Dad's house, totally conspicuous like. *Check*. I'd say they're involved."

"Great. Just stay out of trouble until I get there. I *mean*, stay out of trouble. Period."

"You too. See you in a bit. Oh, and Mom said you are on guard duty, so you are off cake-making duty. I argued with her since I know you like to decorate them,

TERRY SPEAR

but she's standing firm on it."

Tracey laughed. "I'll lick the icing off the spatula and see if you made it properly."

"Hey, baby, who are you talking to?" a man said in the background.

"My twin sister. Just don't get us mixed up when she gets here. All right?"

"No way, baby. I have eyes only for you."

Ugh. Tracey already didn't like boyfriend number, well, she'd lost count. "See you soon, Jessie. Bye." Tracey hung up on her. "Don't you ever call me baby," she said to Hal.

"Huh?"

When they arrived at her parents' home on the outskirts of Loveland, a beautiful two-story, red-brick home with a five-acre forested lot, her sister and Dad walked out to greet her and Hal.

Hal shook Jack Whittington's hand, but before he could offer his hand to Tracey's sister, Jessie, he got a big hug. He hoped Tracey wasn't scowling about the intimacy. He couldn't believe how much the two women looked alike. Though they were different in small ways and definitely they had dissimilar scents, so he would never get them mixed up that way. But their voices too, were very similar. He could see where someone else would think they were the same woman. No matter what, he wasn't interested in Tracey's sister.

The dad was blond-haired, though his hair was starting to gray, but he had the same color of green eyes as Tracey. Jessie's were more amber, and her hair a darker blond. The dad was looking him over as if measuring him for the job of bodyguard. Maybe for more.

Jessie was smiling at him like Tracey had won a prize.

"You're not here to offer to protect Tracey," Jack said, his eyes spearing him, telling him to speak the truth in the matter.

"I couldn't let her come here all alone. Not after all that's happened to her recently."

Jack smiled. "Like I said. You have more of an interest in this than just protecting her."

Tracey said, "Dad, if you keep badgering him, he's going to want to leave."

"Is that right, son?" Jack asked.

Hal caught Tracey's eye, and she looked uncomfortable. Hal smiled at her, not bothered in the least by her father's comments. In fact, he appreciated his frankness. "I think you know the answer to that."

Jack slapped him on the back as though they were good friends, gave a thumbs up to a man sitting in a black car curbside, and then followed Tracey and Jessie into the house. "Mom's baking a cake, crucial stage, and so she couldn't leave the kitchen to greet you."

"And Stan is at a crucial stage in his game and couldn't break free," Jessie explained.

Jack snorted. "The only time he can leave that blasted game is to join us for meals."

"Dad, you're not investigating this business having to do with me, are you?" Tracey asked, joining her mom in the kitchen.

Her mother had blond hair, even lighter than both girls' hair, but her eyes were more of a blue-green. She quickly set the cake pan in the sink and took in Hal's appearance.

"So glad to see you home." Melanie gave Tracey a hug. "Though I wish the circumstances for your visit were different." She considered Hal again. "He looks like he doesn't eat donuts or he works them off."

"I work them off, ma'am," Hal said, patting his belly and smiling at Tracey, who blushed beautifully.

So did Jessie.

Tracey promptly changed the subject. "Dad, you didn't answer me."

"Of course, we're looking into the case. The agency needs every good man it's got to investigate it."

"You're not with the agency any longer."

"I'm not dead either. And this involves both my girls. I'm not keeping my nose out of it. Any more than you are. You can't seriously believe the other guys would, either. So exactly what are we looking at here?"

"We are not looking at anything here." Tracey began washing the cake pan.

Everyone watched her for a moment as if they expected her to change her mind. Then Jack turned to Hal. "So, like I said, you have no intention of just guarding my daughter. You want to solve this case every bit as much as we all do. You and I can discuss it while Melanie brings us some sandwiches and such."

Hal considered the ladies' response to that and Jack smiled. "My wife and Jessie had it all planned out for when you arrived. Tomorrow, you and I get to grill ribs. Not sure about the gamer in there."

"He'll help, Dad, if he comes back tomorrow to join us." Jessie kissed him on the cheeks. "Or he won't get to eat any."

"Good." Jack grabbed a couple of beers and offered one to Hal. "This all right?"

"Yes, sir."

"Call me Jack, if you don't mind. We're on the same team."

"Do you need my help with this," Tracey asked her mother, motioning to the cooling cake.

"No. Go discuss this situation with Hal and your father. And keep your father and his friends out of trouble."

"All right. Thanks." She gave her a hug and raised a brow at Jessie.

"Good with me."

"We'll need to see those photos you took."

Jessie waved in the direction of the other room where her father and Hal had taken seats. "On the laptop in the living room. Dad's got it all set up for you to search through. I looked at the photos, but didn't see anything out of the ordinary. Then again, I wouldn't know what you're looking for exactly, so maybe you'll find something."

"Okay, thanks."

From the loveseat where he was sitting in the living room, Hal watched Tracey and her sister talking.

Both of the women did look similar—smiles, eyes, expressions—but Tracey's hair was longer and she was probably a half inch shorter, unless it had something do with the sandals the ladies were wearing. But the differences would be negligible if one didn't see the women together like this. Would Hal get them mixed up? He didn't think so. He wasn't sure if they'd decide to test him though.

"If you're looking to see the differences between my two daughters, it's easy. Tracey loves blue. She wears it nearly all the time. Jessie loves fluorescent colors, hot pink and the like. Of course, being cougars, we can smell the difference easily enough. But from a distance like this, and upwind, it could be difficult. If you're worried about them trying to pull a fast one on you—you should be. That's how they've broken up with more guys over the years. Oh, and I know you said you're only here as a bodyguard and to investigate this case, but I know differently. You want to make a rancher out of my little girl."

Tracey turned to look at her father and frowned.

Hal laughed.

"If you can do that, you'll have my blessing. She was hell-bent on working for the agency, and I blame myself for it. I used to tell her about all the good cases where we saved wildlife. And so did my friends. Who would have the heart to tell a little girl about all the killings? There's so much more ugliness to this business. Now with this deadly situation, well, I want her out of it. But she's not going to listen to me."

Tracey shook her head as she joined Hal on the loveseat. He was glad he had sat there and not on the couch or a chair. "Stop telling Hal to marry me, Dad, so I'll quit my job. Which I have no intention of doing." She opened up the laptop.

Jack smiled and winked at Hal.

Hal smiled back. He liked her dad a lot too.

With the expanded view of the pictures, Tracey began to look for any clues. "Over fifteen-hundred photos in here. It's going to take forever."

Jessie joined them, bringing the tray of sandwiches, pickles, and chips. "Image 0523 is the beginning of the fifty or so photos I shot in the cave where you had the firefight."

"Thanks." Tracey ran the cursor down until she reached the first of the images and clicked on it.

Hal pressed against her arm, looking for anything also, mainly any hint of more ivory fragments, or the one she had found. But he couldn't help breathing in her scent, and feeling her warmth and softness. She suddenly turned to face him.

He smiled. He couldn't help that sharing the same space with her made him think of being with her earlier today by the waterfall, naked. And he couldn't help that she stirred his libido every time they were touching, even like this.

She rolled her eyes, but the thing of it was, his increased pheromones triggered an increase in hers, so the effect she had on him meant he affected her as well.

"There." He pointed at the screen.

She saw it too. A tip of a tusk mostly hidden in a burlap sack.

"Jessie, you took a picture of the stolen ivory tusks."

"No way." Jessie moved over to see the picture. "Omigod. That was the last picture I took. We were in a hurry to get out of there after I took a picture of the old mining cart, and then we heard a cave-in. I hadn't even had a chance to look in that direction. If you hadn't told me that this was a tusk, I would never have realized what it was. Our guide grabbed my arm and yanked at me to hurry through the tunnel to the shaft. We were covered with dirt and dust from the cave-in and choking on it before we made it to the shaft. The sound was deafening, and to tell you the truth, it was the last mine we went into. After that, I was really spooked about going into another."

Tracey scowled at her. "You said it was safe! That you had a guide who knew what he was doing!"

"Well, yeah. That was the only one in the fifty mines that we visited that we had any trouble in."

"What if these tusks were buried in the cave-in? Were you deeper in the mine?"

"Deeper than what? I don't know where you were exactly when you found the piece of ivory."

"Okay. We went down a shaft, then walked through a tunnel for about five-hundred feet and then down a second shaft."

Tracey studied the picture again. "We only went down one shaft. So either they chipped off a tusk when they went in to hide it. Or broke it off on the way out, which means they recovered their stolen ivory before the cave-in."

Melanie brought in a glass pitcher of a beverage to the coffee table that smelled of bourbon and mint. "Mint julep," she said. "Should we invite Albert in?"

"No," Jack said. "Jessie can take a sandwich and soda out to him. He's on strict guard duty."

Jessie got up and went to get Albert his dinner.

"Hey, Jessie, what about the ghost towns? We were at Anderson when my partner was killed."

Returning from the kitchen, Jessie had a baggie with a sandwich in it and a soda in hand. "There's a list of the images with locations right next to the laptop."

"Thanks. I love how organized you are."

"Have to be if I'm going to write about them. Be right back. Don't find any more clues about this until I return." Jessie headed outside.

Tracey got on the phone to her boss, while Hal opened up the first picture listed for Anderson. "I was looking at Jessie's pictures. The staff you have that are checking them over might have seen it already, but they might investigate and see if there was a cave-in after the second shaft." She explained in more detail what she saw in the photo and what had happened to her sister with the cave-in right after that.

"Nope. I'm not investigating this. Just sitting here visiting with Mom, Dad, Jessie, and Hal, having mint juleps and sandwiches, enjoying my family—like you said for me to do. If I get any other ideas, I'll be sure to run them by you."

She set her phone on the table and began to look at the pictures of the ghost town.

"What did he say about you investigating this further?" Hal was certain Mick knew her well enough to realize she wasn't leaving the case alone.

"He told me to have a nice visit."

Hal's phone rang and he quickly looked at the caller I.D, concerned it was Ted and there was some trouble back at the ranch. Instead, it was Mick. Hal rose from the loveseat and headed for the door. "Be right back," he said to the family. Tracey frowned at him.

He didn't want to hide anything from Tracey, but he didn't want to speak to Mick in front of the whole family. "Yeah? What's up?"

"Are you somewhere you can talk?"

"Uh, yeah, just a second." Hal walked outside and shut the door, but Jessie was still within cougar earshot.

After delivering the sandwich and soda to the retired Special Agent on house watch, Jessie turned and smiled as she headed back to the house and saw Hal on the phone speaking to Tracey's boss. "So what's up?"

"Just needed to take a call in private."

Jessie frowned at him. "You're not seeing another woman behind my sister's back, are you?"

He chuckled. "First, we just met. Second, you would have smelled another woman on me. Tracey would have smelled her first. So no."

"Okay. Just so you know, my dad and sister aren't the only two people in the family who know how to shoot. I don't only use a camera."

He smiled. "Don't think you have to worry about that. Tell Tracey I'll be there in a minute."

"All right." Jessie gave him a look like she meant what she said.

He liked that her sister was protective of her and not trying to make a play for him. It had happened before to him with another couple of sisters, and what a mess that had been.

When the front door closed, he glanced at the middle-aged man sitting in the sedan, who was watching him. Hal waved to him in greeting, and then said to his friend, "Yeah, Mick?"

"Four of my men were down in the tunnel where Tracey found the ivory fragment. I sent word to the man in charge topside. I have four men up there guarding the place. Anyway, he went down to tell the others the news. So we might have some word in a couple of hours about the cave-in."

"You think the men who shot at Tracey were trying

to protect their ivory?"

"Could be. Not that she could have gotten it out if it was buried. But if they knew she'd gone in there and suspected that the ivory was there, they might have concluded that she would be reporting back to us about her find."

"So they thought to kill her and Ricky and dispose of their bodies. She's on administrative leave and was working the case without your approval. So she wasn't giving you any hint of what she was up to."

"Right. She hadn't told anyone. So she was the perfect target. No one would have ever known what happened to her if she hadn't contacted your dispatcher."

Hal heard a window to a room at the end of the house slide up. It had to be the room where Stan was playing the computer games because the game music was suddenly louder. And he wondered then, since the family had said he always came when the food was ready, why he hadn't left the game to eat sandwiches with them. But then again, if he was in the middle of a battle, some games wouldn't allow the gamer to save or pause the game.

Still, Hal listened to what was going on at the end of the house as Mick continued to talk to him concerning what he wanted Hal to do about Tracey and her family. But Hal didn't hear a word he was actually saying. Stan was no doubt just letting some cool, fresh air into the room. Then something that sounded like a screen being removed from that very same window caught his attention, and his curiosity. He moved toward the south side of the house, pulling his magnum from its holster.

"Talk to you in a moment." He hung up on Mick and pocketed his phone. As soon as he headed for the open window still out of his view, the retired agent's car door opened. Damn, Albert was going to screw this up.

Hal turned and waved to the man to stay back. But he had a Glock out and he started across the grass. *Damn it.*

Hal ignored him and continued toward the window, then heard footfalls headed in the direction of the wooded acreage. Hal moved out quicker to catch sight of Stan and see what he was up to. There wasn't any reason for him to sneak out a window, unless he wanted to talk to a girlfriend or something else was going on. Hal didn't even want to consider that it could have anything to do with Tracey.

He heard talking in the woods and stopped to listen. Luckily, Albert had taken his cue and stayed nearer the front door, more in protective mode for the family, which was good.

"Can't stay now. She's here. Yeah. Wait." Footfalls moved toward Hal, Stan's, he thought, and then gunshots were fired.

Hal dove next to the house for cover, hoping to hell Albert was taking his lead. Then he heard the front door of the Whittington's house open. Damn. He knew

Tracey or her father, or both would head outside to help.

Then the man ran off. Hal chased after him.

"No, stay here," Tracey shouted, and Hal knew she couldn't mean him. She had to be talking to Albert. Or her father. Or both.

Then footfalls from behind headed in his direction. The next thing he saw lying on the ground was a gun and clothes dropped all over the place. Stan was in on this business and he was a damn cougar?

"He's shifted," Hal turned to tell whoever was following him and saw Tracey.

"Who?"

"Stan, if that's his name. He came out of that window." He waved his gun in the direction.

Tracey glanced back at the window. "Jessie's bedroom. What are we going to do? We can't let him get away."

"I'm going after him but I want you to stay and watch over everyone." He handed her his gun. "Safeguard it."

"But…"

"You've got to stay and watch the others. And I don't want to leave my gun lying about, or yours either. And while you're at it, grab his revolver."

Hal stripped out of his clothes, pulled Tracey into his arms and hugged her soundly, then kissed her mouth. "Take care of them. If I don't find him, I'll be right back."

He wasn't so much in a hurry to rush off as he was interested in ensuring that Tracey and her family and friends stayed safe.

"Okay, but damn it, don't get yourself killed."

"When you put it that way, how can I do otherwise?"

He kissed her forehead, then turned and called on the shift, his muscles instantly warming, protecting him from the chill of the night air, fur covering his skin, his teeth ready for the confrontation, his body fully cougar and ready to rip into another male cougar. He glanced back at Tracey. She looked so worried for him, he wished he could tell her he'd be fine. Then he took off, ready to take down the bastard, hating that this had been so close to home.

They needed one of these men alive to answer some questions though.

Chapter 13

Hal took off after Stan and chased him out into the wilderness. He couldn't believe the guy working for a trafficker was a shifter. Then again, some didn't care anything more about wildlife than some humans. If it meant money, that's all that mattered.

Cougars couldn't run marathons. They were more for leaping and short sprints. He couldn't imagine where the guy thought he was going. He couldn't drive off in a vehicle all that well without keys, clothes, and he'd left behind his cell and I.D. Then Hal suspected the guy wouldn't have any I.D. on him.

He was glad he had come with Tracey to help protect her and her family. He imagined everyone was shook up about having had the man in their house.

Hal was still trying to locate Stan by scent, but then he heard a car race off in the distance. Damn it to hell. The bastard couldn't have just driven off!

Hal continued to track the cougar's scent and finally reached the place where a car had burned rubber on the dirt road near the woods. And then Stan's scent disappeared.

His cat tail whipping about in agitation as he ensured the man wasn't still here, Hal continued to smell the scents the cat left behind. The cat had been terrified that Hal might catch him. When Hal was certain Stan had left with the vehicle, and it hadn't just been parked in the area for any other reason, Hal loped back in the direction of the Whittington's home. He was furious that he hadn't caught the bastard.

When he arrived at his pile of clothes, he saw no sign of anyone—the family at least. Albert was again sitting in his car watching over things. Hal quickly shifted, dressed, and headed out of the woods to cross the front lawn.

Albert nodded at him. Hal was glad everything had remained quiet here. At least he hoped so. He knocked on the front door and said, "Just me." He opened the door to see every member of the family with a gun pointed in his direction—including Tracey's mother.

"Really, Just me." He smiled a little.

"You didn't get him." Tracey holstered her gun and sat on the loveseat in the living room to look at a different laptop as her mother returned to the kitchen. Tracey's dad sat down again on the couch. Jessie brought in some fresh drinks as Hal locked the door.

"He drove off," Hal said, before anyone could ask.

Tracey glanced at him and arched a brow.

Hal shrugged. "Either he had someone waiting for

him or he had keys in the car and a keyless lock entry. There was no I.D. in his clothes, I take it. But it means he had planned his escape." He joined Tracey on the loveseat.

Jessie said, "Nope. No wallet with his clothes. I checked."

Hal pulled his gaze from the monitor where Tracey was looking through emails and asked Jessie, "How did you meet him and if he didn't have a car parked out front, how did he get here?"

"I gave him a ride from the camera store where I buy a lot of my equipment. His car was in the shop and a friend had dropped him off. He's big into cameras too, and photography, so we were talking away about it. I started mentioning my books about ghost towns and abandoned gold and silver mines. He was dying to see the pictures. I'm a chump when it comes to people giving me a snow job, and I don't even realize it."

Tracey shook her head. "It happens to all of us from time to time." She looked again at the monitor. "I don't see that he did anything on here other than play games, like he said he was doing. He probably was busy listening in on our conversations while he pretended to play games. Or he did that as a cover, but his main focus must have been to listen in on us. I suspect he would have stayed longer if he hadn't realized I was bringing a deputy sheriff with me. And that he didn't know Dad and his friends were all retired Special Agents and would be hanging around."

"Yeah, Albert was the first one to come, but he didn't arrive until this afternoon. I hadn't mentioned who Albert was, or anything about Dad's former occupation. Why would I? Though, I guess Stan might have figured Albert was a retired cop, or something." Jessie sat down on the couch beside her father. "But just the fact that Albert was sitting in the car watching things had to clue Stan in that he was quickly being outnumbered."

"Okay, so he was looking to see if you and Tracey were one and the same person?" Hal asked.

"I guess. He didn't ask me if there were two of us, so I suspect he thought I was Tracey and that the photography was my hobby. Or maybe he believed it was my cover. Anyway, he spent all morning looking at my photos and commenting on them like he really loved them. Now I wonder if he was looking to see if I had any pictures that might have shown anything that revealed any evidence of trafficking. He had breakfast with us, then lunch, and he was really, incredibly nice. I asked him if he'd like to stay for dinner until his car was ready to be picked up. I was going to take him into town and drop him off at the repair shop. He said sure. Then he saw one of my video game boxes and asked if he could check out the game. I said that was fine. I had to help mom bake some cakes."

Hal asked, "Do you know the name of the auto repair shop?"

"Are you kidding? He had to have lied." Jessie

gave him a look as though she couldn't believe Hal would think any of what Stan said was true now.

"Criminals have been known to do dumber things."

"No, he didn't tell me the name of the repair shop. I didn't ask and he didn't say. I figured he'd tell me when I took him to the shop once his vehicle was finished."

"What happened when he learned I was coming?" Tracey asked.

"He said that was really cool. But now that I think back on it, he had a funny look on his face. Then again, he might have thought I just had a sister, and that I was still the one with this other persona."

"But he was still surprised to learn that there were two of us."

"Right. Though if he hadn't taken off like he did, I wouldn't have suspected anything." Jessie lowered her voice. "If Mom catches sight of him, she'll kill him."

Appearing surprised, Tracey's mouth dropped a little.

Jessie motioned to the corner of the house. "The bullets he shot off? They hit the siding on the house, and she's totally fried about it."

Tracey sighed. "Oh. Probably more so when she learns I had to dig the rounds out of the siding so I can send them to ballistics. Mick's sending someone to pick up the gun, Stan's clothes, and the rounds. Did you ever get a picture of him?"

"No. We weren't dating, though with our mutual interest in photography and the fact that he was a cute cougar, you could never tell. He was leaving later tonight, and I really had forgotten all about him when you all dropped in."

"What about his cell phone?" Hal asked.

"Nothing on it. One of those throw away phones. But Mick will have some of our agents on it." Tracey closed down the computer and sat back against the loveseat, looking annoyed.

Jessie frowned. "I don't understand. I thought that if someone had one of those disposable burner cellphones, the government couldn't conduct surveillance on you. That's why the drug dealers are using them."

"Nah. Most of the burner phones buy wireless network space from mobile virtual network operators. So if the burner operates on some of the networks, then they could very well be turning over the data to the government," Tracey said.

"Hell, yeah," Tracey's dad said. "There have been cases of drug dealers or other criminals caught using prepaid cellphones just by triangulating their signals too."

"In the case of a murder conviction, the man was using a prepaid phone, but had his cellphone with him. Even though it was turned off, the police were able to locate him based on his personal cellphone signals," Hal added.

Jessie smiled. "Good one on him."

"Yeah, he was a real cocky SOB too. They were

glad to catch and convict him," Hal said. "So if Stan didn't have a car here, someone had to have met him at a certain location and—"

"He was a cougar," Tracey reminded him. "So if he was supposed to be picked up by someone, he would have to be a cougar also or wouldn't the driver be surprised to see a naked man, or a cougar shifting into a naked man?"

"Hell, Mooney's not a cougar, is he?" Hal asked.

"I don't think so. Then again, he takes hunters on hunts, so for those, he would wear hunter's spray to hide his human scent. Still, unless he knew a shifter was tracking him down..."

Everyone stared at her for a moment.

Hal shook his head. "Damn it, that's it! The connection. He's a cougar shifter. That's why he wanted to get rid of you so badly. You can track him when others can't. He probably knew you were coming for them up in the cliffs. Between the dense, mixed conifer forests with steep, rocky hillsides that climb up to 8,000 feet, it's a cougar's haven. Perfect for a shifter outlaw. But also perfect for a Special Agent working to bring him down. And there aren't that many of you. So the likelihood that a cougar agent would be on his tail would be slim to none. Not since your dad retired. Right?"

"True. Albert and only one other were Special Agents with a decided advantage. Once we retired, that was it. Mick was glad to get Tracey on board," her father said.

"I met with him at a café. He was sure to have worn the hunter's spray then too. That would throw me off his cougar scent."

The doorbell rang and everyone pulled out their guns before Hal went to answer the door. He gave them all a sharp look to stay back. Not that anyone was headed for the door. Tracey was standing in family protection mode, and he was glad for that.

"Yeah?" Hal called through the door, seeing a man dressed in a suit standing on the stoop.

"Mick Sorenson sent me to pick up some evidence. My name is Michael Talbot."

"Either of you know a Michael Talbot?"

Tracey's father smiled. "Yeah. He trained under me when he was wet behind the ears still." He approached the door, looked out the security peephole, and nodded. "That's him. Still looks like a young-un."

"I thought you only said that about me," Tracey said.

"Not just you. About everyone younger than me."

Hal opened the door and asked to see a badge—just in case, and he called Mick also to verify they weren't turning the evidence over to an imposter.

Once they determined everything was on the up and up, Michael said good night and left with the evidence.

Tracey got a call and Hal watched her expression. She glanced up at him. "Okay, boss. Sounds good to me. I'll let them know. Ahh, okay, I'll talk to Hal about it and get back with you." She ended the call and looked at all the expectant faces. "Mick wants Mom, Dad, and Jessie to go to a safe house for the next few days."

Hal realized that due to the severity of the case and that one of the bad guys had been in the house with the family, at least the mother and Jessie didn't object. Thankfully. But Jack immediately said, "I'm not going to—"

"Mick wants you and your agent friends to help with protecting Mom and Jessie. He's really short-handed and he's sending a couple of men. But if you can take turns watching the place along with your friends, that will really help."

Her father frowned, grunted, and said, "All right."

Tracey smiled a little as he got on the phone to his friends.

"Are your cakes all done, Mom?" Tracey asked. "If not, we'll help you finish them. And then you're out of here."

"Three more to go," her mother said.

"Got some extra aprons?" Tracey glanced at Hal, who just smiled right back at her.

He would love to bake cakes or whatever they needed him to help with.

Her father looked a bit skeptically at him as he asked one of his friends to get in touch with the others. Then he finished his call. "Hell, there goes our barbecue. I'll pack some stuff."

"Does Hal cook?" Jessie looked intrigued.

"He sure does. He makes some mean omelets and a great barbecue." Tracey sighed. "Hal, Mick wants you and me to stay here in case the bad guys come back. Are you game?"

"Let me call in some backup." Hal pulled out his cellphone.

"Albert is supposed to stay on guard," Tracey said.

"I'm going to call Dan and see if he can free up Stryker for the night."

"Are you sure?"

"Yeah, I'm sure." Hal didn't want to tell her that he wasn't real sure about their outside backup because he didn't know Albert at all. He knew with Stryker watching out for things, they'd be better off. "Hey, Dan, need to ask a favor if you can spare Stryker, and he's all right with it."

"Sure, what do you need?"

Hal explained what had happened at the house. "Let me know for sure."

"I'll have Stryker call you."

Within minutes, Stryker said, "I'm on my way. So does this mean we get to draw straws for who's guarding her body inside the house and who has outside duty?"

Hal smiled.

They finally finished baking the cakes, let them cool, and iced them, which Hal was having fun doing, though only the women actually decorated them. Tracey knew they didn't have the time to teach Hal the cake-decorating skills her mother had taught both Jessie and her over the years. Then Mick sent an escort for her family.

Her mother said, "I'll be back in the morning to pick up the cakes. I've got to deliver them—"

"We'll help you take them with you," one of the police officers said.

After the family left, and before Stryker arrived, Hal took in the heavenly aroma of sweet cakes filling the air. "So what do you want to do now?"

"I just had a thought." Tracey opened up the laptop again.

"What are you looking for?" Hal sat with her to look at the monitor.

"I noticed Jessie had taken pictures of the cakes mom had made. When she visits, she always does so that Mom can show off her cake designs in posts on her website and sell more."

"Right, so...?"

"So she is always taking pictures."

"Not of me. Or your family. And she said she hadn't taken any of Stan."

"When you were icing the cake, she was taking pictures of the finished ones, but when you were having trouble with the icing sticking to the spatula and not staying on the cake, did you notice she took a shot of you frowning furiously as you concentrated on trying to make it work?"

Hal smiled. "Frowning furiously?"

"Yeah. I motioned for her to get a shot of you."

"So you think she might have gotten one of Stan but didn't remember? Caught him in a reflection, or was taking pictures of something else and caught him in the shot?"

"It's always possible." Tracey began looking at the more recent photos that Jessie had taken and found just what she was looking for. Jessie had taken a screenshot of one of the games that Stan had been playing. And on that shot was a reflection of Stan on the monitor. "Bingo!"

Hal stared at the monitor. "It's hard to see without some photo enhancing to make the picture clearer."

"Okay, so he has brown curly hair like Jessie said. We can't see his eyes, though they appear blue. Then again, he could have contact lenses." She opened a photo processing program and sharpened and brightened the picture. Then darkened it, adding more shadow details, and more contrast.

"There!" Hal made a copy of the picture of the man and sent it to Dan to see if he could run it through their database. Tracey sent it to her boss and just in case, she texted Ricky and sent him the photo. He immediately called her back. "That's Benny!"

"Benny? The guy you said was with your brother and you and talking business?"

"Yeah, it was all a setup. Benny is Stan. Unless he

has a twin like you and your sister." Ricky snorted. "I can't believe you were in another shootout. I should've come with you."

"You stay where you are. Protect Ted and the horses."

"He won't give me my gun back."

"Stay safe, Ricky. I've got to go."

"All right. You stay safe too."

"I will." She ended the call. "Other than being sitting targets in case Stan or Benny—that's what Ricky knew him by—have you anything else in mind?"

"A movie?

She smiled. "Somehow I thought you'd be more mission-oriented."

"In truth, that *is* part of the mission."

She chuckled.

He found an action and adventure movie, and they began watching it. Like watching the movie with Stryker, she cuddled with Hal, but no wine this time, just in case they had any other trouble.

When Stryker arrived, he called Hal. "Okay, good show. Let me know if anything comes up," Hal said. "I owe you one."

Then he ended the call and smiled as he settled back down with Tracey.

"I'm glad the two of you are such good friends," she said.

"The best."

"That's something I love about the two of you. I

think you're both great."

He just smiled down at her, and gave her a squeeze in response. She figured he'd prefer she said that she cared for Hal more than she did Stryker. She liked both men equally—as friends. With Hal, there was a lot more to it, and he had to know that without her saying so.

After the movie ended, Hal said, "Are you ready to go to bed?"

"Yeah."

"I can sleep on the couch, if you'd like. Or shift and sleep on the floor next to the bed." He was being such a gentleman, but she suspected he was trying to be on his best behavior since Stryker was just outside and because of her comment about liking both men.

Tracey slipped her hand around Hal's. "I think that it's important for a bodyguard to be right where the body is that he's guarding. And since we're guarding each other, I think the bed is the perfect place. Besides, now that my parents aren't here, no problem. I just didn't want them to get the notion that you and I were marrying or anything."

He joined her in her bed. "I'll need to relieve Stryker in a few hours."

She figured Hal wanted to know if she'd make the same arrangements with Stryker. After all, she *had* kissed both men. But she had no intention of it.

"Then we better get busy and get to sleep."

The busy part was making love. She always

worried about partners on a mission, but she had really tried hard not to worry about Hal when he took off after Stan, or Benny. She had started looking at the monitor that Benny had used to see what they could learn about him pronto, but her mind had continued to work over what Hal was getting himself into and how much she wished she had been out there watching his back.

And now, for the moment, she wanted to make love to him and fall asleep in his arms, pretending that everything was all right.

Chapter 14

Tracey was about to reach up to kiss Hal, but he wasn't looking at her, and she thought he must be stewing about this situation with her—regarding the case, not as far as their relationship went, for now. She recognized just how much he was like her in a lot of ways. Determined to make this right. Focused, even though she was naked in bed with him. And yet, this really wasn't his case, and she so appreciated that he had the law enforcement and Special Forces background that made him such a great partner—in an unofficial way.

"Who did you put away?" Hal asked, his hand caressing her back as she snuggled against his chest.

"Only a handful of men. Some had up to thirty days in the county jail. Five went to Fort Leavenworth. The rest had fines, lost their hunting license, points removed—minor stuff like that."

"And before the first shootout at Anderson, you never had a problem like that?"

"Minor skirmishes. A trafficker nearly dislocated my jaw when he hit me so hard."

"Is he still alive?"

Tracey didn't answer Hal, and she suspected Hal was angry enough he'd liked to give the trafficker some punishment of his own.

"Tracey?"

"No. He knocked me out. When I came to, my partner had called the agency, police, and ambulance for me, because I'd suffered a concussion. Bill said the man left him no choice. The trafficker didn't want to go back to prison, and he tried to kill my partner. Bill acted in self-defense."

"The trafficker wouldn't be related to Mooney or this Benny guy, would he?"

"Not that I know of."

"Did your partner act in self-defense? I know you were unconscious, but what's your gut instinct on it?"

"I was unconscious." She didn't want to say anything more than that. The trafficker had a knife and two guns, so he wasn't unarmed. Although her gut instinct made her unsure of the matter. She still thought that her partner might have killed the trafficker in self-defense, but she had always wondered if he couldn't have taken the man alive—wounded, sure, but alive.

Then again, the way things were going for her lately, taking these men alive hadn't been a choice.

"Did your partner have previous incidents where no one could corroborate his story and a perp was injured or died as a result of his handling of the case?"

"Not any that I worked with him on. If he had trouble before that, Mick would know."

"Okay, who gives you your assignments?"

"Mick does. That's because I'm a *special* Special Agent."

Hal smiled down at her and kissed her forehead. "You sure are."

Right then and there, he began to kiss her. That was the end of the focus on the case and the attention reverted to them.

Hal knew he should concentrate on solving the case. That he shouldn't kiss Tracey, shouldn't look at her enticing lips, waiting for him to do something. See the gaze in her green eyes, dark with desire. Feel the softness of her skin against his. The fullness of her breasts pressed against his chest. The way her leg and hip were resting against him. So inviting. So willing. When he was trying damned hard to keep his mind on what the hell was going on. And not just what was going on between them. He'd already decided he wanted her for more than just these special moments. He hoped with time he could convince her how much he loved having her in his life and that he wanted her for more.

Her father was right. There was a lot more going on between Tracey and him.

As soon as he cupped her head to kiss her, she moved against his growing erection, and he groaned a little. He kissed her softly at first, and then deepening the kiss, he felt lost in her. In...in the love he felt for her. He broke off the dizzying kiss to take a breath of air and studied her eyes, lovely, aroused, and gazing back at him with hunger.

"Your dad was right, you know."

"Hmm?" She was almost smiling, as if she knew what he was referring to and was amused. Hopefully, she was feeling along the same lines.

Then he began kissing her again, losing himself in the sensuous feel and smell and taste of her. Even her racing heart and soft sighs triggered his need to have her. Everything about her, the way she kissed him back just as tenderly and then passionately, the way she stroked his face and arms and rubbed her lush body against his made him know she wanted him as much as he craved having her.

She continued to rub her lithe body against his erection, punishing him for turning her on—he thought—as he smelled her pheromones kick into action and his played chase with hers, teasing, tantalizing, making him want the whole package.

Burning with white-hot desire, he flipped her onto her back, half straddled her as if he was claiming her, which for the moment he was, and began kissing her deeply again. He stroked her clit with every intent to coax a climax out of her. He relished the way she tensed with need and pleasure, the way she closed her eyes and concentrated on his touch.

Her lips parted and she cried out, just before he inserted his tongue into her mouth and stroked her lovingly. Right before he climbed onto her and pushed his cock into her feminine folds, slowly at first, then deeply and began to thrust.

Her soft caresses over his hips and buttocks made his skin crave her touches even more. She arched against him, welcoming him deeper, thirsting for this as much as he was. He obliged, kissing, licking, and nibbling her sweet lips as she responded in kind. And he tried to hold on as long as he could before he climaxed.

Tracey loved Hal's tenderness, his ruggedness, his body pressed against hers, inside her. And the way he kissed, enjoying the touch and feel of her like she did him. She was burning up as the friction of their bodies ratcheted up the heat.

She was nearing another orgasm, lost in the feel of him rubbing against her, pushing her to the edge, loving how he could make her come apart under his skillful ministrations. The climax hit hard, delicious, and bone shattering. She sank into the mattress as he said her name in a loving and husky way that made her tingle all the way to her toes.

Making love to her ex had never been anything like this. Not even close.

Next time, she'd have to turn the air conditioner on

lower. She realized then how often she was thinking of next times. How much she enjoyed being with Hal. Not just with trying to solve the case, but everything about him. And she knew her family totally approved. Not that they had to, but that made her wonder about his father and mother. What would they think of her and the kind of job she did? She realized then, he hadn't offered to take her to meet them. She sighed. She was way overthinking all of this.

He kissed her soundly again, then moved off her and took her into his arms. "I have to sleep and then relieve Stryker for a while. And then I'm coming back to bed, with you."

"Hmmm," she said, liking that plan and prayed nothing bad would happen during the rest of the night. And beyond.

***

At five in the morning, Tracey's phone jingled, waking her. She recalled that Hal had relieved Stryker sometime in the night and then returned to spoon her for the rest of the morning. Hal stirred and Tracey groaned. She grabbed her phone, frowned at the caller I.D., and said, "Ricky?"

"In two hours, I'm meeting with my brother at that gold mine where you found the tusk fragment."

Tracey sat up in bed. "You can't. Not after what already happened last time."

"He wants to talk, but he's afraid to say something around the rest of the guys."

"No. Ricky. You can't trust him."

"He's my brother."

"Right and he could have had you killed."

"I think it was Benny who set us up."

"It was your brother who sent me looking for the evidence at Anderson. He's been working all along with Mooney."

"You said this Mooney guy takes people on hunts."

"As a guide, yes."

"Well, my brother never did any hunting. Our dad was shot and killed by a hunter who said he thought he was a deer. Anyway, neither my brother nor I ever wanted to hunt after that. We were with him, and I was seven years old and hadn't even used a rifle, but dad wanted us to know how he hunted. Father-sons kind of thing."

"I'm so sorry, Ricky, that you lost your father like that. But your brother doesn't mind hunting people—especially those in law enforcement. And you know how to shoot."

"Yeah, for protection. We'd go to the firing range. Sure. But we didn't hunt any animals. Besides, I think Benny is the guy who's the bad egg."

"But your brother set me up."

"Maybe he didn't know it was a setup. Maybe Benny or Mooney told him to do it, and he was told it was for some other reason. Not to kill you."

"Not to kill you, either?"

"That's different. They had to have been watching

me. Seeing if I got in touch with you. And once I did, they were following us and shooting at us."

"I don't want you going there."

"Your choice." Ricky hung up on her.

Damn. Had it really been Ricky? Or was it his brother?

She explained everything to Hal. "But then I had the notion that it might not be Ricky." She kept forgetting how much the brothers sounded alike.

"I'll call Ted and tell him to make sure Ricky doesn't leave the ranch. Hogtie him if he has to, if that really was him calling, and he has the notion to go to the gold mine." Hal made the call.

"I'll let my boss know." She touched her boss's contact number and put the call through, then waited forever for him to wake up enough to answer the phone. She told him what Ricky had said and waited for her boss's reply.

"I don't want you going into another ambush. I'll send men just in case. You stay out of this."

"Ricky's already left, Ted said," Hal was sitting on the edge of the bed now, looking like he was ready to go with her if they were heading out. "And he's got his gun with him."

"Great." She conveyed the information to her boss.

"Stay put. I don't want you walking into another trap. I'll coordinate with other law enforcement officials and have it checked out," Mick said.

"All right. Your call." But she didn't like it one bit.

"Out here."

Watching her, Hal's body remained tense, ready for action. "Go? No go?"

"We stay here. I hate this and I hate that Ricky could be in danger. But there's nothing we can do about it."

"If it's Ricky's brother and his cohorts, how much do you want to bet the police won't find any of them there?"

"I agree." She laid back down and pulled the covers over her chest, but no way could she sleep.

"Do you want to go out there?" Hal climbed into bed and pulled her into his arms.

She appreciated Hal's offer, figuring he wouldn't want her anywhere near the danger, so he was telling her that they could handle it—together, and she really liked that. "No. I just feel that this all has to do with the ghost town of Anderson somehow. We know that the traffickers had stored the ivory tusks in the town, but it was gone, so nothing for them to try to keep secret there."

"Then your informant calls and says that they'd had illegal stuff there at some time, maybe evidence of wrongdoing, but it's too late for you to really catch them at anything. You said he was murdered because he was trying to backstab his competition and they learned about it. How did he sound? Coerced?"

"Honey sounded like his usual self. Cocky."

Hal stroked her arm, and she pondered the situation

further.

"He knew you'd take the bait. It was New Year's Day, and yet, you'd still run off in a snowstorm and check it out."

"Always."

Hal continued to stroke her with a gentle caress. "You suspected Honey set you up at first, until you found him dead. That he was trying to set up his competition by...?"

Her lips parted, but she didn't know what to say at first, the whole thing becoming muddled. She rested her chin on Hal's chest and looked up at him. "I...thought he was telling me about the site because he knew that they were using it. I'd catch the bad guy's evidence, enough to maybe nail them for their crimes. He would have fed me good information yet again, and I would have paid him. They could have gone to prison, and that would eliminate his competition. That's what I thought once I learned he was dead, and then I assumed his competition nailed him instead. So they knew he had sent me out there and then were waiting."

"But wouldn't it have been better if they killed you, and left Honey alive? Then he was the one who would have set you up and the blame laid on him."

"In this business, they don't want the competition. And if he had tried to gain money by telling on their operation so he could continue his, I could see why they'd kill him."

"What if *he* set you up?"

Tracey frowned at Hal. "Honey? But he was dead. He wouldn't have set me up to have me killed and then what?" She really couldn't wrap her mind around that scenario.

"Why were the men there to ambush you when he only thought there might be a hint of evidence? The stuff had already been moved. It was New Year's Day. Only you and your partner would be dedicated enough to go out there. It seemed like a perfectly safe venture."

"My partner hadn't planned to go."

Hal's brows furrowed as he studied her.

She shrugged. "Like you said, it seemed like a perfectly safe venture. My partner said to wait until the end of the week. I had nothing better to do, and I wasn't waiting. Though he said he wasn't coming, he joined me out there." She took in a deep, settling breath, hating that he had died.

"All right." Hal started to rub her arm again in a soothing way. "Would Honey have known that?"

"He might have. My partner had failed to go with me on several expeditionary missions to find evidence."

"Why the hell was that?" Hal's voice was growly, and he sounded like he would have taken her partner to task if he wasn't already dead.

"He was having a rough time of it. He'd had a recent divorce, and the agency was forcing him to retire out of his position."

"He shouldn't have been neglecting his job and left you to do all the work, and risking your neck because he couldn't deal with life any longer. You should have had an agent who was watching your back like you would his. What did Mick say about it?"

"Are you kidding? I didn't tell him. And don't you dare tell him either."

"Hell, Tracey." Hall took a deep breath, but he still looked angry. "All right, then if Honey knew that, he might have assumed you would be alone. Easier to take down one Special Agent."

"But why would Honey have done it?"

"Maybe the trafficking evidence left in the old schoolhouse wasn't Mooney's, but Honey's."

Tracey shook her head and rested it on Hal's chest again, listening to his heart beating.

"Did you see Honey's dead body?"

"Yes."

"And you're sure it was really Honey? The same guy who had been your informant."

"Unless the guy was acting as the informant for someone else."

"But you discovered he had been involved in trafficking."

"Small time. Not as big an operation as Mooney's."

"What if the small time operation wasn't Honey's? What if it was Mooney's made to look like Honey was into trafficking on a smaller scale?"

"I don't know. And why would he do that?"

"Just trying to come up with far-out scenarios we might not have considered. How did you end up with

Ricky as an informant?"

"He contacted me through the agency. Like Honey had done. They check out the informant's first information to make sure he's not putting agents in danger, or that the 'informant' isn't just a nut case. He was young, so they believed he was working for someone else as a cover for the other guy. He gave them three good leads and then they turned him over to me so that I could work with him since I had lost my informant. But he had nothing to do with this other case."

"He had information about the same site that Honey had. And again, you were ambushed."

"Ricky's brother called me with the information."

"And you know that for certain?"

"No." She hated to admit it, but despite everything, she really couldn't completely put her trust in Ricky. What if he didn't even have a brother?

"I had the notion that Benny might be Mooney. Do you have a picture of Mooney?" Hal asked.

"Yes, and I had asked Ricky already if he'd ever seen Mooney before. He said no."

"Okay, so Benny isn't Mooney. Does Benny have a last name?"

"Smith."

"Figures." Hal wrapped his arm around her. "You're sure that Mooney was there at the scene of the shootout?"

"No. I figured he would be there if he was in

charge of the operation though."

"All right. If you wounded the man who got away like you believe, I wonder how badly he was injured."

"I have no idea. I'm certain that I shot both men. But they managed to get away until I tracked the one and took him down as a cougar. The other couldn't have been too bad off because he got away."

"You were injured yourself by then."

"*Quit* reminding me."

He frowned at her as if he didn't like that she'd been injured, and he'd keep reminding her every time she beat herself up mentally over losing the man. "I tracked the scent of a male for a long time that same day when you saw me in the cliffs running as a cougar, but it was several days after he had left the area. None of us could risk shifting while the Feds were looking into the attempted murder. He had to have had a vehicle parked on another side-road nearby. He probably wanted to make sure Mrs. Blasdell didn't see them."

"Wait. If they were hauling stuff from the schoolhouse, it would have been impossible to carry it over the cliffs."

"It would have been too great a risk to run it by Mrs. Blasdell."

She sighed. "Agreed. Mrs. Blasdell watches everything that goes by her house, unless there's another more recently-made trail. Or if she leaves home on a regular basis at a particular time, and they know her schedule."

"That's entirely possible."

Tracey's phone rang and Hal reached over, grabbed it, glanced at the caller I.D., and handed the phone to her. "Ricky."

Her heartbeat raced as she answered the phone. "Ricky, where are you? At the gold mine?"

"What? No."

"You didn't call me saying you were going to meet with your brother at the gold mine?" She felt ill to her stomach.

"No. *Damn him.* He called you again?"

"Yeah." Or at least she thought it was him. Maybe *this* one was the brother and not Ricky.

Tracey was already getting out of bed. "What horse loves you?"

"What?"

Tracey was struggling to pull her jeans on as she kept the phone tucked between her ear and her shoulder. "The one that you've made friends with because you're scared of horses."

"Who said I was scared of horses? Ted? He doesn't know what he's talking about."

"One of the horses is shy with people. You're afraid of horses, but she likes you, because you're not aggressive toward her. What is her name? If you don't tell me, I'm hanging up on you."

"Ahh, hell, you're testing me. Holly. That's her name. But I'm not afraid of horses."

She smiled, but then frowned. "I got a call about

meeting your brother at the gold mining town where we were shot at. The voice belonged to the same person who said he was you."

"Hell no. Why would I do that?"

Hal was already wearing his jeans, shirt, and boots and offering to talk to Ricky so she could finish putting her clothes on.

"Here, talk to Hal while I get dressed." But she didn't relinquish the phone to him and asked Ricky instead, "Where are you exactly?"

"I just parked at the end of the wagon trail. Tell Ted I'm not afraid of no horse. I'm going to explore around and see if maybe there was something you missed there. You know I'm good at research, but not just on the Net. I can help with this case. But there's a cougar on the prowl out here, and I wonder if it's the one that killed that trafficker."

Because she couldn't let go of the phone as much as she wanted to hear what Ricky had to say, Hal helped her on with her socks and boots. "A cougar," she said half under her breath. "Did it see you?"

As soon as she mentioned cougar, Hal glanced up at her with a wary expression.

"I don't think so. But I got my gun and I'm shooting him if he comes after me."

"Ricky, *listen* to me. Return to your car and go back to the ranch. Let Ted know you're on the way. *Please*, do as I say."

"I'm sorry. I should have told you I was coming out

here. I just wanted to help, and I know you wouldn't let me if I said anything about it to you earlier. You would have made sure Ted was watching me."

"You were supposed to be home taking care of the horses that you're not afraid of. Why are you really there?" She didn't believe Ricky just randomly went there in the dark of night for no good reason.

She held her arms out for Hal to pull her bra on, then fastened it. Then he helped her on with her shirt. She knew Ricky wouldn't listen to her and chill bumps coated her arms as she feared the cougar was a shifter—Benny or his buddy.

"Okay. My brother called me. All right? He said he was scared. I never heard him sound that scared. He's three years older than me and always acts like this really tough dude. But he said he was afraid of Benny. He wanted to talk to me at one of the saloons. He said he couldn't talk to you because you'd arrest him. He wants out of this business. He thought since you and me are friends, I could put in a good word."

Tracey shook her head. "Ricky, don't you see? He told me to go to the gold mine, and he had to have been setting me up again if he's really even planning to meet you."

"He just didn't want you getting word that we were meeting and try to stop me from seeing him. So he sent you in the other direction. I guess. You know. Cuz you worry about me. I'm here now. I'm on the path to the town, and I'm going to check things out. I'll be careful."

"Ricky, go back to your car. Now. It's too dangerous with that cougar running around. Ricky?" She headed out of the house with Hal. "I either lost him because of the lack of reception out there, or he ended the call. He's headed for one of the saloons, supposedly to meet with his brother, but he spied a cougar." She had planned to call the cavalry, but they couldn't. Not if the cougar was a shifter, and she suspected it was this Benny guy.

Hal already had his phone out. "Gotcha." He called Dan. "News alert. Got a call from Ricky that he's at Anderson. We're on our way. A warning—a cougar's running around the place. If it's one of the bad guys, Ricky's in for real trouble. I'll let Stryker know, and he can go with us. Ricky's supposed to be seeing his brother there." Hal glanced at Tracey as she told her boss what was going on. "I know. Someone's lying. Meet us there? That will work. We're on our way."

Hal concluded the conversation and called out to Stryker. He was hidden in the woods and came running. "Yeah, what's up now?"

"We're going back to Anderson. Ricky's there. Alone. Follow us. We might have cougar trouble."

"Like with the bastard who fired shots at you, and then ran off here?"

"Yeah. And if Ricky shoots it?"

Stryker cursed as he headed for his car.

Tracey was already in Hal's truck when he climbed in. She was worried sick about Ricky. Not only for his welfare, but if he shot the cougar? And killed it? It would turn into his human form. No telling what Ricky would do. But she also didn't trust his brother one bit.

"Dan is on his way. He was going to notify your boss, but I take it you already have done so. We can't have anyone out there who's not a cougar shifter in case it's one of our kind."

"I was automatically thinking it was one of the bad guys. What if it's one of your people?" She let out her breath. "Maybe Ricky will go back to his car like I told him to."

"Do you think he will?"

"Fat chance or he would have answered me when I continued to talk to him. He thinks he's going to help us." She explained what Ricky had told her about meeting with his brother. "I think Ricky is relying too much on his brother's sincerity. I don't trust him for an instant."

"I agree. That worries me too."

When they finally reached the wagon trail and Mrs. Blasdell's house, she ran outside with a rifle in hand. Hal stopped his truck to see what was wrong, and Tracey assumed she had heard or seen Ricky drive past the house.

"There's been shooting up there, Deputy Sheriff Haverton."

Tracey's stomach fell.

"Thanks. Deputy Sheriff Hill is right behind me. We'll take care of it. Just stay in your home, and we'll check on you when we've dealt with it."

She nodded, gave Tracey a look like she shouldn't be going into the ghost town on sheriff business, and then headed back into the house.

"You should have showed her your badge," Hal said, driving to the end of the wagon trail as fast as he could on the rutted road, then parked and grabbed a rifle and medical pack.

Ricky's car was sitting there but when they checked it out, they found he hadn't returned to it.

"I have. She thinks I'm just one of the hooligans who used to come here as a teen." Tracey stalked off with Hal down the trail.

Hal smiled at her. "She thought I was too, and the rest of us who ended up being in the deputy sheriff business."

As they hurried down the trail, the whole area was quiet, dark, cool, but quiet. No gunfire and that had Tracey more than worried, thinking of all kinds of scenarios. The cougar had killed Ricky, or he had shot it and it had died, then turned into a man, and Ricky was in shock.

If the cat was really trying to get at Ricky, as it was one of the bad guys, and Hal or Tracey had to shoot it, the same scenario would occur. She could imagine Ricky witnessing it and then what? Humans couldn't see them shift. And shifters had to take matters into their own hands—turn the person or kill him. One or the other. Letting a human know about them and live wasn't an option. That scenario was way too dangerous for their kind.

Stryker hurried to catch up with them as Tracey tried to smell any signs of anyone—cougars, humans, gunpowder. She smelled Benny and immediately glanced in Hal's direction. He nodded, acknowledging he'd smelled him too.

She signaled she was headed around to the first saloon she could reach, smelling for signs of Ricky to learn where he'd gone to. Hal went around the south side of the building. Stryker was following her as if she needed more protection than Hal did.

As if.

Why was it that men always thought women were more vulnerable in a situation like this? She could shoot just as well as any man, keep her emotions under control, and a level head.

Then she heard someone sobbing inside. Her heart nearly quit beating with concern. She motioned to the saloon in front of her, indicating to Stryker she heard someone inside while she searched for an entryway.

Was it Ricky? She feared it was as it sounded like a young man weeping. As long as it wasn't a ruse, but she didn't believe it would be, though she used restraint in any event. She finally found the entryway through the storage room, the same saloon where she and her partner had been ambushed.

"Ricky," she whispered, using her cell phone light. She didn't have a lantern this time. "It's me, Tracey."

"Over here," he whispered back, his voice soaked with tears.

"Are you all right?" She moved toward him, knowing he wasn't all right. Not the way he was leaning up against a wall as if to use it to prop himself up. Not the way his face was ashen, or the way tears were streaking down his dusty cheeks, leaving trails of white skin in their path. Not the way he was holding his shoulder, the gun still gripped loosely in his right hand and his light gray hoody was stained with blood.

"What happened?" She moved toward him using caution, surveying the area around him for signs of anyone else, still concerned she might be ambushed.

"I...I killed it. Him. It."

"The cougar?" she directed her light about and saw a dead man, his naked torso covered in blood, a bullet wound in the head, blood dripping down his cheek. God, it was a shifter.

Stryker was moving inside now, making sure the place was secure before he checked on the dead man.

Hal slipped in the back way too, and stalked across the floor. "I didn't see anyone outside," he said, his voice hushed as Tracey took the medical pack from him.

"There were two of them," Ricky gritted out.

Tracey carefully moved his hand from his shoulder so she could apply antiseptic to the wound. The cougar must have bitten Ricky after he shot it. Otherwise, the cougar would have finished the job before Ricky could have killed him.

"Two cougars?" she asked.

Ricky cried out when the sting of the antiseptic penetrated. "Yeah."

"We've got to get him out of here," Hal said. "We'll take him to our clinic."

Which meant it was cougar run. Not all bites resulted in a turned human. But if it didn't, if they didn't want to kill him, they'd have to bite him again to see if they could change him. What a mess.

Ricky was just staring at the body, his eyes as vacant as the dead man's.

"Anyone you know?" she asked Hal, just to make sure it wasn't someone who lived around there and was one of the good guys. Not that she thought he could be if he had been trying to kill Ricky, but she had to ask.

"No," Hal said, and she thought then it had to be one of the bad guys.

Ricky responded tonelessly, "It's my brother."

And then he began to sob again.

Chapter 15

Hal examined Ricky's brother for vital signs and was disappointed to learn he really was dead, though if he'd still been alive, that would have complicated matters even more. He would have to have been incarcerated for attempted murder, and their kind couldn't go to prison for any length of time when they needed to shift from time to time.

In the meantime, Tracey was binding Ricky's wound to stop the bleeding, and Stryker was checking around the outside of the building, looking for signs of the other cougar Ricky had seen.

"We have to carry him out of here and pronto." Hal joined Ricky and Tracey, and crouched beside Ricky. He squeezed Ricky's good shoulder with reassurance. Ricky was so pale, shaking, his brown eyes dilated and filled with tears. Tears trailed down his cheeks and clung to his eyelashes and scraggly whiskers. He needed medical attention right away. "We need to stick together and head back to the vehicles."

"What about my..." Ricky choked on a sob and didn't say anything further, just stared at his brother.

Hal said, "As soon as we reach the vehicles, we can make a call to have a team out here to investigate—"

"I...I shot him." Ricky cut off Hal's words, as if telling them no one needed to investigate anything further because it was clear that he had killed his brother, and he was ready to plead guilty to the crime.

"Yeah, in self-defense, Ricky. We know. You couldn't have done anything differently," Hal assured him. "It was kill or be killed."

Ricky looked up at Hal with watery eyes. "I...I shot a cougar when he lunged for me. He...he bit me."

He was searching for answers, trying to explain what he'd seen and what he'd done.

"Yeah. We'll take care of everything. We just need to take care of you now and get you some medical attention for the bite wound. Let's go." Hal didn't want to say anything more to Ricky about the cougar not being a cougar. They had to discuss the business with others in their community. They didn't have one leader, but anything of this magnitude had to be discussed with the general shifter population. Not in a public venue, but secretly through a group email, the subject coded for cougar shifters only, in case anyone's email was hacked.

If Ricky had been turned, everyone had to know

about it. If he hadn't been—that would be an entirely different matter altogether. Either they would have to convince him he hadn't seen what he thought he had, which usually wasn't an option, they had to turn him, or they had to eliminate him. Which was why the majority had to agree to it. As for who would turn Ricky if that was necessary? Dan would probably have the task, as sheriff.

"I'm going to carry you out of here," Hal said as he and Tracey helped Ricky to stand.

"I…I can walk." But Ricky really couldn't get far under his own steam.

He was shaking so hard from the adrenaline, fear, the bite wound, and killing his brother, Hal knew Ricky was in shock. As much as Ricky was leaning on them for support, they couldn't allow him to be all tough and macho and try to walk out of here on his own.

"Let Hal carry you," Tracey said, holding Ricky's arm. "You're shaking so hard, we'll never get you to his vehicle. We need to do this quickly. Believe me, if Hal had experienced the trauma you have, we'd have to be carrying *him* out of here."

Hal raised a brow in response to Tracey's comment, and she smiled. But her comment also coaxed a small smile out of Ricky, and Hal was glad she could lift his spirits a bit, despite the circumstances. He could see that she could be a real asset in any crisis.

They heard movement in the storage room and both he and Tracey set Ricky back down on the floor, gently, but quickly, and readied their guns.

"Just me," Stryker called out and stalked into the saloon. "Dan and a few of our men are here. They're at the south edge of town, but I wanted to let you know they're on their way."

"Good. Let them know what the situation is in here." Which meant Hal wanted Stryker to tell them they had a possible newly turned shifter on their hands. And all about the shifter that Ricky had killed and that it was Ricky's brother.

"Yeah. Gotcha." Stryker hurried outside to warn them.

With Tracey's assistance, Hal helped Ricky to his feet again, and then lifted him to carry him out of the saloon.

"Oh," Ricky groaned.

"Hang in there, buddy. We'll get this taken care of, you'll be back at the ranch, and riding horses before you know it."

Ricky groaned again, and Hal wasn't sure if it was because Ricky was still afraid of them, or if he was just in so much pain. Maybe a little of both.

Hal carried him out of the saloon, Tracey sticking close to him. Dan and Stryker stalked through the town to greet them, Dan's gaze on Hal and Ricky while Stryker spoke to Dan in private.

When Dan reached them, he said, "We'll have you in a hospital bed before you know it. We've got an ambulance on the way, but it can't drive over that rutted wagon trail."

"I'll carry him in that direction until the EMTs reach us."

"Okay. He'll be taken good care of. Doc's waiting for him at the clinic."

"Good." Hal wanted Ricky to live. He wanted him to have a normal life.

Changing any person could be problematic, whether he had a family or not. Sometimes, if they hadn't learned to behave as a cougar when they were young, adjusting as a new cougar when they were fully grown could be more than difficult. It could be impossible. If the shifter couldn't be controlled? It wasn't a good ending, but their kind had no other choice. They had to keep their uniqueness secret at all costs.

"Hey, Dan, can you ask Mrs. Blasdell if she has a regular schedule for when she runs into town?"

"Already checked with her late last night. She goes into town on Fridays because they give free samples of food at the grocery store, and on Monday, she runs other errands—post office, drugstore, and the bank. So she regularly makes two trips into town at the very least."

"At a particular time?" Hal asked.

"Always in the mornings and she sometimes has lunch or goes to see a movie with her lady friends."

"So she's gone for several hours. Long enough for the traffickers to move stuff in and out of the place,"

Tracey said.

"Yeah. I would have asked her to vary her schedule, but I don't want her involved in this. Better that she's out of the area when they're moving the goods."

"But they've had the shootouts when she's been home. And she's called us when she's seen people moving about," Hal said.

"Except for New Year's Day. I could have used her call into the sheriff's office that day. I'm going with Hal and Ricky," Tracey told Dan as his gaze switched to her.

"Where do you want me?" Stryker asked.

"Hal and Tracey can watch the EMTs and Ricky make it into town. I need you here to help track down the other cougar. And we'll take care of..." Dan paused until Ricky was out of earshot, though the way Ricky was breathing, Hal thought he had passed out.

Halfway down the path, they heard men jogging on the wickedly rutted trail. The EMTs carrying a litter. They quickly took Ricky from Hal, put him on the litter, and checked his vital signs. Dark haired, Emmett Powell frowned. "He's been bitten by a..."

The EMT didn't have to ask if it was a shifter. His gaze met Hal and he nodded.

"All right. We'll take care of him from here."

"We'll give you a ride to the ambulance and provide protection on the drive back to town," Hal said.

"Sounds good," Emmett said, his partner, Fremont

Gunnison, shaking his head, his green eyes glancing at Tracey as if she caused this calamity.

But then he gave her a smile, and Hal assumed it was more that he was interested in her. Hal growled, "Let's get moving."

It was a long hike to Hal's truck and Hal and Tracey were both armed and ready for a fight while the EMTs carried the litter. Suddenly, Tracey jerked her head to the side, stopped, and peered into the woods.

"Did you see something?" Hal stopped to look in the direction she was studying.

"Stay with Ricky. I'm going to check it out."

"No, you're not. What do you think you saw? Or heard?" Hal hadn't meant to sound that bossy, but she wasn't risking her life, running off into the woods by herself. Not with her track record around these men.

"I saw a cougar."

"He wouldn't come near us with all this firepower." Hal was quickly assessing their options, stay together, or split up, with one of them providing cover for the EMTs and Ricky.

"Someone has to stay with Ricky and protect them." Tracey looked up at Hal, and he could tell that she was waiting for him to agree with her and make a joint decision.

"I'll check out what you saw."

Tracey narrowed her eyes at him, and he could tell she was warring with herself as to whether she'd agree or not. "You could be led into an ambush."

"Better me than you. You have to keep your gun ready and protect Ricky and the EMTs."

"All right, he went that way." She motioned in the direction she must have seen the cougar go. "And don't get yourself killed, or I'll never forgive you."

He smiled a little. "Hell, that sounds like a proposal in the making."

She grunted and took off to catch up with the EMTs and Ricky.

Hal watched her for a moment to make sure she caught up with the other men. He really thought she was beginning to see their relationship as going somewhere, then he headed into the woods. He had no idea what he was getting himself into with the wild cat, but he decided that she needed him in her life. For backup. And for anything else she needed him for. He definitely needed her. He couldn't even imagine seeing a sunrise without her, or visiting the waterfall and not having her with him.

Mind focused where it needed to be, he went into tracking mode. But the cat was on the run and unless Hal shifted and took chase after the cat as a cat, he'd never catch up to him. And he probably wouldn't catch up to him now even as a cat. Hal might as well join Tracey and the others and head back to Yuma Town. Why had the cougar been watching them? Trying to determine if Ricky was dead? Or maybe trying to learn if they were hauling Ricky's brother out instead.

Watching for any sign of trouble, he hurried off to

join Tracey and the others. "It's just me," he said, before Tracey or anyone else could see him. He didn't want her to shoot him, accidentally.

Relief shown on her face, and he smiled. He knew she cared about him.

"Did you learn anything?"

"No. I would have had to have shifted to catch up to him, *if* I could have caught up to him and—"

"You worried about us."

"You're damn right I did." He wrapped his arm around her shoulder, gun still in his hand in case he had to use it, then leaned down to kiss her.

"You know when we're on guard duty..."

"No kissing allowed?"

The two EMTs glanced back at them and smiled a little.

Tracey bumped Hal with her hip in a playful way that said she knew just why he'd said it loud enough for the other men to hear.

The EMTs carried Ricky the remaining three miles to the truck, then put him in the back seat, while one of the men stayed with him and the other rode up front with Tracey and Hal.

"He should sleep for a while," Emmett said. "Doc will stitch him up and give him a blood transfusion."

"I wish we could have checked to see if he was healing any faster." Tracey's voice was filled with worry.

Hal knew it wasn't just because she was worried

about his injury. She was concerned about whether or not Ricky was now one of them.

"We'll know soon enough. I don't think we've met." Emmett smiled at Tracey in that primal way that said he was interested in Hal's cat.

Hal was dying to say she was his, back off, but he was afraid that might not go over too well with Tracey since she hadn't quite agreed to anything that said they were committed to one another. Instead, he gave Emmett a growly look to back off. Emmett smiled knowingly back at him. Tracey shook her head. Hal hadn't thought he'd growled at all, well, not loud enough for anyone to hear. But maybe he had.

When they reached Mrs. Blasdell's house, and the location of the ambulance at the end of the trail, they hurried to transfer Ricky into the ambulance. As late as it was, Mrs. Blasdell's house was dark, and it appeared she must have gone to bed and was sleeping.

"You mentioned you'd tell her when everything was fine," Tracey said as Hal and she climbed back into the truck.

"Dan is here now. He'll take care of it so we can stay with the ambulance."

"I can't believe that Ricky's brother had been turned. What will happen to Ricky?" she asked.

"He's going to have to be watched 24-7. Ted will have to keep an eye on him. Me too. If he has been turned, it all depends on him—whether he can handle being one of us or not."

"Have you ever known anyone who was newly turned?" She hadn't. She couldn't even imagine the trouble that could cause.

"Yeah. Two brothers. One took the change fine as well as could be expected. The other didn't. He ended up committing suicide. Not everyone can handle the differences well."

"Were they living here?"

"No. We have a great support network here. Everyone will become Ricky's new family, if he turns out to be one of us."

"What about his brother? Ricky is feeling really bad about that. Can you imagine shooting a cougar, knowing the big cat is going to kill you, but then learning the cat is a man? And not any man, but your own blood brother? If his brother had tried to kill him when in human form—Ricky probably would have hesitated to shoot him. But not when it was a wild animal."

"He's going to be hurting emotionally all right. We'll all be there for him."

"Who's going to watch over Ricky tonight at the hospital?" Tracey asked as they followed the ambulance into Yuma Town.

"Dan will have men deputized to stand guard. Ricky will be well protected. If he's now one of us, his wounds might heal faster. It's hard to say. It depends on how quickly his body accepts the change. Depending on the individual's immune system, he might not even be changed."

"Okay, so if he is, then what? Return him to the ranch? He can't go into a safe house in protective custody. Not if he has been changed. Besides, someone needs to be with him who knows him. You, me, Ted. Someone he feels comfortable with. Even Stryker because he had dinner with us. Ricky is going to be scared and confused. And so upset that he killed a cougar who turned out to be his brother. That his brother tried to kill him as a cougar. What a nightmare."

"That's why they thought they had to eliminate you. You're a cougar on this case. You could eventually I.D. them through your enhanced sense of smell. It's one thing to keep ahead of the rest of your agents, but you had too great of an advantage."

"How would Mooney have known to hire these guys?"

"What if they have been helping him with his guiding operations already? What if Ricky was wrong about his brother never hunting? Hell, that's something else we can check into. See if he had any hunting gear. If he did, then Mooney learned Benny and Kolby were really great animal trackers. So he hired them. But the reason they're so good at it is because of their cougar senses. Though, of course, Mooney knows nothing about it. Then again, he might be a cougar too. They learn you're a cougar shifter and tracking Mooney, and ultimately them. So they *have* to eliminate you."

"Possibly. I keep wondering if Mooney was there,

watching the whole setup from the first. I can't imagine he wouldn't have been."

"What if you hit him with a stray bullet? If his wound is still giving him trouble, that could be another reason he's after you. The first time ever that he's been hunted, wounded, and then chased further on the hunt."

Tracey smiled. "That would be a good one." She sighed. "I watched him walk into the café after the first battle. He seemed all right, but then that was six months after the shootout. He might have been wounded, still having some discomfort, but hiding it from me to ensure I wouldn't notice."

"Certainly a good possibility. I suppose you're going to want to take first watch after Ricky gets out of surgery. He'll have a private room, but another bed will be in the room, and you can use that to sleep in until he wakes."

"Thanks, Hal. I wasn't certain how your clinic was set up."

"It's mainly for our people. If we get a case of a human who needs care, we send him to the next town to the hospital. Are you sure you want to stay in the room with him? Maybe I should." Hal wasn't certain she could handle Ricky if he were to shift into a cougar in the middle of the night and go crazy.

"He's injured and will be knocked out for the pain. Besides, he knows me. I'm sure I'll be fine with him if he wakes during what's left of the night."

Hal pulled her into a hard embrace, kissed her on

the forehead, and held her tight as they waited for Ricky to get out of surgery. "He should be all right." He couldn't help worrying about him, and Tracey looked up and smiled at him. "What?" he asked.

She snuggled against him. "You're as bad as Chase is about his wife coming in—"

In a rush, Chase ran inside the clinic, his face flushed, but before Hal had a chance to ask what was wrong, it dawned on him. Chase was going to be a dad. Chase grabbed a wheelchair and headed back to the door.

Hal and Tracey hurried after him.

"Is Shannon having contractions?" Tracey hurried outside to open the truck door for Shannon.

"Too close together." Chase sounded flustered.

Hal nearly smiled, only he'd been feeling as anxious about Ricky. And still was.

Tracey held onto the wheelchair as Chase and Hal helped Shannon into it. She was clutching her belly, groaning, and her face was flushed.

Chase turned the wheelchair around and raced up the sidewalk to the clinic. Hal wanted Chase to slow down. He couldn't see why Chase needed to panic so, and he could only make things worse for his mate.

"Get Doc," Chase ordered as he headed for the birthing room.

"She's in surgery, but we'll help you get Shannon into the birthing chair," Hal said. They usually didn't have a couple of emergencies at the same time.

"Her water broke. The babies are coming."

Now *Hal* felt panicked. He rushed off to the surgery room, then paused and returned to help Chase with getting Shannon onto the birthing chair, while Tracey took off, hopefully to let the doc know they had a couple of babies on the way.

A nurse came in to help take charge of the situation as Hal waited for the doc to show up, not that he could do anything, but he planned to stay there to help out if they needed him.

"Dr. Parker's coming," Tracey said. "Ricky's in the recovery room now. She just finished with him."

"We're okay here," the nurse said to both Hal and Tracey.

Hal let out a big sigh of relief and headed out of the room with Tracey. She smiled at him. "Birthing a foal was enough for one week, right?"

He smiled down at her. "Yeah. I didn't have an instruction card for birthing cougar babies."

They checked on Ricky, and he was sound asleep, his neck and shoulder bandaged, his expression sweet and peaceful.

"He'll be all right," Hal said and wrapped his arm around Tracey's shoulder.

"He will. Given time."

After an hour, the nurse moved Ricky into his room, and Hal helped her move him onto the bed.

"Come on. Why don't you get some rest? We were kind of busy half the night. I'll serve guard duty first.

Someone else can spell me in a while." Hal rubbed Tracey's arm.

She kissed Hal's lips, hugged him, and nodded. "I'm exhausted and if I don't get any sleep, I'll be worthless the rest of the day."

"Not to me." He kissed her again, and then left her alone to pull guard duty outside the room.

Tracey felt guilty about sleeping while Hal had to stay up. She thought of going to bed with her clothes on, but what if Ricky shifted and wasn't very agreeable? She'd be better off as a cougar. Not at first, but if she shifted for him to see she was the same as him, it would help reassure him, she thought. She removed her blouse, shoes, socks, and jeans and set them on a chair, and then she climbed under the starched sheets, wishing she was still snuggled in her bed with Hal at her parents' home.

When had she begun thinking in terms of wanting him in her bed to sleep away the rest of the night? She was in deep trouble. She knew their jobs weren't conducive to a relationship that she was already wishing they had.

She didn't think she'd ever get to sleep as she watched Ricky for what seemed like forever, but then some time after that she must have fallen asleep, because the next thing that happened, she heard a low-pitched snarl. She opened her eyes and saw the glow of green cat eyes in the corner of the room.

"Ricky," she whispered, shocked. The bandage on

his wound was stuck to his cat fur, but no longer covering the wound. Though it looked like it was healing quickly and no longer bleeding.

He knew her. He couldn't see her as the enemy. But then he did the unexpected and leapt for her bed and onto it. Startled, she shrieked. If she'd been in her cat form, she would have snarled. But in her human form, she was no match for a violent cougar, and his action threw her heartbeat into double time.

Hal jerked the door open, threw the light switch on, and readied his gun.

But Ricky, exhausted from just jumping onto the bed with her, had collapsed on her and was licking her arm with his sandpaper tongue, half his body on her thin blanketed lap.

"He's fine. He's not going to hurt me," Tracey quickly said, her heartbeat drumming like crazy. She wasn't afraid of Ricky, not after the initial shock of him lunging for the bed, but she was afraid Hal was going to shoot Ricky, thinking the worse.

"Get down off her bed," Hal growled.

All of a sudden the male territorial business was rearing its ugly head. She said, "Maybe he would feel safer and more comfortable—"

"Off Tracey's bed." Hal's hard gaze turned on Tracey. "He gets back in his own bed," Hal said, using a stern, military voice. Commanding, demanding, and he wasn't going to change his mind. "Now."

"Maybe he could curl up with you if it makes him

feel better."

Hal gave her a look that said she was nuts.

She chuckled a little. "Ricky, go back to your bed. I'll be here the rest of the night with you."

"Down," Hal said, as if he was talking to a dog.

Ricky snarled at him, leapt off the bed, and jumped onto his own.

Since Ricky wasn't shifting back, and Tracey wondered how hard it would be for him to get that aspect of his new being in hand, Hal pulled up a chair and sat beside the door, watching both the inside of the room and the outside, this time.

Chapter 16

"Tracey," Ricky said, waking her from a sound sleep. She glanced in his direction, noticed it was nearly noon, and Hal wasn't there, but the door was closed. She pulled the privacy curtain around her bed and began to throw on her clothes. Then she came around the curtain to see to Ricky. His bite wound was again bandaged.

"How do you feel?"

"A cougar bit me."

"Yes." She wondered then if he didn't remember what had happened hours earlier, or maybe he did, but he was in denial.

"But I shot him first."

"Yes."

He had to be trying to process what had gone down because a man shifting into a cougar just couldn't have happened.

He was frowning up at her, looking so lost that her heart went out to him. None of those who had been born as cougars could really understand what he would be going through. And to have murdered his brother on top of that. She squeezed Ricky's hand.

"Are you hurting? Did you need me to get you anything?"

"I...I must have shot the cougar and my brother was standing on the other side of him, and the bullet went through the cougar and killed Kolby." Ricky's eyes filled with tears.

"No, Ricky. Your brother *was* the cougar." She didn't want him thinking that he'd accidentally shot his brother to death. "That's what you saw and that's what you know to be the truth. He tried to kill you as a cougar. You protected your own life by shooting him. You didn't know the cougar was your brother, but it was."

His eyes wide, Ricky shook his head. "You don't really believe that. Nothing like that exists. A wolf-man doesn't exist. Believing that cougar-men do is crazy."

"Werewolves don't exist, but cougar shifters do."

"How come I never heard of one before?" Ricky asked skeptically.

"Because we live in secret. I'm only telling because you turned in the middle of the night. You're one of us. Do you remember shifting into a cougar?"

He just stared at her.

"I'm one. Hal and Ted are. Many of the people

living in Yuma Town and the surrounding area are. You're safe with us. We'll guide you through this. You'll grow to appreciate who you are."

"Who turned you?"

"We were born that way."

He was still staring at her like she was crazy. "I dreamt I was an animal." He glanced at her bed. "I got into bed with you."

She smiled.

"Hal made me return to my own bed. He didn't like it that I was in bed with you."

"Cougars are naturally territorial."

"How…how can you be cougars and work with the horses?"

"They trust us because we live among them."

"My brother tried to kill me."

"It appeared that way. You were only acting in self-defense."

"Why would he want me dead?"

"Money? Lots of it? You were working with me to expose Mooney and Benny Smith. And your brother was working with them. He might have had to prove his loyalty to them by agreeing to take you down. Why don't you get some more rest?"

Ricky shook his head. "He wouldn't have." He squeezed her hand, and released it, then closed his eyes. "Are you staying with me?"

"I might stay again tonight. It depends on how you're doing. If I do and you shift again, for your own protection, don't climb into bed with me."

Ricky smiled at her then. "The boss man won't like it."

"I won't like it. For your protection also, we have someone guarding the room."

"When can I leave here?" He tried to sit up and groaned.

"Take it easy, Ricky. You've been through an awful trauma and had to have a blood transfusion even."

"Maybe if I have enough new blood, it will take away the shifter part of me."

"Would you want it to?" She didn't think that could happen. Though she'd never known anyone to do it, so who knew?

He started to shake his head, but pain reflected in his face. "No. I haven't even tried it out enough when I'm really awake to see what it's like."

"You have to be careful. Really careful. Hunters might try to shoot you, even off season. So you always need to run with one of us."

"I'll run with you."

"I mean, with anyone who's one. Not just me. I have a job to do and you need to stay safe."

Hal came in to check on him. "Hey, buddy. How are you doing?"

"I would have slept better if you'd let me sleep with Tracey." Ricky had the good sense to smile after he said it.

Hal smiled a little in return in a way that said he'd

better not even think it. "Dr. Parker's checking on you in a few minutes to run some blood tests and check you over."

"Will a blood test say I'm different?"

"No. It'll appear as it always has. And when you're a cougar, you'll appear to be only a cougar. They'll feed you breakfast. You can watch some T.V. and sleep a while longer. I've got to take Tracey home to get a shower and a change of clothes. We're going to check out a couple of things and see you later this afternoon."

"Promise?"

"We plan to come back, but if we get hung up, we might be late. Just hang loose, and we'll see you in a while."

"Don't let her get shot," Ricky said as if Tracey wasn't even in the room. "She's always in a firefight. Or something. Just...watch her, will you?"

She shook her head and squeezed his hand.

"Don't I get a kiss goodbye? After all I've been through?"

She grinned at him. "You're *so* asking for trouble. You might not understand our big cat dynamics yet, but—"

"Oh, I understand. It's weird. It's like it's imprinted on my brain. The impulses, the natural instincts. Though I'm not sure I'm ready to bite anyone just yet."

"Good. No biting. That's one of the things we teach our cubs. We don't need you getting ticked off and biting people." Hal folded his arms.

Tracey leaned down and gave Ricky a kiss on the forehead. "Rest well and we'll be back."

Then they left the room and headed to Shannon's room. Two beautiful baby girls were sleeping together in a bassinet next to the bed. Shannon was awake, but looking sleepy.

"We're headed out, but wanted to stop in to see you and the babies," Tracey said, giving her a hug. "They're beautiful."

"Thanks. And thanks for the flowers."

Tracey looked at Hal. He shoved his hands in his pockets and shrugged. "You were watching over Ricky. I ordered the flowers in both our names."

Tracey walked over to the flowers and read the card. "Love from Tracey and Hal." Which sounded a whole lot like they were a couple.

He smiled, not looking in the least bit sheepish. Shannon grinned at them. "Thank you. I love the roses."

"We'll be back after a while and check on you and the twins and Ricky," Hal said.

"How is he doing?"

"Confused. Upset. Chase might not have told you, but he shot and killed his brother last night and so he's pretty torn up about it. And he turned in the middle of the night, so he's one of us for certain," Tracey said.

"Good. I'd hate it if we had to decide his fate."

"It's already been done for us—by his brother. We'll see you in a bit," Hal said.

Then they left Shannon's room and headed outside.

"So what did you have in mind? Besides my showering and changing?"

"We'll check out Ricky's brother's place. I want to know if he was a hunter. Maybe there's some connection to Mooney there. I know everyone would have investigated while we were here with Ricky last night, but we might find something."

"All right."

"I was thinking…you need a reliable partner."

"I've got partners. Had partners," Tracey amended.

"Just my point. I know you're against quitting the work you do and often you have to work with other law enforcement agents to take these men down. So what if I ask Mick to assign you to me?"

She smiled at Hal. "He doesn't assign me to law enforcement personnel. Besides, it won't work if I'm out of your jurisdiction."

"What if I was hired as a Special Agent? And you're assigned to me?"

She chuckled. "As a new trainee, you would be assigned to me."

"That'll work too. We make a great team already."

"You would give up being a part-time deputy and running a horse ranch?"

"Ted and Ricky can run things while I'm out of the area. I've got too big a spread to let all that space go to waste."

"You're inviting me to stay at your place?" She thought there was a proposal in there—like in a marriage proposal, not just a share-the-space offer.

"And watch the sun rise in the mornings, ride the range with me, take care of poachers, and—"

"Play in the waterfall?"

"Hell, yeah."

"And work with me as a Special Agent? You'd do all that just for a housemate?"

"Roommate. We're sharing the master bedroom suite."

"So we have room for guests."

"And we'll have the wedding and reception out of doors on the deck with the view of the Rockies behind us."

She couldn't contain herself and laughed. "Was there a marriage proposal in there somewhere, and I just missed it?"

"Damn, I know I'm going all about this wrong, but yeah. I've been doing a lot of thinking about this, and I know you don't want to give up your job. Maybe if you get tired of it, we can do something else—together."

"You would really do that for me?"

"For us."

"And would be happy doing it?"

"Are you kidding? I'm as much invested in the case as you are, from a different perspective. Mick's down another Special Agent, and what could be better than to team up two cougar shifters together?"

"What if he wants you to work with someone else instead?"

"Absolutely not. If he wants my services, he's got to play by my rules."

Smiling, she shook her head. "The agency decides."

"Mick decides your assignments."

She was still considering the ramifications—what if Mick didn't want to assign Hal to her and was worried he might not be focused on the mission and would get himself killed just to protect her? She didn't want him to give up his life just to please her. What if he didn't like the work? Then he'd quit, they'd be married, and he wouldn't want her to run off on any more of these potentially dangerous assignments.

"What were you doing on New Year's Eve last year before you ended up in a shootout in a ghost town on New Year's Day?"

"I was at home, watching a thriller."

"And New Year's Day? Before the trip to Anderson, I mean."

"I had just started to watch *3:10 to Yuma*."

"And this year? Just think, you could be home with me, watching a thriller, drinking champagne and making love. Not necessarily in that order."

She smiled. In truth, she couldn't see going back to her status quo life after hooking up with Hal at the second shootout in Anderson. Wasn't that a sign anyway? That she needed him in her life as much as he needed her?

"When you put it that way—"

"So, say yes."

"What if Mick doesn't agree to it."

"He will. I already asked."

She slugged Hal.

He grinned at her.

"You're lucky I'm the forgiving type. I can't believe you asked him! And now he thinks we're getting married? What if I said no way?"

"Then I'd have to wear you down, convince you that we were meant to be together. And just for your information, Mick was thrilled. He'd have a highly trained Special Forces service member who happens to also be a part-time deputy sheriff, so trained in law enforcement, who has also worked with you on assignment and is a cougar on the team. Your team. And only your team. I talked to Ted and asked if he could handle it—now that Ricky's a cougar too, and if he could manage that. He said he would do whatever it took to ensure you said yes and became the boss lady. Although he also told me he knew that was where this was heading. Stryker didn't have a chance."

"Poor Stryker."

"Poor Stryker, my ass. He didn't even get you a puppy yet."

She smiled.

"I've been thinking about that too."

"You already have a foal."

"Right. But every horse ranch needs a good dog. Australian shepherds come to mind. I was thinking if we get a puppy—"

She realized at once why Hal wanted to get a puppy. And she didn't believe it was for her. Tears filled her eyes. "You want a puppy so that Ricky can raise him and help him overcome his grief about his brother."

"Yeah. The puppy would be all of ours. Ted loves dogs too. But we could let Ricky name the puppy, and he'd be responsible for him overall. The next foal we have, he can help with the foaling and he can name that one too."

"Speaking of puppies and foals and the like, what about if we have kids?"

Hal smiled down at her. "We'll decide how to handle the situation when the time arrives. I'm not sure that Ted would be willing to take on a couple of kids also."

She laughed. "This seems awfully sudden."

"You don't do anything slow and methodically."

"True." She frowned. "You didn't tell Mom and Dad about this, did you?"

"As a true gentleman, I asked your dad's permission to marry you."

She groaned. "You didn't."

"Yeah, I'm sure your mom is already penciling in the wedding plans. But I didn't have a wedding date to give them."

She shook her head. "Glad I could have some say in this."

"Will you be my mate?"

"What if you hate working with me?"

"I haven't so far and if it doesn't work out, I'll return to the ranch and you keep doing your job."

She smiled. "Somehow I doubt you'll want me out there on my own or with another partner."

"I agree. But it's your decision."

"I married a cougar and we divorced four years ago. We had a big falling out over my job. He didn't like my work ethics."

"I do. Just say yes, and give me a date. That way we can let everyone know, and they can quit guessing."

"Who else knows?"

Hal smiled. "By now? Probably the whole cougar community."

"Hal…"

He hugged her tight. "I thought we could go look at the puppies a breeder has that are ready to go home."

"You already found one?"

"Two, actually. I put the money down on them because I figured one would get too lonely."

She smiled. "Okay, what if we wait to go when we can take Ricky over to see them?"

"I got them for you before all this happened with Ricky. I had to put the money down on them to hold them for us. The others were all sold. So is that a yes on the marriage business?"

"Do you love me?" She loved him with all her heart. Anyone who would give up his work to be with her like that, go through the rigorous training and even ask her dad's permission, and then get puppies for her, that would now help to heal Ricky's shattered heart? Hal was a dream come true.

"Are you kidding? I can't imagine you not in my life, Tracey. I love you with all my heart."

She knew he did both by his words and his actions. "I can't think of a place I'd rather be next New Year's Eve."

"We can't wait that long to get married."

She chuckled. "You said yourself I'm not good with waiting. So no. Whenever you want to do it is fine with me."

"And you love me, right? You're not just agreeing so you can get a couple of puppies, a horse of your own, and get to share the master bedroom with me, right?"

"Hell, yeah."

He laughed. "I guess I should have asked one question or the other. Which is it?"

"I love you." She pulled out her phone. "Okay, when do you want to do this?"

"I'd like to clear this mess up with Mooney first, but on the other hand, if it takes too long, I really don't want to wait."

"In two weeks?"

He grinned. "Yeah, it works for me."

She sighed dramatically. "I can't believe I'm doing this."

"It's for a good cause."

She laughed. "You're perfect for me. You know."

"Ditto, Tracey."

She called her mom, who answered without hesitation. "You're all right, aren't you?"

"Oh, yeah, Mom. We're fine. But you might want to pencil in a wedding cake on the calendar for next Saturday. If you have time."

"For you?"

"Yeah, Mom. I guess Dad already told you?"

"He did, and all his retired friends from the agency, your sister, and everyone's coming, no matter what their other plans are. Though your dad was hoping Hal would talk you into becoming a ranch lady and give up this life of danger."

"Later. When we have kids or we have to retire from our positions."

"Hal said Mick approved his working with you."

"Yeah. But he has to pass all the training."

Hal smiled at her.

"Okay, so nothing really fancy. We have too much work to do and—"

"You're my first daughter to get married. We're doing the wedding gown, the whole business."

"Oh, Mom…"

"Don't oh-mom me. We're doing this right. So pick out a day that you can go shopping, and we'll do this together."

"We're in the middle of a case."

Silence.

Tracey let out her breath. "All right. Monday. I'll pick you up at ten."

"And Jessie too."

"Of course. That goes without saying."

"Any bridesmaids besides your sister being the maid of honor?"

"No. I want to keep this simple."

"And Hal? Will he want his Special Forces buddies to all be groomsmen?"

Tracey growled. "All right, all right. I'll ask some others to be my bridesmaids. Got to go, Mom. We're still running an investigation here."

"Certainly, dear. I'll let everyone know you're taking us shopping on Monday."

When she ended the call, Tracey glanced in the direction of the old bunkhouse and corrals as Hal was driving by it on the road up to the main house. "Hal, don't slow down, but does Ted ever go into the original bunkhouse for any reason?"

Chapter 17

Hal couldn't believe someone would be hiding out in the old bunkhouse. "No, it's not all that stable. In the summer, no telling what might have taken refuge in there. What did you see?"

"Either a ghost or a shadow of someone moving around in there. I might be wrong though," Tracey said.

"Okay, I'm going to stop, we switch places, and you drive the rest of the way to the ranch house. I'll check it out."

"No. If he hears you stop, he's going to assume one of us got out when he hears the truck start up again."

"If we both go up to the house, we might be too late to return to the bunkhouse before he disappears."

"Okay, back up the truck and we both go after him."

"Good call." Hal stopped and put the truck in reverse and headed back to the bunkhouse.

Twisted around in her seat, Tracey kept an eye on the bunkhouse while Hal watched the road and his driving. "No one's leaving it. He can't think he can hide from us in there."

"No. It's more like he'll shoot it out with us." Hal pulled in as close to the bunkhouse as he could get. "Are you ready?"

"Yeah." She had her Glock out and was ready to take care of the threat. "I'll go east."

"Okay, going west. He can't shoot us both at the same time. Stay low."

They climbed out of the truck through the driver's side to use the vehicle as cover. Whoever was inside could hear their footfalls on the dry brush.

But no one fired at them. Maybe he was waiting for them to poke their heads into the doorway or through a window.

"We won't hurt you. Come out where we can see you, hands up in the air," Tracey called out. Hal was already around the other side of the bunkhouse. "Come on. We don't have any reason to hurt you."

"Don't shoot," a man said. "I'm coming out." The floor began to creak as he walked across it, heading toward the front door. Slowly.

Tracey moved back behind the truck, using it as a shield in case the man started firing.

She noticed Hal waiting behind the corner of the bunkhouse as backup.

"I'm armed, but I'm not shooting anyone."

"Come on out," Tracey said.

The man stepped into the morning sunlight, his one hand on his waist, his fingers bloodied, his other hand in the air, holding a gun.

"Put the gun down on the ground," Hal shouted.

The blond-haired guy jumped a little. Hell, Tracey jumped a little at the sound of Hal's commanding voice.

"I'm putting it down. I was planning to protect myself until you arrived." He slowly put the gun on the ground, wobbled a little, and nearly fell.

"How are you wounded?" Tracey asked.

He groaned in pain. She headed for him.

"Move away from the gun," Hal said.

Doing as he was told, the man backed away from his gun and stumbled a little.

"Who are you and who were you planning to protect yourself from?" Tracey asked as she closed in on him.

"I'm Kolby. Ricky's brother."

Both Hal and Tracey stared at him for a moment. She could see the family resemblance, though this man was blonder and his eyes were blue. But he was supposed to be dead. At Ricky's hand. At least, that's what Ricky had said.

Hal hurried to reach him first and tied his wrists together behind his back with plastic ties. Tracey pulled up Kolby's T-shirt. "We've got to get him to the clinic. It's a gunshot wound."

The thing that worried her most was that Kolby

didn't smell like he was a cougar. And now Ricky was one. She got the medical kit and bandaged Kolby, then Hal helped him to the truck. "So who did Ricky kill?"

"Teagan, probably. The guy's been badgering Benny to kill my brother because Ricky's been working for you. In the beginning, I didn't know Ricky was working for you. Until Benny and I overheard him talking to you. I tried to warn you to go somewhere safe—"

So Teagan and Benny were cougars, but Kolby wasn't. Nor was Ricky, until now.

"You thought I would be safe at Anderson where I was ambushed?" She bagged Kolby's gun.

"No. I mean, yeah, I said to go there because they were talking about taking you out at your place. I didn't figure they'd ever believe you'd end up in Anderson. So I figured it would be safe. They must have bugged my phone, or overheard me or something."

"Why didn't you call me and tell me what was going on?" she asked, as she and Hal helped Kolby into the back seat of his pickup, then both climbed in and Hal drove back to Yuma Town's clinic.

"Hell, I figured they had my damn phone bugged."

She raised her brows at him as Hal called in the emergency.

"It has to be. How else would they know to keep intercepting my calls? And learn where you were going?" Kolby asked.

"What about the ambush at the mine?"

"I didn't know anything about that. I...I was going to meet my brother there."

"At the saloon in Anderson, Ricky said he killed you. He must have been protecting you, saying you were dead so that you could get away. Why did you tell him you'd meet him there and then he was ambushed?"

Kolby's blue eyes watered. "Is he all right?"

"Not on account of you." She narrowed her eyes at Kolby. "He said you told him you were going to talk with him. Where were you?"

Kolby collapsed in the back seat of the truck. "Benny shot me and left me for dead. I was going to meet with Ricky and tell him to go someplace far away. I had a wad of cash to give him, but Benny stole it from me and then shot me. I tried calling Ricky to warn him, but he must have already been in the town, and I couldn't reach him. Is...is Ricky going to live?"

"Yes. He's out of surgery and recovering. So what do you know about Mooney's operation?"

Kolby closed his eyes and didn't respond. Her gut clenching, Tracey worried he'd died on them. "I'm climbing into the back seat to check on him."

"Is he okay?"

"I think he passed out or he doesn't want to answer my questions." Tracey crawled into the backseat and felt his pulse. "Pulse is thready. He might not make it, Hal."

"Ambulance is on its way. The guys asked if you were involved in the action again."

309

"Like you don't have any trouble when I'm not around."

"Here they come." Hal pulled over as the ambulance parked in front of them.

To Tracey's relief, the EMTs hurried to carry Kolby into the ambulance.

Once they were on their way, Hal followed them to the clinic. "What do you think? Is he telling the truth?"

"He could be. Ricky said he thought they might have bugged his phone. I figured that was too high tech for these guys, but Mooney's got the money and the resources to do something like that. I just never thought he might."

"Why would Ricky have lied to us?"

"To save his brother. He thought if we believed Kolby was dead, we wouldn't hunt him down. Maybe he planned to leave the area also."

Hal called Dan. "We'll need some more backup at the clinic." He explained the situation with Kolby and the dead man. "He thinks it might be a man called Teagan. We saw a picture of Benny and that wasn't him. We're heading back to the clinic to talk with Ricky."

When they reached the clinic, the EMTs were wheeling Kolby into surgery.

Hal and Tracey went in to speak with Ricky, and Tracey stood next to his bed. He was sleeping.

Tracey said, "We have good news." She was truly glad Ricky hadn't killed his own brother but she was pissed off that he'd lied to them and that he'd faked being so upset over it. She had to give him credit for being really great at giving her a snow job.

Ricky opened his eyes, but he still looked the worse for wear.

"Your brother is alive. But he's going into surgery for a gunshot wound."

His eyes filling with tears, Ricky started to get out of bed.

She put her hand on his shoulder. "No, stay, Ricky. Dr. Parker's taking care of him."

"You—you didn't tell him what happened to me, did you?"

"That you're one of us now? No. And he can't be told. You can't tell him. So who was it that you killed?"

"Teagan. I didn't know it was him when I shot him. I swear it. It's like I said. The cougar came after me, and I killed it, only he turned into Teagan. I couldn't believe it. I thought when the cougar bit me, he somehow made me hallucinate. But he was just lying there. Teagan was."

"Why did you tell us it was your brother?"

"I thought I'd killed him because I'd agreed to see him at Anderson. When Teagan and whoever else came instead, I thought they'd murdered him. And that meant I'd done it. I was responsible. He was going to talk to me about where he was going and—"

"He was going to give you money to run away."

"I wouldn't have. I told him he could ask you if he

could stay with you, but he said we'd both be a target there."

"You said neither you nor Kolby hunted, yet both of you have guns and know how to use them."

"Yeah, for protection. We don't go out and hunt animals. I told you that already." Ricky's eyes rounded. "But then I know you remember that. It's a police tactic, isn't it? To repeat questions and see if you get a different answer." Then he paused. "Is…is he going to be okay?"

"We'll let you know. He's in surgery. Most likely he'll need a blood transfusion, and—"

"I can give him some of my blood."

"You just had a blood transfusion so you can't be giving any blood."

"Would…would it change him?"

"No. It's the saliva in the blood stream that makes the change. But not always. How are you feeling?"

"Like hell."

Tracey squeezed his hand. "Did the doctor say anything about how well the bite is healing?"

"She said it's looking good. But I still feel like hell. Are you going to stay with me again tonight?"

"No," Hal said. "We'll wait until your brother is out of surgery before we leave, and then you can see him. But after that, we've got business to take care of."

"What's going to happen to my brother?"

"We need to know what his involvement has been in all this business, and what he knows. We'll take it from there," Hal said. "Get your rest and no more lying to us."

Ricky nodded, but he still looked so worried.

"I'm certain your brother will be fine. We'll let your guard know to allow you to see him as soon as he's out of the recovery room," Hal said.

Ricky nodded.

They left Ricky's room and once Doc was out of surgery, she met with Hal and Tracey.

"He's going to make it. We don't usually keep humans here because of the cougar situation. But because his brother is here, and he needs to be watched as far as his shifting business and both boys need to be in protective custody, which Dan is providing, we'll make an exception this time." She smiled at Tracey and shook her hand. "I'm Kate Parker and glad to meet you. I gave Dan hell when you were knifed and taken to a different hospital. He should have insisted you come here, but he said it was out of his hands."

Tracey smiled at the doctor. "Next time I need doctoring, I'll be sure to call ahead for a room."

"There's not going to be any next time." As far as Hal was concerned.

Chapter 18

After showering and dressing, Hal and Tracey headed over to Kolby's apartment. Some of Tracey's fellow agents were there, checking everything out. The place was a mess. It looked like someone had trashed it, unless he usually lived like this. The agents greeted her, and she introduced Hal to them.

"Did you find anything related to the crimes this time?" she asked one of the men.

He shook his head. "The place was trashed. It was much neater the last time we checked it out. We've dug around in all this mess and couldn't find any evidence of anything he's done wrong. You still have the lead on the case." He winked at her.

Hal remembered too late that she wasn't supposed to even *be* on the case. He appreciated that the agent would give her the lead anyway.

She smiled warmly at the agent, and Hal was glad

they treated her with so much respect. "Thanks."

He and Tracey searched through the place, but she didn't find anything.

Hal was about to give up the search when he felt a floorboard, half hidden under the couch, tip underneath the weight of his boot. It sounded like there might be a hollow space beneath it. He crouched down and tried to pry it up with his fingers, but he couldn't. Tracey joined him. "What did you find?"

She was pressed up against him, thigh to thigh, and he paused to look into her green eyes and thought of how much he would love to be doing this with her fulltime.

"Might be a loose floorboard like at the schoolhouse in Anderson with a hollow space for hiding things."

Two other agents joined them, one with a flathead screwdriver. "Will this work?" He handed the screwdriver to Hal.

He pried the board loose and found a chip of a bone fragment. "Tusk?"

One of the agents reached down with gloved hands and extracted it. "Appears to be. We'll have it analyzed and let you know."

Hal really hoped that Kolby hadn't been involved in this. But this didn't look good.

When they couldn't locate anything else, they headed back to the clinic. First, they went to see Kolby, but when they reached his room where he was sleeping, they discovered Ricky in there, sitting in a chair.

"You've got to go back to bed," Tracey said. "I'll take you."

"Why can't they move me in here with my brother? You'd only have to safeguard one room then."

"And when you have this other issue?" She help him out of the room, though Hal didn't believe he looked like he needed to use her strength to return to his room. Only that he enjoyed getting close to her.

Hal tamped down his alpha, and very much primal, nature, and sat down next to Kolby's bed. Kolby stirred and opened his eyes. Then they widened. He glanced around the room. "Where's Ricky?" He almost sounded panicked.

Hal realized then how much the boys sounded alike. He wished they could stay in the same room together. But if Ricky shifted again, that would be a disaster.

"Tracey, Special Agent Whittington, took him back to his room. You've been read your rights, but I have a question, if you choose to answer it. When did you store ivory beneath your floorboard in the apartment?"

"You're kidding, right?"

Hal continued to keep his expression stern, and in no way did he sound or look like he was kidding.

"Where?"

"Beneath the couch."

"No. I don't know anything about it. I didn't know there was a hiding spot beneath the floorboards. Ivory?

No way. They only paid me to pretend to be Ricky that one time. I never knew what they were doing."

"Would it have mattered?"

"Hell yeah! That they were trying to murder my brother? And the agent?"

"Agents."

Kolby held Hal's gaze, not flinching, not turning away as if he had nothing to hide. Or he was a habitual liar.

"Did you know that Ricky was an informant?"

"Yeah. I knew he was. He didn't tell me, but he always hangs around me, and I knew he was making money somehow. I work at a grocery store, but Ricky wasn't doing anything. So I listened in on a conversation he was having once. I questioned him, thinking he was dealing in drugs. Our mom died of a drug overdose. I didn't want to see him get into that business. Then these guys offered me good money just to make a call to the agent. When I saw what had happened—heard the news about Tracey Whittington being in a shootout and another agent was wounded—in Anderson, the same place I had sent her, I knew I'd get arrested and charged as an accessory for attempted murder."

"Had you asked them why you were to make the call?"

Kolby lowered his head and looked at his hands clasped together on his lap. "I asked, but they told me they'd already said too much. Either I agreed to do it, or they'd kill Ricky, and then I'd agree to do it. Or I was next. So I made the call."

"And never told anyone about it."

"No. They would have killed me and Ricky. Or the police would have crucified me."

"So why would you have had ivory at your place?"

"A damn plant? If I had gotten out of line, they could have said I was conducting the business they were doing. I didn't know what they were up to, until I saw the news report about Tracey Whittington having lost her partner on New Year's Day. They showed both stories side by side. I'd just been working at the grocery store, and trying to talk Ricky out of helping the agent. I was afraid he was going to get himself killed. When I heard about him at the shootout at the gold mine, I got all the cash together that I could, ransacked my place, and headed out to meet with Ricky. I had called Tracey to ensure she didn't end up in Anderson investigating it again when I went to see Ricky. But Benny must have been watching me."

"Okay, what's the deal with Benny?"

"I knew him in high school. He's older than me, but held back a couple of years. We used to hang out. Then I lost track of him. He popped into the grocery store one day and saw me stocking shelves. He asked me if I wanted to go hunting with him. That he was hunting with some guy who was a hunting guide and it paid better than working at a crap job like I had. I said no. After my dad was killed in a hunting accident, the whole notion makes me nauseous. Literally." Kolby frowned. "He's not illegally hunting too, is he?"

"That's what we're trying to learn. Do you know anything about a man named Mooney?"

"That's the hunting guide's name." Kolby leaned heavily against his pillow. "How much ivory did they leave at my place? Enough to put me away for life?"

"A fragment."

"Hell, because they didn't want to leave enough evidence that would mean money to them."

"Could be." Or it could be Kolby was lying.

"Is Ricky going to be all right? He…he said a cougar bit him, and he killed it and Teagan before Teagan shot him. He…he said I could stay at your ranch."

"Is that why you were there?"

"Benny dumped me on the side of the road. I saw smoke off in the distance and made my way to the old bunkhouse. And then I heard a vehicle coming. I was afraid it was Benny. That he came back to finish me off and realized I'd gotten away. That I hadn't just died on him. Though I had passed out. I guess he thought I had died. Then I recognized the agent from the news reports. From what Ricky had said, she was staying with you at a horse ranch."

"For now, you have to be in protective custody. If Benny learns you survived and could testify that he attempted to kill you, he's going to want to finish the job. Is there anyone else working with him?"

"Just Teagan that I knew of. But then, I wasn't working for them or with them. I just did that one call. God, I'm so sorry. I want the agents to know that."

"All right. We'll talk later."

"Can…can Ricky stay with me here? I thought what he said made sense. That you would only have to post one guard on the door."

"Maybe later."

"How long am I going to be in here?"

"Until the doc says you're ready to go."

Hal stood and was ready to check on Ricky when he saw blood on the sleeve of Kolby's hospital gown.

Kolby immediately glanced at his sleeve. "It's nothing. Picked at a pimple. Bad habit of mine."

Kolby was too worried for it to be something so insignificant. Hal strode around the bed and took hold of Kolby's arm and yanked up the sleeve. A sharp clean bite mark—like a cougar would make.

"Damn it to hell." His gaze shot up to Kolby's. "What happened?" He didn't want to assume Ricky had come in here, told him that he had become a cougar, and bitten his brother so that he could become one of them.

"I was sleeping."

"Don't bullshit me. Did Ricky bite you?" Hal still wasn't saying as what.

Kolby stiffened and Hal released his arm.

"I'm asking him next, but if you want anyone backing you on this, I need for you to tell me the truth."

Kolby snorted. "It sounds crazy."

"Talk. Now."

"Ricky was worried about me. Okay? He came in here to check on me. He was nervous, hiding something from me. I know him. I know when my kid brother has a secret he wants to tell me but is too scared to do so. I figured he'd done something wrong. Something that would get him into trouble with you. I wanted to help him like I've always done. To get him out of the fix he was in. So he finally tells me. And, of course, I don't believe him. I mean, how crazy is it? That you're all a bunch of cougar shifters? And he's one now? That Teagan had been one? Then Ricky starts yanking off his clothes, and I told him probably whatever drugs he was on for the pain was making him crazy. Even having been bitten by the cougar was making him have weird visions or something. No frigging way did I believe him. One minute he was standing there naked, and I was telling him to put his damn clothes back on before they locked his ass away for being a mental case and the next thing I knew, he was a cougar. Scared the shit out of me.

"He didn't even give me a chance to react. He stood against my bed, big clawed paws resting next to my body, and licked my cheek with his hot tongue. Then he shifted, quickly told me he had to turn me so I could heal quicker and work with you or you would send me away, and I never could see him again." Kolby's eyes filled with tears and he looked down at the bed. "He said you couldn't lock me away if I was a cougar shifter. That we had to do it." He looked at Hal again. "We've been fending for ourselves since I was sixteen. I've done the best I could in keeping Ricky out of trouble. This was his way of payback."

Hal shook his head. "Hell."

When Hal left Kolby's room to speak with Ricky, he got a call and he shook his head, then took it. "Mom?"

"You're getting married? And we haven't even met the girl? Come tonight. For dinner. No excuses. We'll see you at six." His mom hung up on him.

"Great." Not that he didn't want them to meet her or vice versa. He did. But things were getting way too complicated with this situation with Ricky and his brother and the rest of the case Tracey was working on. He met up with Tracey in Ricky's room. He gave Ricky a stern look, arms crossed against his chest. "Want to tell me why you bit your brother?"

***

Tracey gaped at Ricky as he explained why he had bitten Kolby. She was glad Hal wasn't furious with the boys. But she could see he wasn't happy with them or the situation. Now they had to see if Kolby turned.

Then Hal said to Tracey, "We'll have them stay together, but I've got to discuss something else with you."

She thought it was bad news, but once they had Ricky situated in the same room with Kolby, and she and Hal walked outside the clinic, he said, "We've got to meet my parents—Roger and Milly Haverton. They're upset that we're getting married, and I haven't even taken you over to meet them. Would you mind seeing them now for dinner?"

"I'd love to." Even though she knew she wasn't marrying Hal's family, she did want to be friends with them, and so she had every intention of putting on her best face.

That evening, Tracey met Hal's parents. Roger began with questioning her all about herself, and she felt she was talking to a law enforcement officer. Then she remembered he was a newspaper reporter.

So she began to question him all about himself—as though she was conducting a Special Agent mission.

From the dining room where Hal and his mother were setting the table, they surreptitiously watched his father and Tracey talking in the living room.

"She's perfect for you," his mother said. She hadn't liked one woman he'd ever brought home for his parents to meet. He thought the world of Tracey, so he worried she wouldn't measure up to their high expectations either. Not that it would make any difference as far as his marrying her.

"She is."

"When are we going to expect grandkids?"

"We have work to do for now. Getting to know each other time. We'll have kids later."

His mother smiled. It was the expression that said

that they'd have kids sooner than later.

"I've never seen anyone question your dad like that. It's great. He'll be talking about how she turned the tables on him forever. Are you sure you want to become a Special Agent like she is though? I thought you loved the ranch." His mother held up her hand. "No. Don't answer that. I know you want to work with her, and I want the best for you. I heard her say her sister is a professional photographer and writing a book. If she ever wants to be featured in the paper, we'd love to do a special interest story on her. I'd offer to do one on Tracey, but she's in the paper quite a lot already."

"Hopefully, future assignments won't be so harrowing."

His mother waved her hand in dismissal. "The two of you can handle it. I hear you're getting a couple of puppies. That's good. It's a great way to learn how to be parents before the babies come."

Hal smiled. He hadn't realized his mom wanted grandbabies so much.

Hal's dad announced, "It's time to eat." He and Tracey joined Hal and his mother and he said, "You've got a damn fine she-cat, Son. If she ever wants to be a reporter, I'm sure your mom would give her a job in a heartbeat."

Tracey smiled and Hal put his arm over her shoulders.

"That's good to know." But Hal figured Tracey's calling was saving and protecting wildlife, and he loved her just the way she was.

***

Later that evening, Dan had assigned other men to watch over Ricky and his brother, though they put Ricky in Kolby's room so they could stay together.

Ricky was glad to be in the room with Kolby, talking with him about what had happened with regard to Benny when his brother wasn't sleeping, ready for him in case he shifted into a cougar and got shook up, like Ricky had been when it had first happened to him.

Even though Ricky thought he was prepared to see his brother shift, he wasn't. For one thing, Kolby suddenly transformed in his sleep and it took a minute for both Ricky and Kolby to register that he'd shifted. Kolby panicked and got tangled up in his hospital gown and sheets, pulled out his I.V. accidentally, and knocked over stuff on the tray next to his bed. It crashed on the floor before Ricky could get out of bed to help him.

A nurse poked her head into the room. "What in the world are you doing?"

Ricky stared at her for a moment, afraid the nurse would run out of their screaming. He still couldn't believe that a lot of the people living in the town were cougar shifters.

"He shifted while he was sleeping."

"I'll go get something for him to help him sleep. He doesn't need to be shifting right now. He needs rest."

She closed the door and Ricky untied Kolby's

hospital gown, then helped him out of it. Then he smiled. "I'm shifting, too." Mainly, because he wanted to get used to shifting so he wouldn't do it by accident. As soon as he was in his cougar form, he jumped from his bed to Kolby's. Kolby snarled at him.

Ricky snarled right back. He had no idea what they had just said to each other, but he had tried to say how cool this was.

Kolby leapt for Ricky's bed. That was one of the things Ricky loved—was the ability to leap such long distances. When Tracey and Hal had left him alone, he had shifted and jumped from his bed to Tracey's, practicing how far the jump would take him.

Maybe because of his injury, Kolby didn't quite make it and with claws extended, he tore Ricky's hospital sheets and blanket as he slipped off the bed. Uh-oh.

The nurse came in the room and started screaming at them. "The two of you, get back into bed at once!"

Kolby and Ricky exchanges glances, showed off their big teeth in a wicked grin, and chased the nurse out of the room, only they quickly stopped when they saw Sheriff Dan and the doctor headed for the room. They were in trouble now.

***

"You would have done the same if you'd had a brother and you were close to him," Tracey said, as she and Ted and Hal sat down to eat dinner outside on the deck that night at the ranch. "How does Kolby feel about Ricky turning him? If he was turned?"

"He was fine with it, I guess. I didn't ask."

Despite that Ted would be the main person who would have to deal with it, he was smiling when he shook his head. "I thought I was going to be ranching, not taking care of two brand new cougar shifters to boot."

"Can you manage? I'm certain someone else will offer to take Kolby in. Even the owner of the grocery store," Hal said, "since he was stocking shelves at another."

"Nah. I'll keep the two of them busy. And we'll have fun too." Ted smiled at Tracey. "I hear we're getting some puppies we'll be raising on account of you."

She looked at Hal. "Does Stryker know?"

Hal chuckled, took a swig of beer, and smiled. "Yeah. He gave me hell for having a foal and buying not only one puppy, but two. Well, three, but one's for Stryker. I haven't let him in on the secret yet."

She smiled. "Are you sure he really wants one?"

"Sure. The puppy will make him even more popular with the she-cats."

"I can't wait to bring them home."

"Two more weeks. We can go see them tomorrow, if you'd like."

"I'd love to. If you all don't mind, I'm going to call my sister. I had a thought about the mines."

"I'm coming with you." Hal said good night to Ted,

left his dish in the kitchen with hers, and walked with her into the living room.

She took a seat on the couch and called her sister. "Jessie, were you ever in the silver mines in Anderson?"

"Sure, the one directly across from the schoolhouse. Have you got a computer handy so you can blow these pictures up and see them more clearly?"

"Do you have a computer I can use?" Tracey asked Hal.

"Yeah. In my office."

She followed him in there and he turned it on.

"Okay, send the pictures to my email," she told her sister and sat down at the desk to access her email.

After Tracey downloaded them, she opened them up in a photo enhancement program Hal had and lightened them up a bit.

"Was this silver mine boarded up?"

"Yeah, but we got permission to go down into the one to take pictures for the book. Of course, we had to at our own risk."

"No one bothered you? And Mrs. Blasdell didn't call the cops on you?"

"She wasn't home. Just from habit, I always look to see if her car is sitting in front of the garage or if she's peeking out her window. But her car was gone and there was no sign of her. I figured she had gone into town for groceries."

"But the mine was safe?"

"'Of course not. It was downright scary down there. But that one didn't collapse. The cave-in was at the other mine. Did they ever find ivory in the one where you found the fragment and the cave-in had occurred?"

"They're still working on it. It's dangerous work. But it's not just ivory that they're looking for but bodies if anyone got caught down there during the cave-in."

"So are you looking through the photos? Do you see anything?"

"Rock walls, rock ceilings, rock floors."

"If they know you're on to them, why would they continue to store the ivory there?"

"Maybe they have them there and haven't been able to get it out without us catching them at it. And investigators have kept them from getting to it. We thought they might be bringing it out somewhere else because otherwise they'd have to get it past Mrs. Blasdell and she'd report them."

"Yeah. No one gets anything by her unless she's not there."

"Okay, thanks, Jessie. Everything all right with you and mom and dad?"

"Yeah, but you be careful."

"I will."

"And congratulations, sis. You couldn't have picked out a hotter cat than Hal."

Tracey smiled, said good night, and turned to Hal. "We need to go spelunking. We could call Mick up, but no way is anyone going to send a team to check out the mine unless we find some evidence. And I don't see any in this mine in the pictures. But what if it's a different mine?"

"They're dangerous."

"Have you been in them?"

"Yeah. We were reckless teens in our youth."

"All of them?"

"A few. We used to look for nuggets of silver. Took pickaxes and chopped away at the rock."

"Are you game? If we can find the evidence to put these men away, when we capture them, that will be the end of this."

"Until the next case." He wrapped his arms around her. "You don't really want to wait to check them out, do you?"

"Nope."

"All right. Get changed into what you want to wear. Contact your boss to let him know you're going to try and find some silver in the mines in Anderson so you can retire from this dangerous job. I'll let Dan know what we're up to. Not sure we'll get any backup at this time of night."

"What are the odds we'd have any trouble with anyone—" She didn't finish what she was saying as Hal raised his brows, shook his head, and stalked off for his bedroom.

Chapter 19

Hal approached the wagon trail leading to Anderson, but to Tracey's surprise, he parked off the road between some trees at another spot. "Why are you parking here instead of on the wagon trail?" It would have been a lot faster, and this way necessitated climbing the rock face.

"Just in case Mooney or Benny or someone else is watching the trail, I figured we'd slip in through the woods. We can see with our cat's sight, so we should be good."

"Great idea." Why hadn't she thought of it?

They climbed out of Hal's truck and started to hike through the woods as quietly as they could as crickets chirped away and the wind shook the tree branches, the cool night air surrounding them with the scent of pine.

Hal touched her arm when they neared the base of

the cliffs and motioned to go up, rather than around them and into the town. She would have much preferred leaping around on the cliffs as a cougar rather than managing as a human. Then she frowned at the cliffs, thinking she'd heard some movement in the rocks up above and said in a hushed voice, "Did you see or hear something?"

"No. I want to take a look around from that vantage point."

She nodded and followed him up. He was as surefooted as when he was climbing around as a cougar. So was she. He was making good time when he suddenly stopped, crouched low against the cliff face, and she nearly ran into him. She waited, listening like he was, and then she heard someone talking in a hushed voice down below, more in the direction of a mine shaft. Up above, someone was smoking a cigarette. She smelled the smoke as it curled about her, and saw the light from the sparks flicked against the darkness. Ass. He could start a fire in the dry brush up there.

Someone began ripping a board off one of the mines below, tossing the boards to the ground, and banging some tool against the next one.

"Hurry it up, damn it. We don't have all night," Mooney growled.

Her heartbeat quickened as she realized he was in on the job. They'd finally catch him in the act of handling the illegally gotten ivory—if that's what they had stored in the mine.

She was both delighted that they'd catch these men red-handed and apprehensive that something bad would go down. They could wait for Dan and the men he was gathering to watch their backs, or chance losing the whole thing if the men moved the goods now, and they weren't able to stop them. She heard three distinct male voices and saw four lights, looked to be headlamps, casting some illumination about down below.

The man on the cliff was still smoking up on the cliff. How many of these men were cougars though?

Hal motioned that he was going after the lookout and for her to stay put.

She did and watched as he began to crawl up the cliff really slow, trying to keep from making a sound, or from sending any loose rocks tumbling, and alerting the man above or the ones below. She had enough of a rock shelf to balance on that she was able to pull out her gun and ready it for a firefight—just in case.

Then disaster struck. The men were still making a racket with the boards, but Hal slammed into the man above, and he cried out. Not loud or long, but enough that it made the guys down below stop what they were doing. One of them called out, "Jessup?"

No response.

She couldn't see Hal or Jessup from her vantage point now. They both had to be lying down on the rock shelf.

"Go check it out. And, you, hurry with the damn boards!" Mooney said.

The one man began ripping at the boards again while another headed up the cliff with his headlamp on so he could see where he was going. Not good. As soon as he reached a certain vantage point, he was sure to see Hal and Jessup. And then the shooting would begin.

"See anything?" the man called out from down below.

"No. He must have taken a stroll. No sign of him."

Tracey was barely breathing, keeping close to the rock face so he couldn't shine his light down in her direction and catch sight of her.

"I'll take care of it," another man said. "Why don't you come down here and help out below?"

Benny? Tracey thought she recognized his voice.

"Don't take long, Benny. You know your way around the silver mine the best of any of us."

Benny. Stan. The cougar. He would track Hal and Jessup, wherever they'd gone to. He'd track her. Damn it. Would he shift?

She needed to shoot him before he shot at her. He had to die. As a cougar shifter, there was no going to jail for him. She readied herself as she heard him make his way up the cliff and the other man made his way down. But Benny wasn't wearing a headlamp. She could see him though, with her cat's night vision. Just like he would be able to see her if he moved just far enough to the cliff's edge once he was on top. He was moving like a cat in human form, carefully, smelling the air, trying to detect their scents.

"How in the hell can you see what you're doing without using any light?" someone shouted from below.

Benny was on the hunt and he wasn't saying anything, just moving quietly, cautiously, searching for his prey.

To her surprise, Benny began to strip. He was going to shift. Had he seen her? Was he going to leap down and kill her? If she didn't get a shot off at just the right angle, he could kill her.

She didn't want to alert the men below by firing off a shot. If they heard her, she could just imagine them all firing a barrage of rounds at her, or attempting to get away. But she was certain they'd want to grab their booty before they took off. And they probably didn't think they had a big police force here to deal with because no one had identified themselves. She really didn't want to scare them off, if they decided to run and didn't take the merchandise. Law enforcement would find the evidence, but she wanted all the men responsible to be caught with the goods. She didn't want any of them to get away this time.

"Go in. Hurry," one of the men said. And she assumed they'd cleared the boards away from the mine shaft finally.

She couldn't see Benny any longer and assumed he'd shifted and was on all four paws. Suddenly, he peered down over the cliff edge and looked straight at her. He must have smelled her. She readied her gun, but another cougar slammed into the cat and sent him flying in another direction. Cougar snarls and growls filled the night air.

One of the men below said, "Damn, a cougar must have gotten Jessup."

"What about Benny?"

"Sounds like two cats fighting over a meal. Benny and Jessup? Come on, let's get the stuff out of the mine. Fewer of us to divvy up the money to."

Mooney. Greedy bastard.

"Go on. Get down there. I'll follow you in."

She was glad the men didn't believe it was anything to do with agents on the case though.

She wanted to help Hal, but she couldn't. Not as a human. She had to keep watch on the other men, but if they were going into the mine, she wanted to be where she could see the entrance. Right now, she couldn't. One headlamp was still shining, the light angling up toward the cliffs, and she assumed the man was trying to see what he could of the cats. But Hal and Benny were well away from the cliff edge that dropped off to the town below.

She needed to take the man out, who was looking up at the cliffs. Then there'd only be two or three left, she thought. Unless some were hiding someplace else, which seemed unlikely.

At this point, it would be safer for her to go back down and come around with the man's attention on the cats up above. She began the climb down, cautiously, watching her foot and handholds, careful of not stepping on loose rocks and sending them flying because it would be coming from a different direction than the two cats and might alert the lookout.

***

Hal knocked out Jessup, who had been smoking while standing guard. Hal hauled him off to a ledge below that area that he'd been standing on and waited while another guard appeared at the same place. Though Hal couldn't see him, only heard him walking around on top of the rock. The man's headlamp had been casting a light over the area, but the overhang prevented the new man from seeing Hal or an unconscious Jessup.

As long as Tracey was quiet and he assumed she was fine, Hal kept still. But he was ready to take out the second man to even up the odds a bit when another man said he'd take a look instead. Hal recognized the man's voice as that of Benny's, and his heart rate picked up its pace by several beats. Benny could smell his and Tracey's scents. Hal had to take him out before he spotted Tracey.

Climbing around the rocks, Hal made his way up to the point where he could see the man. Except Benny had shifted and now was searching for Jessup in his cougar form. He was smelling the air, and then raced across the rock ledge and peered over the edge. Hal raced across the rock to reach him. Hal slammed into Benny and sent the startled cat flying, both of them snarling and hissing in anger.

The cat growls made for great cover for Hal and Tracey, to disguise that they were here if the men below feared law enforcement had taken out their other friend.

For a second, it was a standoff between the two big cats—their ears flattened, their teeth bared, and noses wrinkled in a menacing threat. Hal lunged and bit at Benny's neck, but the big cat scrambled and literally fell off the rock and jumped down to a lower ledge to recover. Hal leapt from his higher perch, not giving Benny the chance to steel himself, and attacked again. But the cat jumped to an even lower rock shelf and saw Jessup unconscious on another and growled.

Hal jumped down and attacked again, growling as Benny hissed back. Benny was more of a runner rather than a fighter, yet he knew he had to kill Hal or be killed.

Claws extended, Benny halfway stood, his teeth bared, trying for a head on bite. Hal jumped away and sent rocks flying over the edge. Then he leapt toward the cougar and bit Benny's neck again, but the cougar fell backward off the cliff and landed on his feet on a rock down below.

Hell. Damn cowardly cougar. Movement up on the rocks stole Hal's attention for a moment as he worried Tracey was coming to help him.

As if he knew he had to finally make a stand, Benny leapt at Hal and this time managed to bite Hal's flank. Distractions could be deadly. Hal shook loose but the rock was too small for the two of them, and both fell off. He landed on a lower rock ledge, while Benny was up above.

A shot was fired from the direction Hal had left Tracey. Glass shattered. A man cried out. A flashlight hit the rocks on the other side of the cliff from where Hal was now. Then a barrage of rounds struck the rocks where she'd been, pinging, chipping, but nothing that sounded like it had hit a soft target. Still, Hal's heart was racing as he feared for her safety. When he jumped onto the rock where Benny had fallen, Hal found he had already taken off.

Heart thundering, Hal bounded off after Benny, fearing the worse—he was going to take out smaller prey—Tracey.

***

No matter how carefully Tracey moved, she felt a few rocks slip under her right foot. Her heart beating out of control, she immediately stopped climbing and held her breath.

Four or five rocks skittered down below her all the way to the bottom and stopped.

She waited for what seemed like forever. If she was in her cougar form, she'd just leap down from her current perch. Even though she moved quieter in her human form than most, she was still limited by what she could do as a human.

The man pulling guard duty crunched on the rocky earth as his footfalls headed in her direction. He was holding a gun in one hand and a high-powered flashlight in the other, pointing the beam all over the cliffs, but mostly below where she was. She didn't have a choice. If the light hit her in the eyes and blinded her, she'd be in damn big trouble. She readied her weapon, aimed, and fired a shot. Glass shattered as the round hit the flashlight, knocking out the light. The man cried out, dropping the flashlight with a clunk on the rocks. And then he began firing rounds that struck the rocks all over the cliff with resounding pings and clunks.

Chips of rock flew everywhere, one skimming her cheek like an arrowhead, and the skin burned from the impact. She moved as quickly as she could, backing away from that side of the cliff. She worried the other men would come running and see what was going on if they had heard the shots fired up above the mine shaft. Or they'd stay put and figure they were trapped. Maybe they'd think the guy standing guard was in a major shootout with the Feds and they wouldn't budge from the mine.

She decided to move up the cliff face again. She'd go to the top and come around one of the miner's huts at the same location that the other two men, Benny and the other, had come up.

She wasn't sure what was going on when the guard stopped firing, and no one came running from the mine.

The guard probably figured she had night-vision goggles and was at a better vantage point to see him than he could see her. He had ducked below the cliff, turned off his headlamp, and she suspected he was waiting in the dark. She couldn't see where he was, but only guessed it from when he had turned off his headlamp, and then his footfalls moved back toward the mine. She reached the top of the cliff, then made her way down. This would be even better. Once she was able to reach the bottom, she would be able to see him, but he couldn't see her without using a flashlight or headlamp. She'd take him down without a fight. As long as he wasn't a cougar shifter, she needed to take him alive for prosecuting.

"What the hell's going on up there?" someone called up from the mine shaft.

The man on guard duty didn't respond, probably scared witless that a sniper would get him as soon as he let out a peep.

She continued down, hoping she wouldn't make a sound this time. She guessed he'd be breathing so hard, his heart beating out of control, that he wouldn't hear much of anything unless she sent a bunch of rocks tumbling.

She reached the ground and saw him half hiding behind a timber to the entrance of the mine.

"Gesner! What the hell is going on? Answer me!" Whoever was in the mine had climbed near the top of the shaft and his voice, much louder this time, startled her, making her jump a bit.

She had to take out Gesner. Either the man in the mine would stay down there, or he would come out shooting, but she'd have a better chance at fighting one, than two.

She shot at Gesner's exposed arm, the one holding the gun. He instantly began firing back in the direction she'd shot him, but she had already jumped away from the location and run off, only this time she had a full view of his body. She fired two rounds, both at his wounded arm and this time heard bone shatter. He cried out and dropped to the ground.

She moved again away from where she had fired the last rounds. She wished she could get hold of the other man's gun, but she figured he wasn't going to be able to use it anyway. He was sitting now on his butt, holding his arm, groaning.

"Hold your fire!" the man in the mine called out. "We're filming a movie and we've got permission to be here."

If she wasn't so anxious about Hal and what a mess she could be in, she would have laughed at the absurdity.

"Gesner, are you all right?" the man called out, still not venturing out of the shaft.

"Wounded. Right arm."

"How many are out there?"

"Not sure. Maybe a dozen?"

She smiled. Anything to save his pride. She still heard Hal fighting with the other male cat, and she was praying he'd come out on top.

There was a lengthy pause and then a gun flew out of the shaft and landed on the ground. "I'm unarmed.

Don't shoot. I'm coming up. You're supposed to identify your damned self. That's the law."

Been there, done that. These guys didn't give officers any chance at survival. Since dozens of officers weren't really here to take these men in, she couldn't chance having them identify her location. Though as soon as the man's head popped up out of the mine, his headlamp would soon reveal her position.

Right before he reached that point, he turned off his headlamp.

He wasn't going to play fair either.

Chapter 20

Hal hoped to hell Tracey was okay. He'd half leapt, half fallen to another ledge, when Benny bit him hard in the shoulder. He wasn't going to be an easy cougar to kill. Every time Hal heard shots fired down below, he prayed to God that Tracey's rounds were finding their destination and the traffickers were missing their mark. But they were firing a hell of a lot more rounds than she was.

When Benny didn't come after him, Hal feared the worst. Benny was going after Tracey.

Hal leapt back into the rocks above, his shoulder burning like it was on fire. Then he followed Benny's trail through the rocks, past the miner's house and snarled a warning to Tracey that the cougar was coming after her if she couldn't smell him in time.

It was Tracey's worst nightmare. She didn't have a choice. She had to shoot the cougar with the intent of killing it. But if she killed Benny, he'd shift into a human. And then the other men would see it and have to be eliminated. Benny knew that. Maybe, he thought she wouldn't shoot to kill. That he'd get her first, and take off.

Tracey fired at the cougar lunging for her, four shots. As soon as she began firing at the big tan cat, a man came out of the shaft and began firing at her. The cat collapsed on her, not dead or he would have shifted. Unable to get Benny off her, she used him as the only cover she could, firing from underneath him.

The man fell back into the shaft. Tracey hoped he took some others with him if they all had the notion to join the shootout.

With Benny seriously wounded, Hal knew he couldn't join Tracey as a cat. He had to shift, dress, and get his gun. He hoped she could hold out until he could join her. She was still struggling to push Benny off her when they heard men's running footfalls coming from the direction of the wagon trail.

"Police! Drop your weapons! Everyone put your hands up!" Dan shouted.

Thank God for big prayers. Hal hurried down the cliff and raced across the ground to reach Tracey. He jerked Benny off her and tossed the cat aside.

Hal pulled Tracey into his arms, but she immediately recoiled. "Are you injured?" he asked.

"No. But I smell your blood. Oh, Hal."

"Just a small bite."

"Like hell it is. We need medical attention over here!"

"How about you?" He touched her cheek that had been cut and was bleeding.

"It'll be healed up in a flash." She glanced back at the men they were pulling from the mine, disarming them, handcuffing them, and reading them their rights. They brought one man out who had apparently died. The man who had been shooting at her and then fell. She wasn't sure what had killed him. Her round or his fall.

"Get them the hell out of here, now!" Dan said.

She knew he wanted to get them out of here before Benny expired and turned into a human.

"Was Mooney among them?" she asked Dan as he headed for them.

"I thought he was the dead man in the shaft. But it wasn't."

"How did the man die?"

"The fall killed him." Dan glanced down at the cougar. "Is that Benny? We didn't see him with the other men."

"Benny." She hugged Hal tight and never wanted to let go of him.

"There's another man up in the cliffs. He's just knocked out, tied up, and not going anywhere, unless a cougar finds him for dinner."

"We'll get him." Dan headed off to get some of the police officers who joined them to pick up Jessup.

"Woohoo, hot damn, Tracey!" Anton called out from the mine.

"Anton?" Tracey squeezed Hal's hand. She couldn't be more thrilled or surprised.

Hal squeezed her hand back. "Go, see him while Emmett's bandaging me."

Tracey kissed Hal's cheek, then ran off to the mine.

"She's not going to abandon you for her old partner," Emmett said.

"You got that right," Hal said.

Tracey glanced over her shoulder and gave Hal a small smile.

When she reached the shaft, she called down. "Anton?"

"You did it! You found it. Hallelujah!"

"What are you doing here? I thought you were still convalescing."

"Typical, partner, you're more concerned about me when here you've been through a hell of a lot all the time I've been sitting at home, doing nothing. Tons of ivory is down here. They hauled it to the ladder and it's sitting there to be picked up and stored as evidence. Over a million dollars' worth, looks to be. Which is why they were trying so hard to get rid of you so they could get it out of here. It looked like it had been buried under an avalanche, and they've been working for months trying to unbury it.

"Just for your information, the boss doesn't know I'm here. I've been keeping up on what you've been doing, and when I heard you thought the ivory might be in the mine, I wasn't staying away. Except Dan wouldn't let me come until all the shooting was over. But it's all here. Every bit of it. Want to see it?"

"No. Thanks. I'll take your word for it. But we still didn't get Mooney."

She didn't want to see all the tusks that meant the death of so many elephants. But she was glad to be able to finally bring these men to justice. "I'm glad you're feeling better. Are you returning to work soon?"

"No, three months convalescence. Heard you were on administrative leave."

She smiled.

"Hell, I knew you wouldn't let the case go."

"How's the wife and your daughter?"

"Great. We're all coming to the wedding. Who would ever have thought it?"

She glanced back in Hal's direction. Who *hadn't* he told?

Anton headed back up the ladder. "Boss will surely take you off administrative now, officially."

"I'm taking some time off, officially."

Anton smiled and looked back at Hal, who was frowning at the EMT. "He looks like he's as reckless as you. Word in the rumor mill is he's applying for a position and wants to work with you."

"That's the rumor."

He laughed. "The two of you will be good together."

"What about you?"

"I think for a while I'm taking a desk job. I'll have to so that I can get back in shape. At least for now, that's the plan."

Stryker joined them and said to Tracey, "Gesner? The man you shot in the arm? He's going to talk to try and get some immunity."

"I wish none of them would get any immunity, but if it means the rest will get some long jail time, I'm glad."

"Amen to that," Anton said.

"Glad to see you doing so well." She gave Anton a hug and he hugged her back.

"Take care, Tracey. You were always my favorite partner."

"Thanks. I've enjoyed working with you too. I'll be seeing you."

"At the wedding," he reminded her.

"Uh, yeah, at the wedding." She still hadn't wrapped her mind around that. Though she wanted to catch Mooney more than anything else in the world, she wasn't delaying her wedding to Hal for anything.

"Come on. Unless Hal wants to ride in the ambulance, I'll drive you to his truck. What made you park over there?" Stryker asked.

"He didn't want them to see us if they were monitoring the wagon trail. Did you find their vehicles?"

"Vehicles?"

"They had to have parked somewhere, then hauled the ivory out, and loaded them somehow into vehicles close by."

"We're bringing men and equipment to haul the ivory to a truck on the main road."

"Right, and so how did they move it here? And how were they moving it out?"

"Maybe in small amounts."

"Where are these men's vehicles? Did you find them anywhere?"

"No. We didn't."

She glanced at Benny's body. The EMTs were putting him in a body bag. She took a deep breath, caught Hal's gaze as he headed for her, all bandaged up. She turned and went to intercept him.

"Are you ready to go home?" He pulled her into his arms and squeezed the breath from her.

"After the doc sees to you."

"She's liable to make me stay over in the hospital tonight."

"Then I'll stay with you."

"Hell, Tracey, I wanted to go home and have you all to myself in the master bedroom."

She smiled and wrapped her arm around his waist as he draped his arm over her shoulders. "Stryker's taking us to your truck. He said there's no sign of these men's vehicles."

"So where are they?" Hal glanced at Stryker.

"Beats me."

"You said that Gesner was going to spill the beans," she reminded Stryker. "So now's a good time."

"Yeah. When we get to the area where we have reception, I'll call and ask him where they are. They might have more evidence in the vehicles."

She was glad Stryker was staying with them, just in case Hal became too woozy. As soon as they reached the area where several vehicles were parked, including Stryker's Jeep, he handed her his phone. "Why don't you ask him?"

"Thanks." She said to Gesner, "This is ATF Special Agent Whittington. I need to know where the vehicles are that you men drove here in."

"We all rode in an SUV. It's parked around the side of Mrs. Blasdell's house."

Tracey climbed into Stryker's Jeep with Hal and Stryker. "She let you?" It was a Wednesday, so not a scheduled day that she'd be away and when they drove down the wagon trail, they saw her Cadillac sitting in front of the garage. She peered out the window, then moved away from the blinds.

"She always lets us use her place to park our vehicles. She gets a certain percentage from Mooney to be quiet about it," Gesner said.

Tracey wanted to strangle the woman. "Anything else you know about her?"

"No. I just know that much because I worried she'd call the police and Mooney said it was covered."

"Thanks." Tracey ended the call and relayed the

information to Stryker and Hal.

"Are you well enough that we can make a stop at Mrs. Blasdell's house?" Stryker asked.

"Hell, yeah. Tracey lost a partner and could have lost another, not to mention being under fire twice because Mrs. Blasdell was acting as an accessory to murder."

They parked behind Mrs. Blasdell's Cadillac and got out.

"She has a rifle," Tracey reminded Hal.

"Yeah."

Tracey and Hal waited by the vehicle, guns readied as backup, while Stryker approached the house.

Stryker knocked on the door. "Mrs. Blasdell, we need you to open up and answer some questions for us."

They heard an engine rev up on the other side of the house. Instantly, Mooney came to mind.

Stryker, Tracey, and Hal took off running to stop whoever it was that was attempting to make a getaway.

Mrs. Blasdell was backing up in a gray Suburban. All three of them fired several times at the tires, taking all four out, but she continued to back up the vehicle.

Dan's police cruiser pulled up behind her, blocking her from escaping.

"Out of the vehicle, now! Hands in the air!" Tracey called out.

The woman scowled at her and then opened the door.

Dan and Stryker ran around the vehicle to take her

into custody, while Tracey stayed with Hal, who was leaning a little against her.

Mrs. Blasdell was sobbing. "They forced me to allow them to park here. They said they'd kill me if I didn't."

"All right. We'll check out your story. But for now, you're going to the police station to answer some questions." Dan read her rights to her and then locked her up in the back of the car. "Are you okay, Hal?"

"Yeah."

But then Tracey thought she heard movement in the garage. She turned her attention to the closed garage. Hal was looking that way too.

She and Hal headed for it, then Tracey hurried around the opposite side. Hal opened the side door to the garage and shouted, "Deputy Sheriff Hal Haverton! Come out with your hands up."

Tracey peered in through a window on the other side of the garage. It was dark inside, but Hal located a light switch and turned on the single naked bulb hanging from the rafters in the unfinished garage.

Wooden crates filled the garage, and Hal wondered if some of the ivory was stored in these crates.

A shot rang out and Hal dove behind a crate for cover, but the round hit the light bulb, shattering the glass and knocking it out.

Tracey broke out a window, but someone fired in her direction. Hal listened for footfalls, thinking the culprit intended to sneak out into the dark. When he saw Mooney heading for the doorway, Hal rushed him. Thankfully, his cougar night vision helped him to see the man before he reached the door, though he assumed Stryker and Dan would be waiting outside, guns ready and would nab Mooney.

As soon as Hal plowed into Mooney, Tracey climbed in through the window and was fired upon.

Damn it to hell. Two men had been hiding in the garage.

Hal heard a thump behind one of the crates as he fought with Mooney over his gun. Hal managed to hit Mooney in the jaw, and he released his hold on his gun. But then Mooney tried to get to a knife, and Hal wrestled with him until he could flip him over onto his stomach and cuff him.

Wherever Tracey had gone, all was quiet. Hal rose to a crouch and studied the dark garage, looking and listening for any sign of movement.

Then he saw Tracey headed for another crate, her light footfalls nearly inaudible. Even so, a man rose to avoid the crate and though Hal was certain he couldn't see Tracey's approach, he was probably listening to her footfalls. He raised a gun, and Hal fired four shots at the man, center of mass.

He went down behind the crate and Tracey raced around behind it, giving Hal a near heart attack. He worried the scumbag was waiting for Tracey to show herself, or at least give away her position.

Hal was running for the crates from the opposite

side and found her crouching beside the man, checking for a pulse.

She shook her head.

Stryker called out, "Coming in!"

"Two men down. Not sure if anyone else is hiding in here," Hal shouted.

Stryker and four other law enforcement officers hurried inside, flooding the garage with flashlights and searching every inch of it.

"I'm innocent of any charges," Mooney said as Dan read him his rights. "I was just here visiting my aunt and came out here looking for a screwdriver to tighten her bathroom doorknob, when the place was overrun by you people. Only we thought you were criminals. Hell, we were here just at the wrong time, got scared, and I stayed here to hide." He glanced back at the dead man. "I didn't even know he was hiding in here."

Tracey frowned at him. "Tell it to the judge."

Hal suspected Mooney's lawyers would be all over the case, trying to keep him from going to jail.

One of the police officers brought in a crowbar, and they pried open one of the sealed crates. It was filled with ivory packed in stuffed animals. Several other crates were empty and plastic bags of stuffed toys made in China were sitting beside them.

"So that's how they were moving the ivory." Tracey took hold of Hal's hand, glad it looked as though they'd finally made a breakthrough in the case.

"One hell of a haul." Hal pulled Tracey into his

arms. "One hell of a very Special Agent."

"You'll make a pretty good partner," she said, hugging him back.

Hal kissed her mouth. "You're damn right, I will."

"I'm taking them to his truck," Stryker told Dan.

When they got there, Tracey ended up driving to the clinic, and Stryker followed them there.

Stryker had to help Hal, who wasn't happy about it in the least, into the clinic.

As soon as they walked by Ricky and Kolby's room, Ricky hurried off the bed and ran after them in his hospital gown and bare feet.

"Ricky, go back to bed," she said.

"What happened?"

"We'll tell you later."

"Is the boss man going to be all right?"

She smiled, amused that Ted's name for Hal had stuck. "Yeah, he's going to be fine."

"Who bit him?"

"Benny."

"Damn. I wish I could have taken him on."

"He's dead. He won't bother you again. Go back to bed."

Ricky looked so serious, then nodded and returned to his and Kolby's room.

When Hal and Tracey saw Doc, she just shook her head, fighting a smile. "Tracey's bringing in more business than we normally get."

"I don't need to be here. I'm just humoring her.

Just do what you need to do, and I'm out of here," Hal said.

"Do you want me to stay with you?" Tracey asked.

"No. I know you want to check on the brothers and Shannon. I'll be done in a minute."

Doc made Hal sit up on the exam table. "All right. What happened this time?"

"It's the end. The bad guys were hauled off to jail. The last cougar shifter involved in the affair is dead. The ring leader is going to jail if his lawyers don't get him out of this one, and the ivory, for evidence to build the case against the rest, was taken in for safekeeping."

"What about Kolby?"

"I think we can prove he was coerced into what he did, and he'll be fine." Hal winced as the doctor cleaned up his bite.

"Except for the shifting."

"Have there been problems?"

"They've been shifting back and forth, trying to get the hang of it. I'm not sure if we're a zoo or a clinic."

Hal shook his head.

Doc smiled. "They chased the nurse out of the room."

"In a dangerous way?"

Kate taped bandages over Hal's bite wound. "No, in a playful way. She recognized it, of course. I had to read them the riot act. No shifting until they're at the ranch. And then they have to be careful around any new horses until they recognize the brothers. Do you think

Ted will be all right with those two?"

"I suspect he's going to have his hands full, what with just teaching them how to care for the horses and now this. He seemed eager to do so. We can always make other arrangements if it doesn't work out. But I'll give him a big pay raise."

"He'll like that. Sure you don't want to take one of the beds for the night? Shannon's going home tomorrow. Ricky could go home tomorrow also. He's healing even faster than I thought he would. But Kolby's injury will take a little longer. He's fine, as far as it's healing more quickly than a human's, but his wound was more invasive. And when he goes home, he'll be limited as to what jobs he can do for a while."

"As long as he's going to be all right, we have no problem with him taking it easy for a while."

"He is. Both he and Ricky seem to be enjoying their cougar status, which can be a great concern."

"Good."

"And you should take it easy."

"Bed rest?"

Kate smiled.

"Am I done?"

"You sure are. And congratulations on your success tonight. I'm so glad Tracey's staying with you and joining the community."

Hal got off the table. "Thanks, Kate. I'm sure she'll love it here."

He dropped first by the brothers' room on his way

to pick up Tracey, who must have been visiting Shannon. Kolby was sleeping and Ricky was watching T.V.

Hal stepped into the room and Ricky immediately muted the T.V. and frowned. "You look like me. What happened?"

Hal explained what had gone down and then added a stern word about the shifting business.

Ricky remained so quiet and looked so serious the whole time, Hal was afraid he'd said too much.

Then Ricky sank against his pillow, looking relieved. "Then we can stay at the ranch still."

"Sure thing." Hal wondered then if Ricky had thought he hadn't wanted to deal with two wayward cougar shifters.

Then Ricky smiled. "Do I get my gun back? You know, to shoot rattlers if they sneak up on the horses."

Hal shook his head. "Dr. Parker says you can go home tomorrow."

Ricky's eyes widened. "I haven't had a real home in years. But..." He glanced at his sleeping brother. "Can I stay with Kolby until he can leave?"

"It may be several days."

"I want to leave, but I want to stay here with Kolby too."

"Are you both okay with the cougar change?"

Ricky just grinned.

"No more chasing the nurses."

"Yes, sir."

TERRY SPEAR

Hal glanced at Kolby. "Make sure he knows the rules."

"He does."

"All right. Check in with you later." Hal found Tracey speaking with Shannon.

Both her babies were asleep in a bassinet, and he smiled at her. "Where's the dad?" Hal figured he was getting some shuteye.

"Sleeping. We're going home tomorrow, and he knows he's going to be busy. Tracey told me all the trouble you've gone through. Chase will be upset that he wasn't able to help out."

"He's had his hands full himself." And Hal was sure thinking how he wouldn't mind being in the same situation as Chase. Then again, he loved the idea of getting to know his mate before...before they added cubs   to   the   family.

Epilogue

With the help of several of the shifters in town, Tracey moved her belongings from her apartment to Hal's ranch. Hal was glad she had moved in with him before the wedding. They had delayed seeing the puppies until he was more healed up. By that time, they'd released Kolby. He, Ricky, and Ted wanted to go too.

Stryker reminded Hal of what he'd said to him about puppies getting in the way of a relationship, but Hal told him he had three puppy sitters who would eagerly take care of that problem. What he didn't tell Stryker was that when the time was right, he'd give one of the ones he had bought to him. Hal couldn't wait to see his reaction.

"They are so adorable," Tracey said, her eyes big with excitement as she cuddled one of the six puppies in the litter.

They were only taking the three of them home in another week, but each of them was holding a puppy for now and smiling. Well, Ricky was holding two so the last one wouldn't feel left out.

Hal knew this was going to work out great. Sure it would be a lot of work making certain the new cougar shifters learned how to cope with their new abilities. Both of the brothers were extremely jumpy when loud noises startled them because they weren't used to hearing so well. And they found it fascinating to listen in on conversations, which Tracey repeatedly told them to quit doing. But it was such a new and fascinating experience for them, they were having a difficult time controlling that aspect of their new enhanced abilities.

But Hal could tell with the puppies, they'd have no trouble taking care of them. Who would have ever thought a cougar family would be so thrilled to take in a couple of dogs. He realized something else too. They truly were a family.

Tracey smiled up at Hal and he smiled back down at her. He suspected their next trip would be to the pet store for toys.

***

The wedding was a fabulous affair—from a sunrise setting and pictures of the bride and groom with the backdrop of the mountains and the colors of the brilliant sunrise and everyone decked out in Western wear. Tracey was wearing a pair of high heeled wedding boots with her wedding dress, special for the occasion, and Hal was grinning at her the whole time.

Following the ceremony, Mick took Anton, his wife, and daughter on a tour of the surrounding area while everyone else ran as cougars through the woods, the first time Ricky and Kolby got to run with so many of the others in the community.

Then they returned for a huge feast out-of-doors. Shannon and Chase were there with their new twin baby girls, the dispatcher, Dottie Brown, with her twin boy and girl, the EMTs who remarked they were glad to be there when no one needed medical attention. The doc, Stryker, and Dan.

Mick was there too, congratulating Tracey and Hal for a job well done and mentioned on the side—though they weren't supposed to be talking business—they'd finally managed to clear away the debris from the cave-in in the gold mine and found more ivory. And a body—belonging to Tobias Mooney.

Tracey stared slack-jawed at her boss. "No."

"Yep. The autopsy revealed he'd been shot a month or two earlier, and had been still healing from the trauma."

Tracey realized then, she hadn't seen Mooney at the café that day, but some imposter who had taken over his home and the business.

"He hadn't lied about being Mrs. Blasdell's nephew. We figured he thought if he mentioned that he was family, we might take his word for it. His nickname is Bear."

"Bear..., wait. Bear Tucker? Ohmigod, he was posing as Mooney at the café and said that a Bear Tucker had quit working for him, but that he didn't think the man was doing anything illegal."

"Right. That's him. When Mooney was caught in the accidental mine shaft collapse at Pine Ridge Gold Mine, Bear, or Leonard, his real name, stepped in to take Mooney's place. He continued to pretend to be Mooney's right-hand man. Mooney was really secretive about what he was up to, so no one suspected that he'd disappeared from the picture for the past few weeks."

"None of them were shifters though?" Tracey asked.

"No. Just Benny and the man who fell to his death in the silver mine shaft. He had to have been the second man who had picked up Benny at your mom's place when Benny was running as a cougar."

She shook her head. "I'm just glad it's all over with."

Tracey's parents and Jessie, with some new boyfriend, and her father's retired Special Agent friends came to the wedding and so did Hal's parents. Even though Ted had been at the ranch that morning, he left early to run an errand as Tracey's dad was about to give away the bride. Everyone turned when they heard puppies yipping and saw Ted had brought the pups to the cougars' wedding. Stryker had been smiling and shaking his head until Ted gave him one and said it was a present from Hal and Tracey.

Hal didn't think he'd ever seen Stryker more surprised and then pleased about something. As soon as Stryker held the ball of fluff in his hands, several young girls from eight to ten years old joined him to pet the puppy. So much for the puppy being a she-cat magnet that included females of dating age.

The wedding proceeded and then Jessie took tons more pictures of the bride and groom, the wedding party, and attendees. Wildflowers had been collected right off the ranch, the horses looking so picturesque in the Western setting for the photos. But most of all, Tracey was beautiful and fit right in at his ranch.

After the wedding and Hal danced with his bride for the first dance, Mick joined him with glasses of champagne and they watched her dance with her father, then Ricky, Kolby, and lastly, Stryker.

"You sure you want to be her partner?" Mick asked.

"Hell, yeah. I'm one of the partners who survived to tell the tale." Hal loved her. He would give up everything just to be with her.

"Anton wanted me to ask."

"He still wants to be partnered up with her?"

"Yeah. She might be a magnet for danger, but she has a lot higher success rate than most of the other agents on the force. I wanted to thank you for taking care of her."

"My pleasure."

"I didn't think she'd agree to marrying you. Or that

you'd want to be an agent just so it would work out between the two of you."

"It's the perfect scenario."

"I think so too."

They watched the two brothers dance with single female cougars.

Hal smiled at the brothers. "You know they both want to be Special Agents with your organization now."

"Kolby's old enough, but I want him to wait a year so that he's got his shifting under control."

"Sounds like a good plan to me. He's enjoying the ranch, and he and his brother are bonding. Both are learning to ride horses too. You can't ask for more."

Tracey finished dancing with Stryker and headed for Hal.

Mick and Hal grinned. "You have your work cut out for you."

After the wedding, everyone left, including Stryker with his puppy in a box, and a farewell thanks as he took the list with him about what he'd need for the pup's well-being.

The boys and Ted returned to the bunkhouse with the other two puppies while Hal and Tracey sat bundled up together on the cushioned bench on the deck and watched the sun set.

"The ceremony, reception, everything was beautiful," Tracey said, snuggling against Hal.

"Agreed. I wouldn't have done anything differently—but mainly *you* were beautiful. You can't know how much I admired you when your dad brought you to stand next to me—giving you to me to love, cherish, and hold forevermore."

"I so wanted to race to your side and get the vows over with, so we could run as cougars—as wedded cougars—and then party the rest of the day. Oh, Hal, I love you so."

He squeezed her tighter. "I couldn't love you more. Are you ready for that moonlit run to the waterfall as cougars?"

Tracey smiled and pulled him in for another hug. "I thought you'd never ask."

They heard a rifle shot fired off near one of the ponds. She turned her attention from the distant pond to Hal. "Do you have your badge on you? I've got mine." She patted her side, and before they could take their cougar moonlit run, they were armed with guns and badges and took off to protect the wildlife.

Before they got back to more pleasurable pursuits.

ACKNOWLEDGEMENTS

Thanks so much to my beta readers, Donna Fournier, Dottie Jones, Bonnie Gill, Maria McIntyre, and Loretta Melvin, who all helped to make the book even better! And to Linda Boulanger for her lovely cover and the banner she created for the two books, for Call of the Cougar and Cougar's Mate.